Romance
on the Rails

*All the Enchantment of Railway Travel
in Four Short Stories*

Wanda E. Brunstetter
Birdie L. Etchison
Jane LaMunyon
Terri Reed

BARBOUR
PUBLISHING, INC.
Uhrichsville, Ohio

Daddy's Girl ©2001 by Wanda E. Brunstetter.
A Heart's Dream ©2001 by Birdie L. Etchison.
The Tender Branch ©2001 by Jane LaMunyon.
Perfect Love ©2001 by Terri Reed.

Illustrations by Mari Goering.

ISBN 1-58660-296-9

All Scripture quotations are taken from the King James Version of the Bible.

Published by Barbour Publishing, Inc., P.O. Box 719, Uhrichsville, Ohio 44683
http://www.barbourbooks.com

 Member of the
Evangelical Christian
Publishers Association

Printed in the United States of America.

Romance
on the Rails

Daddy's Girl

by Wanda E. Brunstetter

Dedication

To my husband, Richard. . .
Thanks for your interest in history.
I appreciate your love and support.

Chapter 1

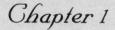

August 1879

Al aboard!" The conductor's booming cry pulled Glenna Moore to her feet. She glanced down at her father, slouched on the wooden bench outside the train station in Central City, Nebraska. His head was supported only by the unyielding plank wall, and his mouth hung slightly open.

Glenna bent down and gave his shoulder a good shake. "Wake up, Daddy. The train's here, and we've got to go now."

Her father groaned and swiped one hand across his unruly goatee. "Leave me alone, Girl. I wanna sleep."

Glenna dropped back onto the bench with a heavy sigh, making no effort to conceal her disgust. "You can sleep all you want once we're on the train." She poked him in the ribs with a bony elbow. "You don't want to be thrown in jail, do you?"

Glenna's harsh reminder of their dire circumstances

seemed to be enough motivation for Daddy. He opened one eye, then the other, yawning widely as he attempted to stand up. His equilibrium was not what it should be, however, and he was forced to grab hold of Glenna's arm in order to keep from falling over.

Allowing Daddy to lean on her small frame, Glenna complained, "If you just hadn't been so determined to finish that bottle of whiskey, you might not be in such a state right now!"

The empty bottle was lying on the floor by their bench, and she sneered at it as though it were her worst enemy.

"Needed it," her father mumbled. "Was dealt a raw hand."

No, Daddy, Glenna lamented silently, *it was you who dealt the bad hand.* Ever since Mama died in childbirth, along with her little brother, Glenna had been Daddy's girl. She needed him as much as he needed her so she would make every effort to bridle her tongue where his problem was concerned.

"If we don't get on board that train heading west, it's going to leave without us." Glenna shuddered. "And if we stay here, the law will either put you in jail or some sidewinder's bound to shoot you."

Her father snorted and gave the empty whiskey bottle a hefty kick with the toe of his sable-colored boot. "Humph! Can I help it if I'm better at poker than most of those snakes in the grass?"

In all her eighteen years, Glenna could never remember her daddy admitting he was wrong about anything—not even cheating at the card tables. She was well aware of Daddy's special vest, with a single strip of elastic sewn inside. She'd seen those marked cards he kept hidden there too. Glenna had no right to complain or judge her father though. After all, he protected her and took care of her needs. Well, most of them anyway.

Glenna glanced down at her dark green, cotton day dress with its form-fitting bodice and tight, short sleeves. The lower part of the gown consisted of both an under-skirt and an overskirt, pulled slightly up in the back, giving it a somewhat bustled look. While it had cost a tidy sum when she'd purchased it a few years back, it was now quite out-of-date. Daddy hadn't done too well at his trade recently, and new dresses weren't a priority—at least not to his way of thinking.

Smoke and cinders belched from the diamond-shaped stack on top of the Union Pacific's mighty engine. The imperious screech of the locomotive whistle and another "All aboard!" drove Glenna's troubled thoughts to the back of her mind. "We've got to board that train, Daddy."

Her father bent down and grabbed his well-worn suit-case, and Glenna followed suit. Due to their rapid depar-ture, they were traveling light. Since they had no additional luggage, there wasn't a need for anything to be placed in the baggage car.

Gripping Daddy's arm, Glenna guided him toward the conductor.

"Tickets, please," the gray-haired gentleman barked, thrusting out his hand.

Glenna set her suitcase down and fumbled in her

handbag. She retrieved the tickets and handed them to the conductor just in time to grab her father's arm before he toppled over.

"Too bad you're not in a private Pullman car," the conductor said with a sympathetic look. "Granger, Wyoming, is a ways off. It appears as though your traveling companion could do with a bit of privacy."

Glenna gritted her teeth and offered the man a curt nod as he helped her board the train. No one wished more for a private car than she. Funds were low just now, and spending what little they did have on something so unnecessary was not a good idea. Until they got settled in the town of Granger, their money must be spent wisely. That meant riding in a dismal, overcrowded emigrants' coach for third class passengers who soon would become a congregation of aching spines and flaring tempers.

Visions of more affluent times flashed into Glenna's mind. Just thinking about their present situation sent a chord of defiance through her soul. She hoped things wouldn't always be like this. Daddy kept assuring her that someday he would hit it really big. Then he'd build a house they could call their own, buy lots of fancy clothes, and give Glenna a horse and buggy fit for a princess. It would probably never happen, but dreaming of better days was all that kept her going.

Her father had already stumbled up the steps and was slouched against one wall when Glenna joined him moments later. "We must find a bench," she said in a voice laced with frustration. If Daddy kept standing there like a disfigured statue, they'd not only have trouble securing a seat, but they would probably be the laughingstock of the entire coach!

With another one of his pathetic groans, Daddy pulled away from the wall. Grabbing Glenna's free arm, he began shuffling down the aisle.

Glenna felt, rather than saw, the curious stares from the other passengers as they awkwardly made their way toward a vacant wooden bench. She kept her eyes focused on her goal so she wouldn't have to view the pity or disgust from those nearby. Why couldn't Daddy have stayed sober today? Why must *she* suffer the humiliation of his actions?

She drew in a deep breath, then blew it out with such force she felt the tiny curls across her forehead bounce. As far back as she could remember, things had been this way where Daddy was concerned. She hated to admit it, but barring some unforeseen miracle, she knew things would probably never be any different.

Daddy dropped his suitcase and gave it a good kick under their seat, then he flopped onto the hard bench. Glenna placed her own piece of luggage next to his and slid in beside him, thankful they would no longer be viewed by the entire car. Maybe now she could find a few moments of peace.

David Green pulled methodically on the end of his recently trimmed beard as he studied the young woman in the seat directly across the aisle. Dark ringlets framed her oval face, and her high-necked dress, though slightly outdated, fit just right. He couldn't help but notice her flushed cheeks, wary expression, and the obvious tension in her body. She probably had her hands full with that man who sat beside her. Was the drunkard her father, perhaps an uncle, or even a much too old husband?

David shook his head. Surely this delicate beauty could not be married to such an uncouth fellow! Those long, tawny curls and fetching brown eyes could easily have wooed a younger, more distinguished, and pleasant man than the one sitting next to her. Why, the paunchy, middle-aged man was slouched in his seat as though he hadn't a care in the world.

How despicable. Then a verse of Scripture popped into David's mind. *"Judge not, that ye be not judged."* He swallowed hard. *Thank You for reminding me, Lord. But for the grace of God, there go I.*

David's thoughts were pulled aside as the man who shared his seat spoke up. He blinked. "What was that?"

"I said, 'when do you think the train will pull out?' " the young man asked. "We've already had several delays today, and I'm getting anxious to see this trip to an end."

David turned his full attention to his chum—a name given to those who shared seats on the emigrants' coach. The man was already on board the train when David got on in Omaha, Nebraska. He'd introduced himself as Alexander P. Gordon, a Scottish author and poet. He boasted of having a modest reputation as a "travel writer."

Before David could open his mouth to reply to Alexander's question, the train whistle blew three quick blasts, and their humble coach began to rock from side to side. The swaying motion was almost gentle and lulling at first, but as the train picked up speed, David could hear the familiar *clickety-clack, slap-slap-slap* of the wheels. Soon their car began to bounce like a rolling ship at sea.

David tried to ignore the distraction and smiled at his companion. "Guess that answers your question about when we'll be leaving Central City."

Alexander nodded. "Yes, indeed."

A boisterous hiccup from across the aisle pulled David's attention back to the lovely young woman and the inebriated man whose head was now leaning on her slender shoulder. She looked so melancholy—almost hopeless, in fact. His heart went out to her, and he wondered what he might do or say to make her feel better. After all, it was his calling to minister to others.

"Tell me about this place where you have been called to serve, Reverend Green."

David turned back toward Alexander, but the man's attention seemed to be more focused on his red, irritated wrists, which he kept scratching, than on what he'd just said to David. Alexander had told him earlier that he'd acquired a rather pustulant itch. Probably from the cramped quarters aboard the train he'd ridden before meeting up with David.

"I'll be shepherding my first flock in a mining town known as Idaho City," David replied, averting his gaze from Alexander's raw, festering wrists back to the woman across the aisle.

"Hmm. . .that would be in Idaho Territory, if I'm not mistaken."

David nodded. "Quite right."

"And you said you recently left Divinity School?"

"Actually, it was Hope Academy in Omaha. I just finished my training a few weeks ago."

"Ah, so you are what some Americans refer to as a 'greenhorn'?"

David chuckled. "Some might say so. However, I have had some experience preaching. In fact, I spent a few years as a circuit rider before I decided to attend the academy and further my ministerial studies."

"I see. So, are you married or single?"

David's eyebrows shot up. "I'm single. Why do you ask?"

Alexander frowned. "Most men of the cloth are married, aren't they? I would think it might even be a requirement."

"Why's that?"

"Too many temptations. The world is full of carnal women who would like nothing better than to drag a religious man straight to the ground."

David chewed on his lower lip as he pondered this thought. Perhaps Mr. Gordon was right. It could be that he'd been too hasty in accepting this call from the good people of Idaho City Community Church. He thought about the letter inside his coat pocket. It was from one of the church deacons, and as he recalled, it made some reference to him being married. In fact, the deacon's exact words had been: "The ladies here are anxious to meet your wife. I'm sure she will feel quite welcome in our church and soon become a part of our growing community as well."

I wonder what could have given them the idea that I'm married, David reflected. *Perhaps Alexander is right. It could be an expected thing for the shepherd of a church to have a wife.*

A deep rumbling, followed by a high-pitched whine, drew David's attention back to the young lady across from him. The man's loud snoring was clearly distressing to the woman, and she squirmed restlessly in her seat.

If only my chum would keep quiet a few moments, I might think of something appropriate to say to her.

Though more than a bit irritated, David listened patiently as Alexander began a narration of the many illnesses which had plagued him all of his twenty-nine years. David was twenty-six, and he hadn't had half as many ailments as this poor chap.

As though by divine intervention, Alexander suddenly became quiet. David cast a quick glance in his direction and found that his chum had drifted off to sleep. Drawing in a deep breath and sending up a quick prayer, David made a hasty decision. He would get out of his seat, walk across the aisle, and see if that young lady was in need of his counsel.

Chapter 2

Two men dressed in dark suits sat in the seat directly across from Glenna. One seemed intent on scratching his wrists while the other man kept staring at her. At least she thought he was looking her way. Maybe he was just watching the scenery out her window. *But why wouldn't he watch out the window nearest him?* she wondered. *Surely there's nothing on my side of the tracks which would hold any more appeal than what he can see over there.*

Glenna swallowed hard as she glanced across the aisle again. This time she studied the man's features. They were strong and clean—a straight nose, dark brown hair, parted on the side and cut just below the ears, and a matching well-trimmed beard. She couldn't be sure of the exact color of his eyes from this distance, but they appeared to be either green or perhaps a soft gray. They weren't dark like hers, of that much she was certain.

Her heart did a little flip-flop when he nodded slightly and offered her a pleasant smile. He was easily the most handsome man she'd ever seen. She returned his smile with a tentative one of her own.

Daddy was snoring loudly now, and she elbowed him in the ribs, hoping to halt the irritating buzz. How would she ever catch the eye of an attractive man if her father kept making such a spectacle of himself? If Daddy appeared disagreeable, then so did she. At least, that's the way Glenna perceived it. If only she had a jar of canned tomatoes to cure the hangover he would undoubtedly have.

Her mind wandered back in time as she remembered how they'd been staying at Prudence Montgomery's Boardinghouse in Sioux City, Iowa. Daddy had come back to their room late one night. He'd been "working" and had guzzled a few too many glasses of whiskey.

Glenna shuddered as she thought about the scene he'd made, yelling and cursing at poor Prudence for not keeping his supper warm. When he'd finally ambled off to bed, Prudence had turned on Glenna. "Gambling is evil—spawned by the devil himself." She sniffed deeply and lifted her chin. "If you don't watch yourself, young lady, you'll grow up to be just like your drunken daddy. Like father, like daughter, that's what I have to say!"

Maybe it's true, Glenna thought ruefully. *Maybe I'll never be anything more than a gambler's daughter.*

"Excuse me, Miss, but I was wondering if you might like to borrow a pillow."

A melodic, deep voice drew Glenna back to the present, and the distinct fragrance of bay rum cologne tickled her nose. She jerked her head and looked up at a pleasant face with a pair of soft green eyes. Her heart jumped into her throat when he sent her a melting glance.

"A pillow?" she squeaked.

"For your companion."

Glenna swiveled back toward her sleeping father, whose head drooped heavily against her shoulder. Daddy would probably be more comfortable with a pillow, and so would she. Should she accept anything from a complete stranger though? Despite his present condition, Daddy was well-learned, and among other things, he'd taught her to be wary of outsiders—especially men.

As if the young man could read her mind, he extended a hand. "I'm Reverend David Green." He motioned toward his seat companion. "Between the two of us, my sleeping chum and I possess three straw-filled pillows, so we can certainly spare one."

Glenna shook the offered hand, though somewhat hesitantly. Even if he was a man of the cloth, she was still a bit uncertain about speaking to Rev. Green. "My name's Glenna Moore, and this is my father, Garret." She tilted her head in Daddy's direction. His mouth was hanging slightly open, and she felt the heat of embarrassment creep up the back of her neck, then spread quickly to her face.

"It's nice to meet you, Glenna. May I use your given name?"

She smiled shyly and nodded. "Yes, Rev. Green."

"Then please be so kind as to call me David."

Glenna had only met a few ministers, and those had all been "fire-and-brimstone" parsons who stood on the street corners shouting out warnings of doom and gloom. As she looked into David's kind eyes, she decided there would be nothing wrong with calling him by his first name. After all, he had asked her to, and what could it possibly hurt?

She lifted her chin and smiled. "David, then."

David's throat constricted, and he drew in a deep, unsteady breath. He hoped Glenna didn't realize how nervous he was. He'd met lots of attractive women in his life, but none had held the appeal this young woman did. He'd noticed how breathtakingly beautiful she was from the moment she had boarded the train. Was it her long, curly, dark hair or those penetrating mahogany eyes? Maybe it was her soft, full lips that made his palms begin to sweat. Perhaps it was her forlorn expression that drew him like a moth charging toward a dancing fire. He imagined how she might feel held securely in his arms. What would it be like to bury his face in her deep brown hair? How would her ivory skin feel beneath his fingers?

David shook his head, trying to clear away such errant thoughts. He shouldn't be thinking this way. What had come over him all of a sudden? Maybe he was merely in need of more pleasant company than Alexander—the poet with itchy wrists, stories about ill health, and tales of lengthy journeys.

The train made a sudden, unexpected lurch, and David grasped the back of Glenna's seat to steady himself. His ears burned at the thought of being pitched into her lap. As it was, the disconcerting jolt had brought his face mere inches from hers.

Garret Moore's eyes popped open before David had a chance to right himself and gain his composure. "I say there," the man sputtered. "And who might you be?"

"Daddy, this is Rev. David Green," Glenna answered, before David could even open his mouth. "He's seated across the aisle."

David extended one hand, while hanging onto the seat back with the other. "Nice to meet you, Sir."

Garret wrinkled his bulbous, crimson nose and made no effort to shake hands. "What's your business, Son?"

"I–I'm a minister of the gospel."

"Not your profession, you idiot!" Garret bellowed. "What business do you have with my daughter?"

Taken aback, David began to stutter—something he hadn't done since he was a young boy. "I–I–w–was–just—"

Obviously aware of his distress, Glenna came quickly to the rescue. "David was kind enough to offer me one of his pillows, Daddy."

One dark eyebrow shot up as Garret tipped his head, apparently sizing David up. "Is that so?"

David nodded. "The pillow was actually for you, Sir. I thought it might be more comfortable than your daughter's shoulder." Feeling a bit more sure of himself now, he smiled. At least he was no longer stuttering like an addle-brained child.

"Just what do you know about Glenna's shoulder?" Garret shouted at the top of his lungs.

David dipped his head. "N–nothing at all."

Glenna's father squinted his glassy blue eyes and waved a husky hand toward David. "We're not some kind of charity case, you know. If either Glenna or I have need of a sleeping board or pillow, I'll hail the news butcher and purchase one."

Glenna offered David an apologetic smile. "Thank you for the kind offer, but we'll manage just fine."

David felt sure this was her way of asking him to return to his seat. From the irritated look on her father's face, he was also quite certain the unpleasant man would probably create a nasty scene if he didn't leave soon. He nodded slightly, looking only at Glenna. "If you need anything, you know where to find me."

She smiled. "Thank you, I'll remember that."

David shuffled back to his seat, feeling much like a whipped pup coming home with its tail between its legs. Groveling went against his nature, yet he knew it would be wrong to create a scene. *You're a new man in Christ now,* a small voice whispered. *Let Me fight your battles.*

Glenna glanced at her father, hoping he wouldn't say anything about her making conversation with a complete stranger. *Surely he must realize that David, being a man of God and all, wouldn't cause me any harm.*

Daddy gave her a grim frown, followed by a raucous yawn. "I can't believe you, Glenna. I lay my head down to take a little catnap, and what do you go and do behind my back?" Before she could reply, he continued his tirade. "You started getting all cozylike with some man, that's what you did. And a black-suited, Bible-thumpin' preacher at that!" He shook one finger in her face. "What's gotten into you, Girl? Have you no more brains than a turnip?"

Glenna cringed. Daddy's deep voice had raised at least an octave, and the last thing she wanted was for David Green to overhear this ridiculous tongue-lashing.

"I wasn't getting cozy with the preacher," she defended. "I was merely being polite after he so kindly offered us one of his pillows."

"Humph! That man has designs on you," her father snapped. "I know the look of a man on the prowl. Why, I oughta speak with the conductor and have the cad thrown off this train!"

Glenna grabbed her father's coat sleeve. "Please, don't. David. . .I mean, Rev. Green has taken his seat. I'm sure he won't bother us again."

Her father gave the end of his scraggly goatee a few sharp pulls, then he shrugged. "I'll let it go for now, but if that scoundrel bothers you again, I'm going to report him immediately. Is that clear?"

Glenna nodded solemnly. She knew Daddy meant what he said. He was not a man given to idle threats. If he said he would do something, he most certainly would. She scowled. *Of course, that doesn't include winning big. Sometimes, when the cards are in his favor, he makes a real killing. Other times, like last night, Daddy gets caught cheating, and then . . .*

Glenna clamped her teeth tightly together. She wouldn't dwell on last night's happenings. Daddy had been cornered by those professional gamblers, threatened with his life, then run out of town. Their brief time in Central City, Nebraska, had come to an end, and that was that. It wasn't the first time something like this had happened, and it probably wouldn't be the last. Glenna knew she should learn to accept things as they were and quit wishing for a miracle which would probably never happen. She closed her eyes and tried to relax. She wouldn't think about that good-looking man across the aisle, and she wouldn't keep hoping for Daddy to change!

Chapter 3

David had just closed his eyes and was about to doze off when his chum spoke up.

"Would you like to hear one of my poems?"

The last thing on David's mind was poetry, but he nodded agreeably. "Sure, why not?"

Whipping a crumpled piece of paper from his coat pocket, Alexander opened it with a flourish. There was obvious pride on his face as he began reading. When he finished, the poet turned to face David, a questioning look in his eyes.

Never having cared much for poetic rhyme, David offered a forced smile. "That was. . .unique." It was the kindest thing he could think of to say.

Alexander's face broke into a smile. "You really think so?"

David nodded, feeling much like a rabbit caught in a trap. "Unique. . .yes, very."

Alexander refolded the piece of paper, this time being careful not to rumple it. David's encouraging words must have bolstered his confidence, for the twinkle in his eyes gave indication that he was a man with a mission. Alexander placed the poem back into his pocket. "I've written an essay, too. It's entitled 'Travels in the Mountains on Foot.' "

David raised his eyebrows. "A rather unusual title, isn't it?"

Alexander nodded. "Perhaps, but it's an account of a journey I made about a year ago. It took me through the mountains in southern France."

I can't imagine this sickly little man making such a trip, David mused. *There must be more to him than meets the eye.*

"The adventures from this train trip will also become an essay," Alexander continued. "I believe I shall call it 'Across the Plains.' "

David smiled. "An appropriate title for now, but once we leave Nebraska, our journey will take us through some rugged mountain ranges."

Alexander frowned. "At least I won't be overtaking it on foot."

"The train is much better transportation," David agreed.

"Even with all its irritating stops and starts. I couldn't believe it when the train was held up for nearly an hour because a silly cow was standing stubbornly on the tracks." Alexander squirmed uneasily. "And these uncomfortable benches are far too short for anyone but a child!"

David chuckled. "You must have a powerful good reason for going all the way to California in an overcrowded, unsanitary emigrants' car."

Alexander's eyes opened wide. "Did I not tell you my mission?"

"I don't believe so." The truth was, ever since Glenna

Moore and her disagreeable father had boarded the train, David's thoughts had been detoured. Often while Alexander was talking to him, he'd been watching the lovely young woman across the aisle instead of listening.

He glanced her way again, but she seemed to be engrossed with the passing scenery out her window. Her father, on the other hand, was holding a deck of cards. Every few seconds he would shuffle them with bravado, using his battered suitcase as a kind of table balanced on his knees.

"So, in a few weeks, I hope to be married."

Alexander's last words brought David's attention back into focus. "Married? You're getting married soon?"

"Yes, to Annie Osgood. I just told you, she lives in California and hasn't been well. I'm hoping my presence will bring her around. As soon as she's on the mend, we plan to be wed."

David clamped his mouth shut, afraid he might burst out laughing. A sickly man, traveling all the way to California, on a train he detested, in order to marry a frail woman? What sense did that make?

"I love Annie very much," Alexander said, as though he had some insight as to the questions swirling around in David's muddled brain.

David smiled. "I wish you all the best."

A cloud of black smoke curled past the window as the train moved steadily down the tracks. Glenna leaned close to the glass, studying the passing scenery with interest. Here and there, scattered buildings dotted the land, but mostly there was just prairie. . .miles and miles of dusty earth reaching up to the blistering sun high overhead.

Glenna repositioned herself against the stiff, unyielding wooden bench, cutting into her backside. Feeling the need for a walk, she stood up and stretched her arms over her head, hoping to dislodge a few of the kinks. Maybe a stroll to the front of the narrow, box-shaped car would help. Daddy was engaged in a game of poker with a group of rowdy men near the back of the coach where the water closet was located. She craned her neck and noticed he was engrossed in his work, as usual. He'd never even know she'd left her seat.

Glenna glanced candidly at the two distinguished-looking men who shared the seat across from her. They both appeared to be sleeping. She wished she could speak to Rev. Green again. . .maybe offer some kind of apology for her father's earlier rude behavior. She rotated her shoulders a few times, then started up the aisle. It soon became apparent that she would need to grab the back of each seat as she proceeded up the corridor. She could only hope the train wouldn't jerk suddenly, sending her toppling to the floor. Glenna would be so relieved when the train made its next stop. It was hot enough to pop corn inside this stuffy car! Some fresh air and a chance to walk on solid ground would be a most welcome relief, not to mention an opportunity for a quick bite to eat.

By the time she made it to the front of the coach, Glenna's legs felt like rubber, and rivulets of perspiration ran down her forehead. She stepped through the door and onto the small platform which separated their car from the one ahead. Gulping in the only fresh air available, she steadied herself against the metal railing. In spite of the day's heat, the continual breeze from the moving train seemed cool and inviting.

Glenna licked her dry lips and swallowed hard. Her throat felt parched, and she wished she'd had the good sense to bring along a canteen filled with water. What had she been thinking of? She'd ridden the train before. She knew there were times when endless stretches of uninhabited land meant no stops at all.

She moistened her lips again. At this very moment she'd have gladly given away what few possessions she owned in order to have something to quench her thirst. To maker matters worse, she'd forgotten to pack a linen duster to wear over her traveling dress. She knew how dust could filter through the open windows, sifting, penetrating, and finally pervading everything in sight. No amount of brushing or shaking would ever remove it all either. After a few days on the train, Glenna would probably hate herself, as well as the cursed dust.

"Are you all right, Miss Moore?" A deep, male voice, whose words were spoken loud enough to be heard over the noisy *clickety-clack* of the train's steel wheels, caused Glenna to jump. David Green stood a few feet away, a look of concern etched on his handsome face.

"I saw you come out here," he explained. "When you tarried, I became concerned."

Glenna's stomach reeled with nervousness. "It's kind of you to worry about me, Rev. Green, but—"

"David. Please, call me David."

"I needed some fresh air, and I'm thirsty as a hound dog." She moistened her lips one more time. "Other than that, I'm perfectly fine."

He chuckled, and there was a distinctive twinkle in his emerald eyes. *He really is a charming man. Why would Daddy object to me speaking with someone as kind as David?*

"Have you anything to drink?"

Glenna shook her head. "Daddy and I were in such a hurry to leave Central City, neither of us thought to fill a canteen." She sighed deeply. "I don't think clearly when I'm under pressure, and Daddy wasn't in any condition to think at all."

David's twinkle was gone now. In its place was obvious compassion. "I have a listening ear, if you'd care to talk about anything."

She swallowed hard and sucked in her lower lip to keep from blurting out her frustrations. This man seemed honest and genuinely concerned for her welfare. Maybe she should swallow her pride and open up to him about some of her troubles. *He might even be able to help somehow. After all, he is a preacher, and men of God are supposed to have words of wisdom to offer, aren't they?*

Glenna was on the verge of telling David why she and Daddy were on this particular train when the door of their coach flew open. Her father, red-faced and sweating profusely, lumbered onto the platform.

"Daddy, what is it? You look upset," Glenna declared. Was he angry with her for coming out here alone? Or were his labored breathing and crimson face due to the rage he felt at seeing her and David together?

With a sense of urgency, Daddy grabbed Glenna's arm. His face was pinched, as though he were in pain. "I love you, Glenna. No matter what happens, please remember that."

Before she could respond, Daddy gave her a quick hug, threw one leg over the metal railing, and plunged off the train.

Chapter 4

Glenna let out a scream that echoed in her ears. *"Daddy!"*

She leaned over the iron railing, her eyes scanning the ground below for any sign of her father. The train was moving too fast. She could see nothing but the blur of trees and thick dust swirling through the air. There was no sign of Daddy anywhere. Had he fallen under the train? Was he lying wounded in the dirt somewhere? Was he. . .dead?

David grabbed Glenna by one arm and pulled her away from the railing. She buried her face in his chest and sobbed. "Daddy! Daddy! Oh, why would he jump from the train like that?"

David patted her gently on the back. "I have no idea, but—"

His comforting words were halted when two burly-looking men came running onto the platform. One of them was dressed in a dark suit with a plaid vest. The other wore a Stetson and a tooled leather belt.

"Where is he? Where is that scum? I oughta lay him

out like a side of beef!" the taller man bellowed.

"He came though this door!" the other one shouted. "Now where's he hiding, anyways?"

When she noticed the guns nestled at both men's hips, Glenna's heart began to pound. Unable to answer, she merely swallowed and hung her head.

The shorter man's fingers danced in a nervous gesture over the trigger of his weapon. "I'll bet that low-down snake ran into the next car. He's probably lurkin' behind some poor old lady's skirts, thinkin' she'll save his sorry hide." The man squinted his beady, dark eyes. "I'll blow the hair off anyone's head who's dumb enough to protect the likes of Garret Moore!"

Glenna pulled back from David. Her chin was thrust out defiantly, but it quivered, nonetheless. "You needn't bother looking in the next coach. My father is gone."

"Gone? What do ya mean, 'gone'?" the taller man asked.

"He jumped off the train," David explained.

The shorter man peered over the railing, as if he expected to see something more than the passing scenery. "You'd better be tellin' the truth about this."

"Why would we lie about something so awful?" Glenna's voice shook with raw emotion, and she covered her mouth with the palm of her hand.

David reached out to clasp her hand. "Miss Moore is right. We have no reason to hide anything from you."

The taller man shrugged. "If that simple-minded sidewinder jumped off a train goin' at this speed, then he got his just reward."

Glenna shuddered. This was her father they were talking about. Daddy had more than his share of faults—even cheated at the card tables from time to time—but he was no simple-minded sidewinder!

"You take that back!" she cried, jerking her hand free from David's. She began to buffet the shorter man's chest with her small fists. "My daddy loved me! He'd never have jumped unless he'd been forced into doing such a terrible thing."

"Ha! He was forced, all right!" the big man blustered. "He either had to give our money back or take a bullet in the head."

Glenna trembled, realizing her father's choices had been limited—either die at the hand of another gambler or jump to his death from a moving train. Of course, he could have given the men their money. Better yet, Daddy should have resigned his unsavory lifestyle and gotten a decent, law-abiding job years ago. *He could have given up drinking too,* she thought bitterly. His addiction to the bottle had only brought them untold grief.

The shorter man snorted. "Guess there ain't no use hangin' out here, Sam. The girl's daddy is gone, and so's our hard-earned cash."

Glenna's heart was thumping with fury now. "Hard-earned?" she shrieked. "If you two make a living the same way my father did, there was nothing *hard-earned* about the money you lost!"

Sam sneered at her. "You're pretty feisty for a little slip of a gal." He moved aggressively toward her. "Why, I oughta—"

David stepped quickly between Glenna and the gambler. "I'm sure the lady meant no disrespect."

Glenna's lower lip began to twitch. "I can speak for myself, thank you very much."

Sam snorted again and turned to face his buddy. "Come on, Rufus. Let's get back to our game. I'm sure we can recoup some of our losses if we find a few more saps to play the next hand." He glared at Glenna. "This little filly ain't worth us wastin' no more time on."

Rufus nodded. Then, brushing past them, his elbow bumped David in the back as he sauntered into the coach. Sam was right on his heels.

David drew in a deep breath. "Whew, that was close."

"Close? What do you mean, 'close'?"

"Those men had guns, Glenna. If your father hadn't jumped off the train, they would have shot him." David looked her straight in the eye. "And if I hadn't stepped in and softened them up a bit, they might have shot you."

Glenna's mouth dropped open like a broken hinge. She'd been so upset about Daddy jumping from the train, she hadn't realized her own life might be in danger. She chewed her bottom lip and winced when she tasted blood. "What does it matter? Without Daddy, I have no life."

David followed Glenna back to their dreary coach, wondering what he might say or do to help ease her pain. He'd been preaching and counseling folks for a few years now, so he should know how to help her. The only problem was, most of those he'd helped weren't as appealing as young Glenna Moore. At least none had conjured up the protective feelings he was experiencing right now. Was there more to this than just concern for her unfortunate circumstances?

Glenna reached her seat and stopped short. Her whole body began to shake as she bent down to pick up a deck of playing cards, lying on the bench. David figured either her father had dropped them there before his great escape or one of the other gamblers had decided to return them. Either way, the last thing Glenna needed right now was a reminder of her father's folly.

He watched her study the cards as tears welled up in her eyes. Her chin began to quiver, and like a tightly coiled spring, she suddenly released her fury. "These cards are evil! They've brought us nothing but bad luck!" With a piercing scream, Glenna dashed the cards to the floor and fell in a heap beside them.

David looked around helplessly, wondering how Glenna's display of unbridled emotions was affecting those nearby. He prayed fervently for the right words to offer in comfort. To his surprise he noticed that Alexander was still asleep, as were several other passengers. A woman and her husband, who sat two seats away, were openly staring. An elderly gentleman shrugged as though he couldn't understand what all the fuss was about. David glanced toward the back of the coach. The men who'd confronted them a few moments ago were already absorbed in another round of poker, uncaring or unaware of the hysterical young woman on the floor.

David dropped to his knees beside Glenna, then

scooped up the deck of cards. "The cards in themselves are not bad," he said softly. "It's the way they're often used which causes folks to sin."

Glenna hiccupped loudly as she looked up at him, her dark eyes brimming with tears. "Those cards are the reason my daddy jumped from this train."

David stuffed the cards into his jacket pocket and gave Glenna his hand. Once she was on her feet, he offered her a drink from the canteen he'd taken out from under his bench. When she calmed down some, he helped her into her own seat, then sat down beside her.

She sniffed deeply as he handed her the handkerchief he'd pulled from another one of his pockets. "Thank you. You're very kind."

He smiled in response. "You know, Glenna, the deck of cards can have a double meaning."

"It c—can?"

He nodded and pulled the cards back out of his pocket. "I've been thinking about using cards such as these for one of my upcoming sermons. It might help some who are more familiar with worldly ways to better understand the Bible."

Glenna's interest was obviously piqued, for she tipped her head slightly to study the cards.

David fanned the deck and retrieved the ace. "This stands for *one* and reminds me of one God, who loves us all." When she made no response, he continued. "Now the two makes me think about the fact that the Bible is divided into two parts—the Old and New Testament." David withdrew the three of hearts. "When I see the three, I'm reminded of the Triune God—Father, Son, and Holy Spirit."

"And the four?" Glenna asked, touching a fingertip to the four of clubs.

"Four stands for the four evangelists—Matthew, Mark, Luke, and John." He held up the five of spades next. "Five makes me think of the five wise virgins who trimmed the lamp."

Glenna's forehead wrinkled. She obviously knew little or nothing about the Bible.

"The six of hearts is a reminder that God created the world in six days," David said. "On the seventh day, God rested." He tapped the seven of diamonds with his thumb.

"And the eight? What does it stand for?" she asked, leaning closer to David. In fact, she was so close, he could smell the faint aroma of her rose-water cologne.

David drew back slightly, afraid he would lose track of his thoughts if he didn't put a safe distance between them. "Eight represents the eight righteous persons God saved during the great flood. There was Noah, his wife, their three sons, and their wives."

Glenna nodded. "Mrs. Olsen, a woman who ran the boardinghouse where Daddy and I once stayed, often told Bible stories. I wasn't that interested then, but I do remember her telling about Mr. Noah and the big boat."

David chuckled. "Guess that's about right, though I've never heard it put quite that way before." He tapped the nine of spades with one finger. "This one makes me think of lepers. There were ten of them, and when Jesus healed them all, only one of the ten bothered to even thank Him. The other nine neglected to do so."

Glenna frowned. "Jesus healed men with leprosy?"

"Yes, and He made many others well too."

"What does the ten stand for?"

"The ten represents the Ten Commandments, which were God's law. He gave the laws to the children of Israel through His servant, Moses." David picked up the king of hearts. "This one reminds me of one special King. . .the One who died for each of us so we could have the gift of salvation and forgiveness from our sins."

Glenna chewed thoughtfully on her bottom lip but said nothing.

"The queen," David continued, "makes me think of the virgin, Mary, who bore our Savior, Jesus Christ."

"There's one card left," Glenna said, pointing to the jack of diamonds. "What does that stand for?"

"This card," David said, emphasizing each word, "represents the devil himself."

Chapter 5

Glenna's brown eyes grew huge as flapjacks. "The devil?" she rasped. "Mrs. Olsen said the devil is man's worst enemy."

"Mrs. Olsen was right." David shuffled the cards thoroughly and held up the deck. "These can be used in a bad way, by the devil, or they can serve to remind us of the fact that there truly is a God, and He loves us very much."

Glenna blinked rapidly. "God could never love someone like me."

"That's not true," David was quick to say. "Why would you even think such a thing?"

"My daddy was a gambler. He cheated people out of their money."

David shrugged. "That was your father's sin, not yours."

"But—but, sometimes I covered for him. I often told lies in order to protect him. Daddy was all I had. He watched out for me, and I took care of him." Her eyes pooled with fresh tears. "Some days, when we had no money, I begged or stole things. Daddy's gone now, and I'm all alone with no way to support myself. I hate stealing, but I may not have any other choice."

"You're not alone," David argued. "God's with you, and so am I. You don't need to lie or steal."

Her eyes drifted shut as she drew in a shuddering breath. "You're here now, but you have your own life. My ticket only takes me to Granger, Wyoming. When the train stops there, I'll be forced to get off. You'll go on and forget you ever met me."

David swallowed hard. She was right, of course. He did have a life—obligations to the church in Idaho City where he'd been asked to pastor. He could hardly take Glenna with him. Besides the fact that he barely knew Glenna Moore, she was not a Christian. By her own lips she'd admitted she was a sinner.

"He that is without sin among you, let him first cast a stone at her." The Scripture passage from the book of John reverberated in David's head. He, of all people, had no right to point an accusing finger at anyone. Not after all he'd done in the past. He wondered if Glenna might question him about his earlier days now that she'd revealed some of hers.

"Your silence only confirms what I said," Glenna moaned. "Once we part ways, you'll never think of me again."

David knew that wasn't true. Though he'd only known the young woman a few hours, she'd made a lasting impression. He turned slightly in his seat so he was looking her full in the face. "I assure you, Glenna, you are not a woman to be easily forgotten."

He resisted the urge to kiss away the tears streaming down her flushed cheeks. Instead of acting on impulse though, he merely reached out and took her hand, giving it a gentle squeeze. "Would it be agreeable for me to share some passages from the Bible with you? I believe God's Word will act as a healing balm, if you're willing to let it."

For a moment she said nothing, her eyes shut and her breathing labored. Finally, she spoke. "I suppose it would be all right. I have nowhere else to turn, and all the steam has left me. . .like vapor rising from wet boots."

"There is only one place to turn. God's love can ease your pain." David removed a small Bible from his pocket and began to read some Scripture verses pertaining to man's sin and the need for salvation. Then he went on to read the account of Christ's death and resurrection. "It's about as clear as cold water, Glenna. You can be released from sins by a simple prayer of faith."

"I—I don't know how to talk to God. I used to pray when I was very young—when my mother was still alive, but I haven't uttered a prayer since her death. I wouldn't even know how."

"I'll help you, Glenna. I can lead you through the sinner's prayer."

She drew in a deep breath. "Sinner—yes, that's what I am."

"We've all sinned and come short of God's glory," David murmured. He admired her willing spirit. He wished everyone he preached to would be so eager to admit their shortcomings.

Glenna had never known such a feeling of freedom as when she finished her heartfelt prayer and confession of sin. A new creature, that's what she felt like now that she'd asked God's forgiveness and accepted Jesus as her Savior. She didn't have her real daddy anymore, but David had reminded her that the heavenly Father would always be with her.

She brushed an errant tear from her cheek and sniffed deeply. God's Spirit might be here, but physically she was still alone. Her ticket would only take her as far as Granger. Then what? Daddy had all their money. Glenna had nothing but the clothes on her back and a few more personal belongings in her suitcase. *I may have my sins forgiven,* she mused, *but I'm sure in a fine fix!*

"For a lady who's just been reborn, you look a bit down in the mouth."

David's deep, mellow voice drew Glenna out of her musings, and she shifted in her seat. "I'm glad I found Jesus, but it doesn't solve my immediate problem."

He lifted one eyebrow in question.

Her shoulders drooped with anguish and a feeling of hopelessness. "Daddy's gone, and I have no money—only a train ticket to Granger."

"Do you have any other family?"

She shook her head. "Mama died giving birth to my brother. He died too. That's when Daddy started drinking and gambling. He never mentioned any relatives either."

"What did your father do before that?"

Glenna had only been five at the time, but she still remembered. "Daddy used to run a mercantile up in Sioux City, Nebraska. We had a house of our own and everything."

David offered her a sympathetic look. "After your mother died, did your father sell his home and business?"

She nodded. "He sold out to the first man to make an offer."

"And then?"

"We left Sioux City and traveled from town to town. Daddy gambled in order to make a living, and I remained in the care of the boardinghouse keepers when he was gone."

"Did the women who ran the boarding homes educate you?" he asked.

Her forehead wrinkled. "Educate me? In what way?"

He smiled. "The three R's—reading, writing, and arithmetic. Your manner of speech indicates that you are not uneducated."

Glenna shrugged. "We never stayed anywhere long enough for me to go to school with other children. Daddy was an educated man though. He always took time out to teach me reading and sums." Lost in memories, she stared down at her hands until they blurred out of focus. She'd always felt as if Daddy loved her. At least until today when he'd jumped off the train. How did he think she could care for herself? Why hadn't Daddy ever gotten a *real* job so he could be a *real* father?

A shallow sigh escaped Glenna's lips as she continued her story. "Once, when I was about ten years old, I thought Daddy might actually change."

"In what way?"

"He met a lady. I think she really loved him."

David smiled. "Many a good woman has been responsible for helping tame a man." He patted his jacket pocket, where he'd replaced the small Bible. "Of course, no one but God can ever really change a person's heart."

Glenna grimaced. "Daddy needed Jesus. Not even Sally Jeffers could heal his hurting heart. When she started making demands, Daddy packed our bags, and we left Omaha for good."

"Demands? What kind of demands did she make?"

"Asking him to settle down, get a job, and marry her." Glenna's eyes clouded with fresh tears, and she turned her head toward the window. There was no point in talking about all this now. Daddy hadn't married Sally, and he sure enough hadn't settled down. She drew in a deep breath. Life was so unfair.

David shifted uneasily in his seat as he glanced across the aisle at the poet whose nose was stuck in a book. The events of the last hour had been a bit too much. . .even for someone like himself. Maybe he should have remained in his seat, listening to Alexander go on and on about his writing and many ailments. Perhaps he shouldn't have involved himself in Glenna's life at all. The pastor part of him was pleased as honey that she'd responded to his invitation to accept Christ as Savior. The only fly in the ointment was the fact that Glenna's father was gone, and she had no other family to turn to. The man part of him felt responsible for someone who obviously could not care for herself. How could David abandon this woman? Glenna had relied on her father all these years, and she really needed someone now that he was gone.

David's thoughts drifted to the letter he kept tucked in an inside jacket pocket. The letter from the deacon at his new church. The congregation at Idaho City Community Church thought their new pastor was married. If he showed up without a wife, it could affect his standing in the church and maybe even the entire community. A wife could be a real asset in the home, as well as the ministry.

For several moments David sat there quietly, thinking about a way to solve both of their problems. Then, impulsively he reached for Glenna's hand. "I—I've been thinking."

She turned to face him, an eager, almost childlike look on her face. "Yes?"

"I was wondering—how would you like to get married?"

Chapter 6

David didn't know what Glenna's reaction to his question might be. He thought she would probably say she wanted to think about it awhile. After all, they'd only known each other a few hours. The last thing he'd expected was for Glenna to throw herself into his arms, but that's exactly what she did.

"Yes, yes, I'll marry you!" Glenna sobbed. "Thank you, David. Thank you so much!"

Just as she pulled away, the train gave a sudden lurch, and David nearly fell off the bench. He gripped the edge of his seat to steady himself. The jolt was enough to get him thinking straight, and the sudden realization of his surprising proposal hit him full in the face. What had he been thinking? Glenna was no doubt in shock over her father's unexpected actions. She probably only agreed to marry him because she wasn't rational right now.

David glanced her way. She was looking at him as though nothing was wrong. He had to admit, he was intrigued with the young woman, and he did find her beauty to his liking. There was another concern though.

What was he was going to do with a wife he barely knew?

The hint of a smile tweaked Glenna's lips. "I know what you're thinking."

"You do?"

She nodded soberly. "You think I accepted your proposal too readily." Before David could respond, she rushed on. "I know we don't really know each other yet, but I'm sure this will work out for both of us. I'm all alone now, and I need a man." She leaned over close to him and whispered, "I will be a good wife, I promise."

David swallowed hard. Glenna Moore was pleasant and rather easy to talk to, but was this the right thing for either of them? Another concern he had was over her ability to fulfill the role of a preacher's wife. She'd only been a Christian a few hours. What did she really know about God's ways or the expectations which would no doubt be placed upon her?

"When will we get married, and who will perform the ceremony?" she asked, breaking into his troubling thoughts.

"A close friend of mine is a minister. He lives in Granger, Wyoming, so we can get married when the trains stops there."

The mention of Granger caused Glenna's heart to ache. Daddy had a friend living there too. That's why he'd purchased their tickets to Granger. *How ironic,* she thought. *Soon I'll be leaving Nebraska far behind and marrying a man I've only just met. Then we'll be going to Idaho City, where I'll begin a whole new life as a pastor's wife.* Glenna sucked in her breath and pressed her nose against the dust-covered window. It wasn't as if she had many other choices right now. Daddy wouldn't be going to Granger or meeting up with his friend. Daddy was dead—probably crushed under the iron wheels of the train. Glenna had to think about her own needs now, and Rev. David Green was willing to take care of her. Getting married may not be the perfect situation, but at least she had somewhere to go and someone to look out for her.

Daddy cared more about himself than he did me, so now I'll do what I think is best, Glenna fumed. She bit back the bile of bitterness threatening to strip away her newfound faith. She was no longer Daddy's girl, and she never would have been again.

David and Glenna spent the next few days learning a bit more about one another. He shared a seat with her during the day and slept beside his chum, Alexander, at night.

The eccentric poet often complained about the feeble illumination of the small oil lamps, glimmering at intervals along the walls of their car. At least there was enough light for David to keep an eye on Glenna. Once they were married, he would worry a whole lot less about her safety. That wouldn't stop him from worrying about his new ministry, however. Was he really ready to take on the responsibility of full-time pastoring? From what he'd learned so far, Glenna had experienced a lot of pain and emotional trauma in her past. Her newfound faith was weak yet, although she did seem eager to learn. While David felt it was God's leading that caused him to propose marriage, he could only hope and pray that she would be an asset and not a hindrance to his calling.

David glanced over at Glenna, sitting beside him now. It was another warm day, and she was fanning herself with one hand as she stared down at his Bible, lying in her lap. He was pleased that she'd asked to read the Scriptures. As a new Christian, she needed to be fed with the bread of life.

"Would you care for a paper, Sir?" the freckle-faced news butcher asked as he sauntered up the aisle, peddling his wares.

"I believe I will take one," David answered with a friendly smile. "I can catch up on the local news and help my lady friend to cool off at the same time."

The young boy wrinkled his forehead, but agreeably he gave David a newspaper.

As soon as he'd paid the lad, David got right down to business. He glanced quickly through the paper and found the page full of advertisements. He ripped it out, then began folding the sheet, accordion-style, until he'd made a suitable fan. When he finished, he handed it to Glenna with a smile. "Here, this might work better than your hand."

Glenna reached for the handmade contraption and immediately began to fan her face. "Ah, much better. Thank you."

"You're welcome," he said with a wink. *I wonder if she'll always be so easy to please. It gives me pleasure to make her happy. Maybe my worries about our future are totally unfounded.*

The conductor moved swiftly down the aisle, calling, "Next stop. . .Granger, Wyoming!"

As the train slowed, then jerked to an abrupt halt, Glenna felt her whole body begin to tremble. This was where she and Daddy were supposed to be getting off. This was where they would have begun a new life, in a new town, with new people—and the same old problems—Daddy's gambling and erratic drinking.

That wasn't going to happen though. Instead of searching for a suitable boardinghouse, Glenna and David would be seeking out a preacher. From the moment Glenna said "I do," her life would never be the same. Could she really go through with this crazy plan to marry a man she barely knew? But what other choice did she have? She had no money, no job, and no place to go. David offered security and a home. He was a good-looking man, not to mention pleasant and easygoing. He'd shown no signs of a temper or even any bad habits. *David would be easy to love,* she thought wistfully. *But can he ever love me? I'm a gambler's daughter, and I've only recently found forgiveness for my sins. What if I do or say something to embarrass David in front of his new congregation? What if I don't measure up?*

David grabbed his suitcase, and Glenna carried hers. He reached for Glenna's free hand, and the two of them picked their way down the narrow aisle toward the door. "Everything will be fine, you'll see," he whispered.

When they stepped inside the church, a middle-aged man

with bright red hair and a mustache to match greeted David with a warm smile and a hearty handshake. "My friend, it's so good to see you." His gaze lit on Glenna. "And who is this lovely creature?"

David slipped an arm around Glenna's waist, and her face turned crimson. "Pastor Jim Hunter, this is Glenna Moore. We plan to get married and want you to perform the ceremony." He grinned sheepishly. "That is, if you're willing and have the time."

Jim slapped David on the back. "For you, I always have time." He glanced at Glenna again but spoke to David. "I'm surprised to see you. I thought you were on the way to your new pastorate."

David knew his old friend well. The look on Jim's face said volumes. He was a lot more curious about the sudden appearance of David's fiancée than he was about his whereabouts. He knew too that Jim wasn't about to perform any marriage ceremony until he'd heard the details of this unplanned stop in Granger.

"If Alice is at home, maybe Glenna could go next door and freshen up a bit," David suggested.

Jim nodded. "She's home, and I'm sure my dear wife would be most happy to meet Glenna. She'll no doubt offer us all some refreshments, then Glenna can bathe and rest awhile." He began moving toward the church's front door. "I'll walk the two of you over there, we'll say howdy to Alice, then David and I can come back here for a little chat while you get ready for the wedding. How's that sound?"

Glenna smiled and tipped her head. "I'm coated

with dust from head to toe, so a bath sounds absolutely wonderful."

A short time later, they were all at the parsonage, sitting around a huge wooden table. A slightly plump, middle-aged Alice was happily playing hostess. After a cup of hot coffee and a slice of gingerbread, the men ex-cused themselves to go back over to the church.

David wasted no time telling his friend the story that led up to his betrothal, and soon the two men found themselves on their knees in front of the altar. While Pastor Jim hadn't actually condoned David's unconventional behavior, he didn't lecture him either. Prayers went up on David's behalf, and both men beseeched the Lord for young Glenna and her new role as a minister's wife. David felt certain that Alice was probably giving his wife-to-be a few pointers as well.

Glenna felt her eyelids flutter as she forced a mind full of doubts to concentrate fully on the words Pastor Hunter was saying. She glanced nervously at her groom and sucked in her breath while he offered a reassuring smile. David had shaved off his beard and bathed before the wedding. His dark hair was still slightly damp, and as he stepped closer, the clean, fresh smell of soap assaulted her senses. This man she was about to marry was a handsome one indeed! But was she worthy of such a man? Her past life had been full of sin and lies—being forced to move from one town to another, watching Daddy drink and gamble, then making excuses for his disgusting behavior.

Glenna glanced down at the pale yellow gown she'd

changed into after her bath. Made of pure silk, with a touch of lace at the neck and sleeves, it was the only nice thing she owned anymore. When she looked to her left, Alice Hunter, who stood as her witness, smiled sweetly. To David's right was Richard Hunter, the pastor's sixteen-year-old son, who was acting as David's attester. There were no flowers or music, and no one else was in the audience to share in this unusual, yet auspicious occasion. Pastor Hunter stood before them, holding a Bible in his hands and wearing a solemn expression on his rotund face. As he shared several Scriptures and some insights on marriage, it was obvious to Glenna that he took his job quite seriously.

A surge of panic rushed through her veins, and she nibbled on the inside of her cheek, wondering if she could really go through with this wedding. It was too late for second thoughts, though, so she forced herself to concentrate on the remainder of the ceremony.

"And now, whom God has joined together as one, let no man put asunder. I do here and now pronounce them to be man and wife," the minister said in a booming voice. "David, you may kiss your bride."

Glenna swallowed hard, steeling herself for what was to come. It was done. She was married to Reverend David Green. Would her husband's kiss be as gentle as his melodic voice? Would it send shivers of delight up her spine, causing her knees to go weak? She'd seen many women swoon after being kissed by a man, yet she'd never experienced any such thing herself. In fact, except for her father's quick pecks, Glenna had never known any man's lips.

Much to her surprise, and yes, even to her disappointment, David merely bent his head and brushed a fleeting kiss across her cheek. She was sure he had his reasons for marrying her, but love was obviously not one of them. *Does he find me unattractive or too unappealing to kiss me on the mouth?* she cried inwardly. *Did he marry me only out of obligation?*

Taking her by surprise, David bent down and whispered in Glenna's ear, "You make a beautiful bride."

Self-consciously, she lifted a hand to touch the soft curl that lay next to her ear. She'd pulled her long hair away from her face and secured it with the tortoise shell combs she often wore. However, unruly curls had a mind of their own, and a few had managed to escape.

"How would you like to have dinner in the hotel dining room before we check into our room?" David asked.

Her head jerked up. "Hotel? Are we spending the night in Granger?"

A soft chuckle escaped his lips. "Of course. There won't be another train heading west until midday tomorrow."

Glenna nodded, feeling suddenly foolish and more than a bit flustered.

A short time later, David and Glenna said good-bye to Pastor Hunter, his wife, and their son. Soon they were seated at a table for two in the Hotel Granger's dining room. A gold-colored tablecloth, graced with a cut glass vase full of daisies, created a cozy, yet romantic scene.

Glenna had been subjected to some luxuries over the course of her eighteen years, but that was only when Daddy had been winning big. *Winning or cheating?* a little voice niggled at the back of her mind. *Did Daddy ever win any money in a fair game of cards?*

"What appeals to you?" David asked, breaking into her disconcerting thoughts.

She shrugged and stared blankly at the menu lying before her. "Whatever you're planning to have is fine."

When the waitress came, David placed each of them an order for pot roast, with potatoes and carrots on the side, along with a plate of fresh greens. They had coffee and tall glasses of water to drink, and a basket of freshly baked bread was brought before the main part of the meal.

"You seem rather quiet and withdrawn this evening," David noted with a look of concern. "Is everything all right? You're not having seconds thoughts about marrying me, are you?"

Glenna took a sip of coffee, then glanced at him over the rim of her cup. "It's not that. I'm just missing Daddy. If he hadn't jumped to his death, the two of us would have been here in Granger right now. This is where we'd planned to get off the train, you know."

David reached across the table and placed a gentle hand on top of hers. "I know you're still grieving, but remember, you have a new life with me now. We have a church and people waiting for us in Idaho City."

Glenna stared into his green eyes, so sympathetic and full of understanding. She swallowed past the lump in her throat and was about to reply when some boisterous voices caught her attention. Her gaze darted to the left. Two men were heading toward their table, arms draped across each other's shoulders, bodies swaying carelessly.

One of the men was looking directly at Glenna, and her mouth dropped open. Disbelieving her eyes, she looked down at the table, then quickly back again. *Daddy?*

Chapter 7

Daddy's eyes glazed over, and he stared at Glenna as though he'd seen a ghost. "Glenna? Baby, is that you?"

Trembling, she could only nod. This had to be some kind of a dream. She'd seen Daddy jump from that train. Even if by some miracle he had survived the fall, there was no way he could have made it to Granger on his own steam—not to mention as quickly as the train had brought them there.

"Mr. Moore, we thought you were dead," David said, scraping his chair away from the table but still remaining seated.

"It would take a lot more than bailing off a train and rolling down a prickly embankment to kill someone as ornery as me," Daddy replied with a hearty laugh.

"But—but—how did you get here?" Glenna stammered.

"Some good folks came by in a wagon and picked me up." Daddy leaned against his friend for support and riveted David with a hard gaze.

David's face was a mask of suspicion, and Glenna noticed the muscle in his cheek had begun to twitch. "I hardly think a wagon could have beat the train here, Mr. Moore," he said evenly.

"And what about your injuries?" Glenna interjected. "Surely you must have been hurt after that fall."

Her father grinned and gave his goatee a few tugs. "I was kind of banged up but not too much worse for the wear." He took a few steps closer to their table, then leaned his weighty arms on the corner nearest Glenna. "Those folks with the wagon had an extra horse. They were kind enough to let me borrow it. That's how I made such good time."

For the first time, the man beside Daddy spoke up. "That's right. My old friend, Garret, galloped into town yesterday afternoon, and we've been havin' ourselves a good old time ever since." He pounded Glenna's father on the back, causing them both to wobble unsteadily.

"Yep," Daddy agreed. "Alvin and I go way back."

Glenna knew Alvin must be the friend Daddy had planned to link up with when they arrived in Granger. From the looks of things, Daddy cared more about his drinking partner than he did her. He hadn't even asked about her, nor had he seemed that interested in the fact that she was sitting in the hotel dining room having dinner with a man.

Swaying slightly, Daddy leaned over and stared David right in the eye. "Say, you're that preacher fellow who was on the train, aren't ya?"

David nodded and opened his mouth, but Glenna cut him right off. "David's my husband now, Daddy. We were married today. . .by a *preacher* here in Granger. . .in a *church.*" Why Glenna was emphasizing the words "preacher" and "church," she wasn't sure. Maybe it was to be certain Daddy knew the marriage was legal and binding, and there was nothing he could do about it. If he cared so little about Glenna that he would jump off the train and leave her all alone, then he had no right to interfere in her life now.

"You're what?" Daddy bellowed.

She lifted her chin and held his steady gaze. "I'm a married woman."

Daddy's fist came down hard against the table, jostling the silver and nearly upsetting the vase of daisies. "You can't be married!"

David jumped to his feet, quickly skirting the table to stand beside Glenna. He placed one hand on her trembling shoulder. "Glenna's my wife. We'll be leaving on the train tomorrow, heading for my new pastorate in Idaho City."

Daddy's face reddened further, and he shook his fist in front of David's nose. "Glenna is *my* daughter, and you can't have her! She's staying here, not traipsing off to Idaho with some high-and-mighty Bible-thumper!"

Glenna's ears burned, and her eyes stung with unwanted tears. Her father and her new husband were arguing over her. She'd been Daddy's girl for eighteen years. She'd only been Rev. David Green's wife a few hours. Anxiety gnawed at her insides, but she knew she had a choice to make. Who should she stay with? Her chin quivered as she considered her options. "David is my husband. I'm going with him."

David tensed protectively when Garret Moore grabbed Glenna's arm. "Have you taken leave of your senses? You're my daughter, and I've always met your needs."

"The way you did on the train?" David asked between clenched teeth.

"Glenna wouldn't have a father right now if I hadn't jumped," Garret snarled, though he did release his grip on Glenna's arm. "Those card sharks were gonna kill me. I had to make a quick escape, and I figured I'd make it to Granger, then meet up with Glenna when the train stopped here. How was I to know she'd go and do something so foolish as gettin' hitched up with the likes of you?"

David stepped closer to Garret, nearly knocking him into his buddy, Alvin. "I'm sorry about all your troubles, Mr. Moore, but if you hadn't been gambling in the first place—"

"Don't you go preachin' at me, Sonny!" Garret shouted. "I've made a fair enough living at my trade, and my daughter's never done without." He perused Glenna a few moments and frowned. "Are ya comin' with me or not?"

David's spirits slid straight to his boots. What if Glenna had changed her mind? What if he had no wife to take to his new pastorate after all? Relief bubbled up in his chest when she shook her head, but it ripped at David's heartstrings to see her so shaken and torn. He knew she'd always been "Daddy's girl," and deciding to stay with him rather than go with her father could not have been an easy decision.

Garret shrugged his shoulders. "Suit yourself, Daughter, but if you change your mind, I'll be at Mrs. O'Leary's boardinghouse." With that, he grabbed his pal's arm and practically pushed him out of the room.

As Glenna stood staring out their hotel room window, her thoughts became a tangled web of confusion. She hadn't been this upset since Daddy jumped off the train three days ago. It was hard to find any joy over her marriage, especially after learning that her father was alive. Knowing that she and David would be leaving tomorrow and she'd probably never see Daddy again didn't help her mood either. Even if she and David ever returned to Granger for a visit with David's friend, what were the chances that Daddy would be there? Daddy never stayed anywhere very long. He'd get bored and decide to move on to the next town, or someone would catch him cheating, and he'd be run out of town with the threat of jail or a bullet in his back.

Glenna wished Daddy could find forgiveness for his sins and know the sweet sense of peace she'd found by asking Jesus into her heart. She knew there was nothing she could do for Daddy now but pray.

Forcing all thoughts of her father aside, Glenna concentrated on her new husband. David had seemed a bit distant since they'd left the hotel dining room and come upstairs to their room. Was he sorry he'd married her? Had Daddy's unexpected appearance marred their future? Maybe David thought she really wanted to go with Daddy and was only staying with him out of obligation. Despite the fact that she hardly knew David Green, Glenna was certain of one thing—her husband was a good person. He was a man of God, not some drunk who thought nothing of gambling away his money as though it were no more than a jar of glass marbles.

Goose bumps erupted on Glenna's arms as David stepped up behind her, wrapping his comforting arms around her waist. She'd thought he was still sitting in the cane-backed chair across the room, reading his Bible.

"Glenna, I think we should talk." David's words came out in a whisper, caressing her ear with the warmth of his breath.

She leaned into him, relishing the closeness of his body and the way his embrace made her feel so protected. She drew in a deep breath, letting it out in a lingering sigh. She knew it was ridiculous because they barely knew one another, but she had fallen hopelessly in love with this man. The question was, did David return her feelings or was he merely being kind? Did David see her as a woman he could love or just a needy person he felt obligated to care for?

"I appreciate your being willing to marry me," she murmured. "I know it wasn't in your plans, but I'm very grateful."

"I think we need to talk," David repeated.

She nodded mutely and allowed him to take her hand. He led her over to the bed, and they both took a seat. "I realize seeing your father today was quite a shock," he said softly.

"I never thought he could survive such a fall," she admitted.

"Glenna, I—"

"He abandoned me on that train," she said, cutting him off. "Now Daddy thinks I should abandon you."

"And would you?"

Unwanted tears rolled down her cheeks. "Daddy doesn't care about me anymore." She sniffed deeply. "And I care nothing for him."

David's fingers clasped her own, and warmth spread quickly up her arms as she savored the feel of his gentle touch. She relished the feeling of safety she had with David and was confident she could trust him never to abandon her the way Daddy had.

"You must forgive your father, Glenna," David said.

She shrugged. The motion was all she could manage, given the circumstances. Talking about her father was too painful right now. Besides, she didn't want to forgive Daddy. She was angry with him. Could it be that she was staying with David only to get even with Daddy?

David draped an arm around her shoulder, pulling her close. He bent his head slightly, and she was sure he was about to kiss her. To her disappointment, he pulled away suddenly and stood up. "We'd best settle down for the night and get some sleep." His words trailed off in a yawn. "You can have the bed, and I'll sleep on the floor." He dipped his head, refusing to make eye contact with her. "Good night, Glenna."

Glenna awoke the following morning feeling as though her head had been stuffed with a wad of cotton. Last night had been her wedding night, and she hadn't slept well. Visions of Daddy and David had danced through her head like storm clouds. Did either of them love her at all? Did anyone love her? David said God loved her, but God was a spirit. How could He ever meet all her needs?

She was thankful when they went down to breakfast and found that Daddy was nowhere around. Since David obviously didn't love her, she'd actually been having some thoughts about staying in Granger with Daddy. If she saw him again, she might weaken. Glenna knew in her heart that a marriage without love would be preferable to her previous life as a gambler's daughter. She'd made up her mind. As difficult as it would be to board that train, she was going to Idaho City with her husband!

A short time later, she and David were seated on a wooden bench in front of the train station. Glenna glanced about, tugging nervously on the strings of her handbag. *I'm doing the right thing,* she kept telling herself. *I am a new creature in Christ now. I can never go back to my old way of life, no matter how much I might miss Daddy.*

"You look pale. Are you all right?" David asked, eyeing her with a look of concern.

She gave a slight nod and kept her voice strong. "I'll

be fine once we board the train."

Gazing down at the open Bible in his lap, David offered a half smile. "I hope so."

When a familiar voice called out her name, Glenna jerked her head up. Daddy was heading their way. She jumped to her feet, clenching her fists in anticipation for what he might say or do.

"Glenna, I'm so glad I caught you before the train left," Daddy panted. "I have something to give you."

David was at her side now, and she felt his hand at the small of her back. "We have no need of tainted money, Mr. Moore," he said evenly.

Her father laughed, shaking his head and reaching into his jacket pocket. "It's not money I wish to give. I want my daughter to have her mother's wedding ring." He held up a delicate gold band and handed it to Glenna.

She stood there, mouth hanging open and eyes filled with tears. "This was Mama's ring?"

His head bobbed up and down. "I've been holding it until you got married. Please take the ring, Glenna. Your mother would have wanted you to have it."

Glenna glanced briefly at David. His brows were furrowed, and his lips were set in a fine line. "I had no ring to give you on our wedding day," he mentioned. "I think it would be a good thing if you wore your mother's ring, don't you?"

She accepted the gift then, letting her father slip it on the ring finger of her left hand. The fact that Daddy had sought her out, offering such a fine present and not making a scene about her being married or going to Idaho City made Glenna feel guilty for her bitter feelings. She swallowed past the lump in her throat. "Thank you, Daddy. I'll cherish this ring for the rest of my life."

Daddy's eyes filled with tears. She'd never seen him cry before and was taken by surprise. He opened his mouth as if to say something, but the words never came. With no warning whatsoever, an ear-piercing shot rang out. Daddy dropped like a sack of grain at Glenna's feet.

Chapter 8

Glenna screamed, then collapsed to the ground beside her father's body. Daddy wasn't breathing. Dark blood oozed from a bullet wound that had obviously penetrated his back and gone clear through to his chest.

David spun around and raced off toward the gunman. There was chaos everywhere. Some nearby folks screeched in terror, others ran about calling for help, and a few stayed to offer comfort to a very distraught Glenna.

It was inconceivable, but in the short span of a few days, she'd lost her father twice. First, when he'd jumped from the moving train and now from a bullet in the back!

"How could this have happened?" she sobbed. "How could God be so cruel?" She observed the faces staring down at her with apparent pity. They were all faces of strangers. Where was David? Had he abandoned her too?

Glenna sat in her seat, ramrod stiff, barely aware of the irritating sway of the train, and not noticing any of her surroundings. She felt cold and empty inside. Even the warm hand placed upon her own did nothing to console her anguished soul. Everything was so final. Daddy was gone, and there had been no chance to make amends or even say a proper good-bye. There hadn't been any possibility for her to witness about God's redeeming love either. She'd failed Daddy, and God had failed her. She would probably let David down as well. How could she possibly go to Idaho City and be a pastor's wife when she felt so dead inside? Why had she ever agreed to this marriage of convenience in the first place? She'd been foolish to get caught up in the silly notion that her life could be better. Her hopes and dreams for the future had been buried, right along with Daddy's lifeless body. The words Pastor Hunter said at the grave site this morning had done little to comfort Glenna's aching heart.

She glanced down at the golden band on her left hand. It was all she had left of her mother, and giving it to her had been the last good thing Daddy had ever done. Maybe it was the *only* good thing he'd ever done.

Glenna's thoughts swept her painfully back to yesterday. She could still see Daddy racing eagerly toward her. In her mind's eye, she saw his apologetic smile, heard the words of love, and felt his warm hand as he slipped Mama's ring onto her finger. Glenna tried to stop what came next, but it was to no avail. She could hear that fatal gunshot echoing in her head as though it were happening again. The image of Daddy's pale face and blood-soaked shirt would be inscribed in her brain for as long as she lived. She had known he was gone, even before the doctor came along and pronounced him dead.

There had been no train trip that afternoon. Instead, she and David spent the next several hours in the sheriff's office, giving him the sketchy details of the unexpected shooting. David had seen the murderer, and he'd even chased after him. The gunman had vanished as quickly as he'd appeared. Quite possibly her father's killer would never be caught or punished.

David had sent a telegram to one of his church members, letting him know they were going to be detained another day and, Lord willing, would leave for Idaho City the following afternoon. Rev. Hunter agreed to do the graveside service for Daddy the next morning, and they would be spending another night in the Granger Hotel.

Glenna swallowed against the lump in her throat. Their second night had been even worse than the first. David slept on the floor again, and she'd refused to even look at him or say a single word. There was a part of her that blamed David for all this. Had he not suggested they get married, she would have simply gotten off the train in Granger, gone looking for a job, and sooner or later would have run into Daddy. If she hadn't married David, Daddy might still be alive.

As frustration and exhaustion closed in like a shroud, Glenna shut her eyes. Leaning her head against the window, she let much-needed sleep claim her weary body.

David watched the rhythmic rise and fall of Glenna's steady breathing. He was glad she'd finally given in to sleep. She had been too distraught to sleep much of the night before and had withdrawn into a cocoon of silence. His heart ached for her, yet he had no idea how to draw Glenna out. It would probably be most appropriate to leave her alone for now, letting grief run its course in whatever way she chose. During his ministerial training, David had been taught about the various stages of bereavement a person went through when losing a loved one. The first was shock. Later came denial or a great sense of loss, often accompanied by depression. Glenna appeared to be in the first stage right now, which was no doubt for the best. David needed time to read the Scriptures and pray, asking for God's wisdom in helping her through this grieving process.

It was interesting, he noted, that she hadn't been nearly as despondent when her father jumped off the train and she thought he'd been killed. Perhaps this "second death" was more traumatic since Garret had been murdered in cold blood, right in front her. His death was final. No more wondering if he might have survived, and no more anger because he'd taken his own life. This time he'd been killed by an assassin, plain and simple. Who the man was, why he'd fired the fateful shot, and where he had gone was still a mystery which might never be solved. David's job as Glenna's husband was to help her through this difficult time, no matter how long it took. He owed her that much.

David ran his fingers through his sweat-soaked hair, as troubled thoughts took him back to the last two nights spent at the Hotel Granger. It had been a difficult decision, but he'd chosen to sleep on the floor, not wanting to rush his new bride into something she might not be ready for yet. Perhaps it had been a mistake to do so, but it was in the past and couldn't be changed.

He released a deep sigh and glanced over at her again. The truth was, David wasn't sure about his feelings for the sleeping woman who sat beside him. Was it love or merely a sense of obligation that invaded his senses every time she looked his way? There was no point in leading her on. They both needed more time. Time to get to know one another. Time to grow in their relationship. For some reason she hadn't asked about his past, and he hoped she wouldn't hate him once she learned the truth.

Glenna awoke from her nap feeling a bit more rested but still deeply troubled. She peeked over at David. In one hand he held his Bible; in the other was a deck of cards. They were Daddy's cards—the same ones he'd left on the seat before he jumped off the train. She'd thrown the cards on the floor, and David had retrieved them, later using the deck as some sort of parallel to things written in the Bible. Glenna was surprised to see that David still had those cards. Why hadn't he thrown them away? What would a God-fearing, Bible-teaching preacher need with a deck of cards?

David must have caught her staring at him, for he turned in his seat and smiled. "Good, you're awake. Did you rest well?"

Her only reply was a stiff nod. What did he care—this husband who slept on the floor and had spoken only a few words to her since Daddy's death?

David stuffed the Bible into his jacket pocket, but he

kept the cards held firmly in one hand. With the other hand he reached out to touch Glenna's arm. "You've been through a horrible ordeal, but in time God will heal your internal wounds."

Glenna scowled at him. "I'm not so sure. If God makes bad things happen to people, then He's no better than Daddy! How can I count on Him to heal anything?"

David averted his gaze to the deck of cards. "God doesn't *make* bad things happen to His children, Glenna. He *allows* them."

"Why? Why would a loving Father let bad things happen to His children?"

David fanned out the deck. "These cards are an example of God's love for me."

She tipped her head in question.

"I haven't told you much about my past, and you've been kind enough not to ask." He pinched the bridge of his nose and frowned. "There are some things I think you should know. Especially since I've taken you to be my wife and to share in my ministry."

"I don't understand."

David cleared his throat and shuffled the cards on his knees. "There was a time when I was no better than your father." His eyes glazed over as he stared out the window. He appeared to be transported to another time. . .another place.

Glenna waited patiently for him to come to grips with whatever he needed to say. It was hard to imagine David Green being anything like Daddy.

After several moments, David turned to look at her

again. "I—uh—used to be a gambler."

Glenna's mouth dropped open and she gasped. "You what?"

"I gambled and cheated people, just the way your father did."

Glenna felt her whole body begin to sway, and she knew it was not from the motion of the train. Her head felt light, and her vision began to blur. She needed fresh air. She had to get away from David. Bounding from her seat, Glenna started down the aisle.

"Where are you going?" David called after her. "Please come back and let me explain."

Glenna kept moving as fast as her wobbly legs would allow. By the time she reached the end of their car and had stepped through the door to the platform, Glenna was sure she was going to lose the little bit of food she'd eaten before they boarded the train.

Grasping the cold, metal railing, she leaned her head over the side and breathed deeply. Since the weather was warm and humid, it wasn't fresh air, but at least she was away from David—her gambling husband. He'd lied to her. He'd led her on and made her believe he would take care of her. David was right—he was no better than Daddy. She had no one now. A little voice in the back of her mind whispered, *You have Me, Glenna. I will never leave you, nor forsake you.*

Scalding tears streamed down her face, and she cried out in anguish, "Dear Father, is that You?"

"No, it's me! Your old man's dead." A deep, grinding voice sliced through the air like a knife.

Glenna whirled around to confront a stocky, red-faced man. He wore a patch over one eye and held a gun in his hand. She opened her mouth to scream, but it was too late to cry for help. One beefy, moist hand clamped across her mouth as the man jerked her roughly to his chest. "Where is it?" he growled. "Where's the money?"

Chapter 9

With the man's clammy hand planted firmly over her mouth and his foul-smelling body pressing her up against the hard railing, Glenna could neither move nor speak. She wiggled and squirmed, but it was to no avail.

"Hold still, or I'll toss ya over the side," he hissed.

Glenna stiffened, unable to understand what was going on or why. She'd come out for some air and to get away from David. She never expected something like this to happen.

The man held the tip of his derringer at Glenna's back, squishing her against the iron rail. "I'm gonna take my hand off your mouth now. If ya cry out, I'll pitch ya on over, is that clear?"

Glenna could only nod. Tears of frustration coursed down her flaming cheeks while icy fingers of fear crept up her spine. She'd made another unwise decision. She should have stayed in her seat and let David explain about his past life. No matter how much it hurt to hear that he'd once been a gambler, it was nothing compared to the way she was feeling now. Gripping the rail, she stood motionless, waiting for her captor to remove his hand.

In one quick motion, the man jerked his hand away, then pushed the gun tightly into her back. "I wanna know where that money is, and I need to know now!"

"Wh—wh—what money?" she stammered.

His hand went to her throat, and he gave it a warning squeeze. "Don't play coy with me. Your daddy had my money, and I saw him give it to you before he died."

"No, no, he didn't. All Daddy gave me was my mother's ring." Glenna held up her hand. "I know nothing about any money."

"Ah—hem! Is there some kind of problem here?"

Glenna turned her head toward the sound of a man's deep voice. It was the conductor. She breathed a sigh of relief. Everything would be all right now. She'd be safe, and this horrible man with putrid breath would soon be locked away in the baggage car until the train stopped at the next town. Then he'd be hauled off to jail, which was exactly where he belonged!

"Nope, there ain't no problem here," the evil man said to the conductor. His hand went to Glenna's waist and he swiveled around, pulling her with him. "Me and the little lady was just havin' a friendly chat whilst we got us a whiff of fresh air."

Glenna felt the tip of his gun and wished it could be seen by the conductor. She nodded at the man in uniform, offering him the weakest of smiles. "Everything's fine."

The conductor hesitated, but a few seconds later he

tipped his hat and opened the door to enter the car.

A sense of relief washed over Glenna, but it was quickly replaced with one of fear. The man wearing the eye patch wanted his money, and he was convinced she had it. Not knowing what else to do, Glenna sent up a quick prayer. *Help me, God. I need You now.*

David reached into his vest pocket, drew out a gold pocket watch and flipped it open to check the time. It was a little after four. Glenna had been gone nearly half an hour. How much more time did she need to cool down? David knew it wasn't her body that needing cooling though. Glenna had been madder than a wet hen when she'd stormed off without a word of explanation. Had he been a fool to believe he could divulge the secrets of his past and not have her react unfavorably? After being drug from town to town all her life, never knowing the security of a real home, how else would Glenna have reacted? He thought she'd found a sense of peace when she accepted Jesus as her Savior. Had he undone all that by his untimely confession? *If only she'd allowed me to explain,* he fretted. *I really believed I could tell my story and make Glenna see how God changed me. I'd hoped she might even see how a simple deck of cards can be used for good, to teach others about the Lord.*

David rubbed his fingers along his chin, suddenly missing the beard he used to hide behind. *I haven't gambled in years and wouldn't dream of using marked cards now, much less cheat anyone out of their money.* He leaned to the left, trying to see up the aisle. He could see nothing through the small window of the door leading to the open platform. He glanced down at his timepiece again. If Glenna didn't return to her seat in the next five minutes he was going out there!

Held at gunpoint, up against the railing again, Glenna felt as helpless as a pitiful baby bird caught between two cats. If only she could make the man believe she had no money. Maybe then he would leave her alone. *God, if You see me safely through this, I promise to go back to David and let him explain things about his past,* she prayed. *Perhaps David really has changed. Maybe he isn't like Daddy at all.*

Glenna leaned her head as far away from the man as possible. She could feel his hot breath against the back of her neck. She could hear his heavy, ragged breathing. "I don't know who you are, Mister, and I don't understand why you think I have your money, but I can assure you—"

Slap! The man's fat hand connected to the back of Glenna's head.

Her head snapped forward. Stinging tears streamed down her burning cheeks, and she clamped her mouth shut in an effort to keep from crying out. Where was God, her Father, now? It appeared as if He had abandoned her too.

"Garret Moore cheated me outa all my money at the gamblin' table a few nights ago," the man sputtered. "I seen him hand it over to you, then I shot him."

Glenna gasped. So this was her father's murderer! The one David had chased. The one who'd vanished as quickly as he'd appeared. Apparently the man had followed them when they boarded the train. He'd obviously been hiding out somewhere, waiting for the chance to accost her. If she didn't give him what he wanted, there was a good chance he would kill her too. But how could she give him what she didn't have? It was an impossible situation. Unless. . .

"My mother's ring is made of pure gold," she rasped. "Might I give that to you, in exchange for the money you lost?"

"I didn't lose it," he snarled. "It was stolen from me, plain and simple."

"I'm sorry about your misfortune, but I have no money, and Mama's ring. . ."

"Hang your mama's ring!" he bellowed. "I didn't kill a man or board this train for some stupid circle of gold that probably ain't worth half what your old man took from me." He squeezed Glenna's arm, and she winced. "Now, what's it gonna be, Sister? Are ya ready to talk, or do you wanna join your daddy in death?"

Glenna opened her mouth to reply, but she was cut off by a voice she recognized. "What's going on here?"

The would-be killer whirled around, pulling Glenna with him. "This ain't none of your business! Now get back in that car and be quick about it!"

"I'm afraid you're wrong," David said evenly. "I'm married to the woman you're holding at gunpoint. That makes it my business."

The sight of David standing there snatched Glenna's breath away, and she shot him a pleading look. David didn't seem to notice though. He was holding a Bible in one hand, and his mouth was set in a determined line. He may not love her, but he obviously cared for her safety. Perhaps she'd been wrong about him being like Daddy.

"Your little woman has somethin' that belongs to me," the sinister man growled. "I aim to get it back, so you'd better not try to interfere."

Glenna's eyes filled with fresh tears, and her voice quavered. "I don't have his money, David. The only thing Daddy gave me was my mother's ring."

"That's right. I was there when he did. Garret Moore never gave her any money at all." David waved the Bible. "I'm a minister of the gospel. I wouldn't lie about something like this."

"Humph!" the man scoffed. "You would say that. All you Bible-thumpers want is money. Why, you'd do most anything to wangle some cash outa good folks."

"That isn't true. I'm sure David would never try to take people's money," Glenna defended. With her newfound faith in him, she offered her husband a weak smile, and he responded with one of his own.

David's gaze darted back to Glenna's captor. "I'm asking you nicely to let my wife go." He took a few steps forward, but the evil man lowered his head and charged like a billy goat. The blow caught David in the stomach, and it left him sprawled on the wooden platform, gasping for breath.

Free of the gambler for the first time, Glenna seized the opportunity at hand. With no thought for her own safety and feeling a need to help David, she began railing on the man's back with her fists.

At first, the fellow just stood there, grinning as though

he was amused at her feeble attempts. After a few seconds, he grabbed one of Glenna's wrists and jerked her to his side. "Take one last look at your woman, preacher-man, 'cause I'm about to shoot her dead if she don't tell me where that money's hid."

David struggled to sit up, then lifted the Bible over his head. "In the name of Jesus, I command you to reconsider."

Much to Glenna's surprise, the gunman dropped his weapon to the floor and extended both hands in the air.

A slight shuffling noise drew Glenna's attention off her husband's astonished face to the man standing directly behind him. The tall, brawny sheriff, wearing a gold star pinned to the front of his brown leather vest, stepped forward to apprehend his prisoner.

David stood up, and Glenna rushed into his arms, nearly knocking them both to the floor.

Chapter 10

With the aid of the conductor in front and David behind, Glenna stepped wearily from the train. They had finally arrived in Boise City and would be traveling by wagon to Idaho City, their final destination. The trip from Granger had taken two days, climbing steep mountains, threading their way through dark tunnels, and creeping along dizzying shelves, hundreds of feet above the river. Glenna was exhausted and wasn't relishing the bumpy ride in a hard-seated buckboard, but at least they could stop whenever they pleased, and there would be plenty of fresh air.

Their last days on the train had been rather quiet. Glenna wanted David to tell her more about his past, but he thought it best to wait until they were heading to Idaho City in the wagon. David had spent a lot of time reading his Bible and praying, and she'd done the same. Maybe it would make a difference when they did take the time to talk things out.

Glenna found a seat inside the train station, where

she would wait with their luggage while David went to the livery stable for a wagon. Butterflies played tag in her stomach whenever she thought about the days ahead. Would she and David ever be able to communicate? Could she find the courage to tell him what was truly in her heart? Would their pasts always lie between them like a barbed wire fence, or could they use those terrible things to build a firm foundation for their marriage and David's ministry?

Glenna's head jerked up when David touched her arm. "Ready to go?"

She offered him a hesitant smile. "Ready as I'll ever be."

David loaded their suitcases and the supplies he'd purchased for the trip into the back of the wagon, then covered it all with a canvas tarp. He went around to help Glenna into her seat, but to his surprise, she was already sitting there with a strange look on her face. He cast her a sidelong glance as he climbed into his own seat and took up the reins. "All set?"

She merely nodded in reply.

They rode without conversation for nearly an hour, the silence broken only by the steady *clip-clop* of the horses' hooves over the rutted trail leading them northward. The warm afternoon sun beat down on their heads, and David began to pray for traveling mercies on this trip which would take a day and a half.

"The landscape here in Idaho is much different than the plains of Nebraska," Glenna said, breaking into David's prayer.

"That's right. Lots of tall, rugged hills surrounding the area."

A gentle sigh escaped her lips. "I've never been this far west. It's beautiful."

He smiled. She liked the land. That was a good sign. Yes, a very good sign.

"Will you tell me about your past now?" Glenna asked suddenly. If their marriage was ever going to work, she really did need to know more about this husband of hers, even if it wasn't all to her liking.

David tipped his head. "I suppose it is time I tell you."

Glenna leaned back in her seat, making herself as comfortable as possible, while David began his story. "I was born in Ames, Iowa. When I was sixteen, my parents and younger brother, Dan, were killed."

"What happened?"

"There was a fire. Our whole house burned down, and they were all inside."

Glenna gasped. "How awful! Were you in the house too?"

He shook his head. "I was spending the night at my cousin Jake's. I didn't even know about the fire until the next morning. I came home expecting some of Mom's delicious buttermilk flapjacks for breakfast. Instead, I found nothing but the charred remains of what used to be our home."

Even from a side view, Glenna could see the grief written on David's face. The tone of his voice was one of regret too. She knew what it felt like to lose both her parents and a little brother. She and David had that much in common.

"What did you do after you found your house burned and knew your family was gone?" she prompted, laying a hand on his arm.

David gripped the reins a bit tighter, and a muscle in the side of his cheek began to twitch. "I lit out on my own, and I never went home again."

Glenna's mouth fell open. "But you were only sixteen. How did you—"

"Support myself?"

She nodded.

"I learned the fine art of gambling," he replied tersely. "I traveled from town to town, cheating people out of their money, lying, stealing, cursing the day I'd been born, and blaming myself for my family's deaths."

"How could you be held accountable for that? You said you weren't even at home when the fire started."

David blew out a ragged breath. "I didn't start the fire, but if I'd been there, I might have saved a life or two."

She studied him intently. "Maybe you would have been killed too. Have you ever thought about that?"

He shrugged. "There were days when I wished I had been."

Glenna sat there awhile, letting his words sink in. Hadn't she felt the same way after Daddy was killed? Maybe it was part of the grieving process to think such thoughts. "How did you get away from the life of gambling?" she finally asked.

He turned his head and offered her a heart-melting smile. "Pastor James Hunter found me, and I found the Lord."

"He *found* you? I don't understand."

"Some men—gamblers I met on a riverboat in Mississippi—beat me up real bad and dumped me in the river. Jim was fishing nearby, and he saved me from drowning."

"But Pastor Hunter lives in Granger, Wyoming," she reminded.

David chuckled. "True, but he didn't always live there. He used to pastor a church down south."

"So, he saved your life and told you about Jesus, much like you did for me."

"That's right. I saw the light—like Paul in the Bible on his trip to Damascus. Shortly after my conversion, I felt led to become a minister. I traveled as a circuit riding preacher for a few years, then finally went to Hope Academy in Omaha, Nebraska, for more training. That's when the church here in Idaho called me to be their full-time pastor."

"God changed your heart," she said softly. "I should have known by your actions that you were nothing like Daddy."

"Glenna, about your father. . ."

"Yes?"

"I really believe it might help if you talked about your feelings toward him."

"There's nothing to say," she snapped. "Daddy's dead, and the only good thing he ever did was give me this." She held up her left hand to show him her mother's wedding band.

"I believe there's some good in all men," David

murmured. "After all, your father married your mother, didn't he?"

She only nodded in response.

"Through their union you were created, and that was a good thing."

A small, whitewashed wooden structure, which David referred to as "the parsonage," stood next to a tall white church. This was to be their new home. Glenna swallowed back the lump which had formed in her throat. One week ago she had no home at all. Now, thanks to her impetuous decision to marry Rev. David Green, Glenna was about to take up residence in Idaho City—as a minister's wife, for goodness' sake. Never in a million years had she expected her life to take such a turn. Even if David didn't love her the way she loved him, she would at least have a sense of belonging.

As they stepped down from the wagon, a short, middle-aged man with a balding head came bounding out of the church. His smile stretched from ear to ear as he extended one hand toward David. "So you're the new preacher." He looked Glenna up and down, then nodded in apparent approval, grinning at her too. "This must be the little woman. A bit younger than we expected, but I'm sure she'll fit in with some of our ladies."

David shook the man's hand. "This is my wife, Glenna. And you are—"

"Deacon Eustace Meyers," the little man said with a flutter of his eyelids. "You need anything done around the church, and I'm your man. You need a meeting called, and I'll get the word spread, quick as a wink."

Glenna bit back the laughter threatening to bubble up from her throat. She had no doubt about the ability of Deacon Meyers to get something done."

"I'll show you the house first," Eustace said, nodding toward the smaller building. "I'm sure you're wantin' to get settled in and all."

David grabbed two suitcases from the back of the wagon, and Eustace carried one of the supply boxes. Glenna followed, wondering if all David's church members were as friendly and helpful as the deacon seemed to be.

Once inside, Glenna wandered from room to room, inspecting her new home. It was small but quite service-able. Besides the living room, there was a homey little kitchen, one bedroom downstairs, and a modest loft overhead. This would no doubt serve as David's office or perhaps be used as a guest room, should they ever have overnight company.

As David and Eustace talked about the church, which members he should get to know right away, and how many places of business were in this mining town, Glenna relished her new surroundings. She sent up a silent prayer, thanking God for being so good as to give her a place to call home. Her only concern was whether she could be the kind of wife David needed. As long as she harbored resentment toward Daddy, Glenna knew her ability to minister to others would be impaired.

"I'll leave you two to get settled in now," she heard the deacon tell David. He moved toward the front door, then just as he was about to exit, he turned back around.

"Oh, I almost forgot to give you this." He reached inside his shirt pocket and pulled out a piece of paper. "It's a telegram. . .for you, Mrs. Green."

"For me?" Glenna couldn't imagine who might be sending her a telegram.

"Are you going to read it, or should I?" Eustace asked, stepping up beside her. "I've had an eighth grade education, you know."

"I can read it myself, thank you," Glenna replied.

The deacon nodded and stepped outside.

Glenna's hands began to tremble as she studied the telegram.

David pulled her to his side. "What's wrong? Is it bad news?"

She shook her head. "No, quite the contrary, it's good news."

"Are you going to share this good news?" he prodded.

"The telegram says there's money waiting for me. . .at the bank here in town."

"Money? From whom?"

She shrugged. "I don't know. It just says I should go to the bank and ask about a bank draft made out in my name." She moistened her lips with the tip of her tongue. "Do you think it's a joke?"

"I don't know," David replied. "I guess the only way to find out is to make a trip over to the bank. Would you like to go right now?"

She nodded. "Yes, please."

The bank president greeted them enthusiastically, stating

that he and his family attended David's church and would be in service on Sunday morning. When Glenna showed him the telegram, Mr. Paulson beamed. "Yes, indeed. I have a bank draft in my safe, made out for quite a tidy little sum. There's a note attached to it as well."

Glenna and David took seats, while Mr. Paulson went in the back to get the money in question. When he returned, he handed the legal paper to Glenna, along with a handwritten note. It was Daddy's handwriting! She'd have recognized it anywhere. But how? When?

"David, this draft is from my father," she squeaked. "The letter's from him too. Daddy says he was once a God-fearing man. After losing Mama and my little brother, Daddy walked away from God and turned to whiskey bottles and the gambling table for comfort." She swallowed against the tide of tears threatening to spill over. "Daddy says he kept Mama's dowry all these years. He never spent any of it. . .not even when he'd gambled everything else away. When Daddy left the hotel in Granger, he decided to wire Mama's dowry money here, knowing this was where I'd be living with you."

David lifted a finger to wipe away the tears streaming down Glenna's cheeks. "There *was* some good in your father. It could be that he turned back to God before his death too."

David's tender words and warm smile made Glenna's heart beat so fast she thought she might fall right out of her chair. She smiled through her tears. "I was Daddy's girl all my life. Now Daddy's gone, but my true father is God. I know you're not in love with me, David, but I believe God sent you to me."

As they left the bank, Glenna leaned into David. "I love you, Pastor Green, and I'm going to try to be the best wife I can." She moved to stand in front of David, then boldly wrapped her arms around his neck. With no thought of their surroundings or who might be watching, she kissed him full on the mouth.

David responded by returning her kiss, sending a cascade of glorious shivers down her back. "I probably haven't shown it too well, but I do love you, Glenna," he whispered. "I've been asking myself for the last several days why God put us together on the same train. The answer He put in my mind kept coming back the same—we were meant for each other."

Glenna released a sigh of relief. Until this very moment, she'd never felt more loved or cherished.

"I found you, and you found God," David whispered against her ear.

"Yes, and since God is my Father, I'll always be Daddy's girl."

WANDA E. BRUNSTETTER

Wanda lives in Central Washington with her husband who is a pastor. She has two grown children and six grandchildren. Her hobbies include doll repairing, stamping, reading, and gardening. Wanda and her husband have a puppet ministry, which they often share at other churches, Bible camps, and Bible schools.

Wanda writes stories, articles, poems, and puppet plays, but her main emphasis is on inspirational romance. She's had two Heartsong novels published, and this is her second Barbour novella. Wanda invites you to visit her website: http://hometown.aol.com/rlbweb/index.html

A Heart's Dream

by Birdie L. Etchison

Dedicated to my sister,
Barbara Ann Rutledge,
though gone from this life she will continue
to be a source of inspiration for me.
She loved trains.

Chapter 1

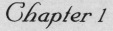

June 1900—Creston, Iowa

Charlotte stood at the end of the lane, looking back one last time. The house, the only home she'd ever known, now stood empty. Sunshine cast shadows on the old clapboards badly needing paint. Perhaps the new owner would paint it and make it beautiful once again. She bit back the tears.

The furniture, linens, dishes, and pots and pans had been sold at an auction; she'd packed clothing and a few personal belongings in the trunk. Her heart ached with the loss. She'd hoped to find space for Grandfather's favorite painting. It was by a local artist and showed a boy on a riverbank, fishing. Done in blues and reds, it had hung in her bedroom since she could remember and was the first thing she saw each morning. It brought a handsome price from a lady who said it had "great depth." Whatever that meant.

Money was needed for the train trip. A teaching

position waited in Traer, Kansas, a small farming town on the Nebraska border. Charlotte wanted to stay and teach in Creston. She didn't care that the house looked shabby, the roof leaked, or that the fence was leaning. It was home, and she would never forget all that was so dear to her.

The trumpet vine blooming on the side of the house was one memory she would take with her. Just that morning she snipped a bit of vine and tucked it into her carpetbag. She'd put damp shredded paper around it to keep it moist and then wrapped it in a strip of oilcloth. If she watered it often, it might make it all the way to her new home in Kansas. It would take two days—one on the train and one by wagon.

So much change, too fast. First losing Grandmother, then Grandfather, obtaining a teaching certificate, now the journey. Cousin Lily, whom Charlotte had met but once before, had offered to board Charlotte and her brother, Robert, until Charlotte had enough money to find a place of her own. Lily's mother and Charlotte's mother had been sisters.

How could this have happened? Grandfather had not once said he didn't own the land or the house. Even on his deathbed, three months ago, he hadn't revealed that the bank had a lien. He'd either forgotten or simply had no money. She thought of how she'd held his hand when he was dying with a raging fever, his lips parched and bleeding. "Take care of Robert," he'd said. "You're all he has, Charlotte."

Not one word of love. No warning they'd have to

move on because neither the house nor the land was his. Mr. Anthony told her that the day after the funeral.

Once again tears threatened, but it wouldn't do to let Robert see her cry. He was only nine and seemingly had not experienced the sadness or loneliness Charlotte felt. He was excited about the adventure of traveling on the train.

"Robert!" she called now. He had hurried to the pasture to see his beloved pony. He was sadder about leaving Brown Beauty than he was about leaving the farm. Brown Beauty was named after the horse in the book *Black Beauty*. Robert was pleased that a nearby farmer had bought the pony for his daughter who was Robert's age. Still, he had said good-bye twice this morning.

She felt an arm on her sleeve. "It's all right, Lottie. We'll like it in Kansas."

He'd caught her wiping her cheeks with the back of her cotton glove. She ruffled his hair and leaned over to kiss his forehead. He was all she had, and she'd do any-thing to protect him, keep him safe.

"Isn't the wagon supposed to be here now?"

"Soon." Charlotte looked at the freckled face and concentrated on his eagerness, not the hole in his best shoes or his threadbare jacket. "Put your hat back on. You know how easily you get sunburned."

He stuffed the round-brimmed straw hat back on his head and looked up the road. Their dear neighbor, Mr. Farnsworth, had promised to take them to the train sta-tion in Creston. If they didn't leave soon, they'd miss the connection.

"I'm sure he's on his way. Don't you fret now," she said more for her own benefit than his.

A relentless sun beat out of a blue sky as she took one last look, then turned to the sound of approaching horses and wagon.

Mr. Farnsworth brought the team to a halt and tipped his hat. "Nice morning, isn't it now?"

Charlotte nodded. "It's more than a fair morning, Sir!"

"The missus sent a basket for you, something to eat on the trip. I hope you have room in your bag." He held up the small straw basket.

"Oh, thank you very much. It was so kind of her." Charlotte knew there was no room in the bag so she'd have Robert carry the basket aboard the train. Her stomach growled, but she paid it no never mind.

"Here, Robert, help me with this trunk," Mr. Farnsworth said.

They took the handles and lifted it high, setting it in the back of the wagon, then Robert climbed in.

Mr. Farnsworth turned to Charlotte. "Let me help you up!" She rode in the seat next to him, the bag on the floor by her feet, the basket of food in her lap. She'd worn her best calico, and the wide-brimmed, navy blue straw hat that had been Grandmother's Sunday-go-to-meeting bonnet. The gloves had a hole in the left palm, but she could hide it.

"It's going to seem mighty strange not to have you living next door."

Charlotte tried to smile. "I will write once I am settled," she said with a lift of her chin. "We are looking forward to this, aren't we, Robert?"

"Oh, yes, Lottie," Robert said in agreement. "I can't wait to ride the train."

Twenty minutes later, when Mr. Farnsworth pulled up to the station, it was not a moment too soon as the train whistle sounded in the distance.

Charlotte took deep breaths and murmured a short prayer. "Yes, we can do this; yes, we can do this; Lord, help us do this."

Robert had already hopped down and stood watching the giant steam engine chug slowly up the track. A big puff of steam rose as it came to a halt, mere feet from the wagon. Charlotte watched in dismay, shouting for Robert to stand back.

"The boy is excited," Mr. Farnsworth said from the ground as he held his arm up to Charlotte. "May I help you down?"

Steam still rose from the smokestack, and she wondered how she could have agreed to ride on such a monster.

From the window of the arriving train, Franklin Hill III watched as an older gentleman helped a young, slim woman from a farm wagon. She was pretty, but it was her spunky look that caught his eye. The man now beckoned to a small boy to come help with a trunk. The lad sat his basket down and ran over. It was a large trunk, and Frank sensed it was more than the two could handle. He sat his coat on the train bench and got off the train.

"Could I be of some help?" he asked.

"Yes," the man said, "thank you very much."

The trunk was hoisted onto the baggage car, and Frank, in turn, offered his assistance to the woman with eyes as blue as cornflowers while the lad climbed the steps, shouting, "Where do we sit, Lottie? Where do we sit?"

"Robert! Wait!" But the boy had disappeared inside the train, and her look of distress caused Frank to say, "I'll help you board, Miss."

The frown deepened on her face as their gazes met, then a slight smile turned up at the corners of her mouth.

"I must get on this train," she said.

"I know." Frank grabbed the satchel with one hand and offered his arm. Introductions could come later.

Charlotte had noticed the stranger light from the train and wondered if he would continue on the train, or was this his final destination? Dressed in a bowler hat, white shirt, and dark trousers and jacket, the man had a kind face and dark, warm eyes fringed with long lashes.

"Thank you," she said, her chin trembling. She lifted the skirt of the faded calico and boarded the steps.

"Where do we sit?" Robert asked again, his cheeks all red from the sun because he never kept his hat on.

"I expect anywhere we can find."

"That's one excited boy. Could see that right off." The man tipped his hat. "Name's Franklin Hill."

"And this is Lottie, and I'm Robert." Robert was all smiles, the cowlick sticking up on top of his head. The sight made Charlotte think again of Grandfather. He too had had a problem with a cowlick. "Lottie's my sister, and our last name is Lansing," Robert continued.

"Pleased to make your acquaintances," he said. "I'm sitting right across the aisle from you."

"Are you going to Kansas too, Mr. Hill?" Robert asked.

"Not as far as Kansas. I'm staying in McCook, Nebraska. And please call me Frank."

Charlotte flushed at the sound of his deep voice and withdrew her lace handkerchief. She suddenly felt faint, then remembered she'd been so busy packing the last few items and saying good-bye to the house that she hadn't eaten yet today.

"Are you okay?" Frank was there, standing over her protectively.

"Oh, my, yes. The feeling has passed."

"What passed?" Robert was suddenly interested.

"My feeling of dizziness."

"I'll just wager that you didn't eat a proper breakfast this morning," Frank said.

"I, well, it's been such a busy time, getting ready for this trip—"

"And we had to leave the farm and my pony and all our furniture, and—"

"Robert! That's quite enough."

Charlotte rarely chastised him; he looked bewildered.

She fluttered her hanky again. "We're off to stay with dear, dear Cousin Lily, and things are going to work out just fine."

"I have candy to share," Frank said, nodding as he sat back down across the aisle from Charlotte and Robert.

"Oh, goodness, no," Charlotte said. "We have this lovely lunch from Mrs. Farnsworth." She held the basket protectively to her chest.

The train gave a lurch and began rolling forward.

"We're going!" Robert yelled, holding onto his hat.

Charlotte cast him a reproachful look, then smiled. "He's been looking forward to this," she said, turning to look shyly at Frank. "We've not been on a train before."

Robert jumped up again. Charlotte wanted it to stop. She wanted more than anything to get right off this train and return home. How could she possibly go to a place she'd never been and teach school? It was almost unthinkable, but there was no turning back. God said in His Word that He would never forsake those He loved, and Charlotte was certain that God loved her. What would she do without God's love and caring spirit?

"I have something for Robert, with your permission, of course." Frank extended a long stick of peppermint candy.

"Oh!" Robert's eyebrows rose. "May I have it, Lottie? Please say yes."

"Well, maybe just this once." Charlotte knew she was far too easy on Robert. How was he to learn discipline when she always let him have his way? He was so lovable.

The train's whistle sounded again as it chugged slowly out of the station, leaving the town behind. The smell of smoke drifted into the open windows, and Charlotte held her hanky to her nose and began praying.

"I'll close the window," Frank offered. "It's open due to the summer heat, but the soot and cinders are bothersome when we first start off."

Charlotte nodded in agreement while Robert brushed

off a cinder. "That was hot," he claimed, then looked down at the tiny hole in his jacket.

"Yes, that happens every time I ride the train," Frank said.

Frank was a soothing sort of person, one a person could lean on, and Charlotte was surprised at the sudden fluttering feeling that seemed to take over her being. This feeling had nothing to do with hunger.

"I'm going to make this candy last and last." Robert had licked it to a long point. "I may make it last the whole day!"

A chuckle sounded from across the way. "No need for that, Robert. I have more where that came from." Frank produced a brown bag and opened it for the boy to see. "I never go anywhere without candy. Here, do you want one, Miss Lansing?"

"Oh, my no. But thank you. It's very kind of you." She looked at the basket Mr. Farnsworth had given her earlier. "I have something to eat right here."

Thick, white chunks of bread and slabs of ham and cheese were in one wrapper. Charlotte's stomach lurched. Two apples and cookies, the kind Mrs. Farnsworth was noted for—oatmeal raisin with pecans—were in another.

"Would you like a cookie?" Charlotte said then. "Our neighbor is one of the best cooks in Pottawattamie County."

"Why, thank you very much." He leaned over and took one of the large, round cookies.

His presence seemed to disarm her, and Charlotte wondered why she was feeling this way. A man had never come calling, but at eighteen she wondered what it might be like. Would she ever have a chance now? The last two years had been spent taking care of her sick grandparents. And, of course, Robert. Their mother had died when an influenza epidemic hit their community the year after Robert was born. Their father had left after burying his wife because, in his words, he was "dying of a broken heart."

Charlotte had tugged on his coat, begging him not to leave her and Robert, but he had gone anyway. She remembered the little cloud of dust the horse made as he galloped down the lane and out of sight. The only memento she had was a faded photo of her father as a young man before he'd married her mother. She kept the picture in a locket around her neck.

"This cookie is delicious," Frank said, shaking her out of her reverie.

"I'm glad you like it." She looked over and smiled.

His dark eyes twinkled. "I suppose you bake cookies every bit this good."

"Lottie does," Robert said. "She does all the cookin' and baking." Robert had finished his candy stick and wiped his mouth with the back of his sleeve.

"Robert! You said you were going to savor it."

Frank grinned, as if he remembered what it was like to be a little boy with a candy stick. "Don't scold the lad," he said then. "We'll get more if need be."

The train *clickety-clacked* over the tracks at a smoother pace, and suddenly Charlotte felt weary. She wanted to forget all that had transpired, forget the worries that crowded her mind though she knew and fully believed that God was in charge. She had said so many prayers this morning, and somehow she knew more would be forthcoming. If only she knew that Cousin Lily would be waiting at the station for them. Her eyelids began to close just as she heard Frank say that he was heading west to be a cowboy.

Chapter 2

Frank had no idea what a cowboy did or why the words slipped out like that. Charlotte suddenly jerked forward and stared at him as if he said he was going to be a thief or a pirate on the high seas or something equally notorious.

He had often thought about going west, but to pursue a career as a cowboy was far-fetched. Only lately had he considered it, since he wasn't sure about continuing in the medical field. If he could just forget what happened back in Ohio. . . .

"You're a *cowboy?*" Robert jumped up and down. "A cowboy ropes cows and rides big, huge bulls and rides on the range all day." He wrinkled his nose. "And what else does he do, huh, Frank?"

Frank couldn't keep from smiling. "You're thinking of a rodeo cowboy, Robert. They rope cows and ride on bucking broncos and other such feats. That's not for me." Frank did not look at Charlotte again. Her disdain was obvious.

Robert wasn't ready to let it go though. "But you could do those things, and it would be fun." Robert twirled his straw hat. "You could give up that hat you got on and have a *real* cowboy hat."

Frank laughed at that image. He certainly was not wearing anything that would fit on the open range. He'd have to add cowboy boots and one of those fancy shirts with a fringed yoke. But he had never thought of being in a rodeo. He just wanted to see what the Wild West was like.

"You do have an imagination," Frank said.

"It's from all the books he reads," Charlotte said with a nod.

At least she was looking his way again, but he knew she was not pleased with the turn their conversation had taken. Why hadn't he just said he was a doctor? Why the sudden cowboy fascination? In his travels of the past, he had discovered that people treated doctors differently. He would be asked all sorts of medical questions and expected to know the answers. Doctors were also expected to be perfect. He was not, nor could he ever be, like that. He was far too impetuous, just like the cowboy remark. Though he had in all honesty entertained the idea, he didn't plan on going through with it. It had been a whim, but now he needed to explain.

"Where are you going?" Robert asked.

"Robert." Charlotte's voice stopped him in the middle of yet another question. "That's enough talk about this going west. Leave Mr. Hill alone now."

Frank didn't want to be left alone. The child was a wonderful diversion, a blessing to be with.

He leaned forward, taking in Charlotte. She was

young. Frightened. Alone and going on a train for the first time. Anyone would be scared in those circumstances. Then too, she had the responsibility of her brother, and it had to be difficult to mother the boy when she was not much over being a child, herself. Offhand, he'd guess her to be nineteen, maybe twenty.

From the first moment he'd laid eyes on her, he knew his being on this train was definitely God's leading. When one prayed each morning for guidance and direction, God was there to help, to lean on. Frank believed that wholeheartedly.

Rest wasn't necessary, but Frank had some thinking to do. He nodded in Robert's direction, took his hat off, placed it carefully on top of his valise, and leaned back.

"Words hastily spoken cannot be taken back," Grandmother Julia had told him. He supposed he was Robert's age then. He'd never forgotten, but his quick tongue had gotten him into trouble more than once. A trip to the woodshed was often the answer, but on this particular occasion he had to go apologize to his mother for asking why she didn't get out of bed and fix him pancakes for breakfast. Illness meant nothing to him. Dying was a word in a book, something that happened to others, but not to Frank. Not until that fateful day six months later when the sheet had been pulled up over his mother's eyes after he'd been summoned in to say good-bye. Could his mother have been saved? The doctor said it was consumption, and most people died from it.

Charlotte did not want to think about what lay ahead. A

month ago she'd been secure with a house and a grand-father who was ill, but still someone for her to care for, to love. How dear he had been to her, and even when she discovered the house and farm were no longer hers, she had forgiven him. Whatever happened had happened, and God promised to provide. A verse came to mind, 2 Corinthians 9:8, one of many she had memorized sitting on Grandmother's knee: "And God *is* able to make all grace abound toward you; that ye, always having all sufficiency in all *things*, may abound to every good work."

In a dreamlike state, Charlotte thought of the daffodils and hyacinths that sprang to life each spring, the cherry and apple trees that budded and lent shade during the hot summers, bearing fruit in the autumn. She wondered if Cousin Lily lived on the prairies of Kansas, or would there be hills and trees as there had been at home? What would happen when Lily met them? Would they be wanted in this new town, or had Lily sent for them out of duty? Charlotte sighed. Time would tell. By tomorrow morning they would reach their destination and a new life would begin. . . .

Frank's voice stirred her back to the present.

"I rather think cowboys are like farmers," he was saying. "They raise cattle, grow wheat and corn. . .and it's a lot of hard work."

"But if you go west, they just have cattle," Robert said, as if he were the voice of authority.

"That could be," Frank said with a nod. "Guess I've been missing out on the exciting part of it."

"So you really *are* going out west?" Charlotte looked

at Frank. He was handsome, his smile pleasant. She thought of her father who had left Iowa and headed west. He too had been handsome and had a nice smile, and he had yearned to be a cowboy. What lured men to that kind of life? Why hadn't he stayed in Iowa or nearby in order to at least see his children? Why had he felt the need to go so far away? No, cowboys were not to be trusted.

"I like traveling," Frank said. "There's lots of country I've never explored."

"Do you know some rope tricks?" Robert looked hopeful.

"Not really. All I know is how to make a monkey out of a handkerchief and make him talk."

"Make him talk?"

Charlotte turned in her seat to stare.

"Yes, I'll show you."

In no time Frank had formed a figure out of the hanky and made it move. Robert stared in fascination at the object, knowing it couldn't talk, then back at Frank. Frank's mouth wasn't moving. Robert's jaw dropped, and Charlotte laughed at the look on his face. Ventriloquism. She'd read about it, but she had never met anyone who could throw his voice.

"That's very good," she said.

Frank turned in her direction, now using a falsetto voice. "You really think so, Ma'am?"

Charlotte laughed again. "Yes, I really think so."

"Do it again," Robert begged. "Do it again, Frank."

And so Frank told a story about a man who went on the train and then met a young boy. He spoke with a deep voice as the man and changed it to a younger sounding voice for the boy.

"Are you talking about *me?*" Robert asked.

"Could be," Frank answered in his normal tone. "What do you think?"

"Yes, I'm the boy." Robert held his hand up and tried to make it sound different, but it didn't work. "How do you do that?"

"It's something I learned many years ago."

"Do you perform anywhere?" Charlotte asked.

"No. Just do it for my own enjoyment."

"I'm with Robert. I don't see how you can talk and not move your mouth."

"It comes from within." Frank pointed to the back of his tongue. "It takes practice, of course, as all things do."

The conductor came down the aisle, interrupting their conversation as he collected tickets. Frank said something, making it look as if the conductor had said it.

The man turned and stared at Frank, then over at Robert. "That's some trick. Now which one of you did that?"

Robert pointed. "Him."

Chuckling, the conductor shuffled on past and Charlotte stifled a giggle. It had been so long since she'd had anything to laugh about, and it felt good. Her heart seemed lighter than it had when she first boarded the train back at Creston. Had God brought this man, a cowboy, into their lives for a reason? Even if only for a day, it was a blessing. She believed that one prayed for safety, for an unblemished life, and to be of service to

God. Teaching was going to be her service. The school-children would become her children. She might never marry, and that would be all right. She would raise Robert, for he had been entrusted to her care, and he mattered the most right now.

There had been a boy once. Charlotte remembered him watching her at school. He had taken her home, but when he asked to come calling, she had said no. She had no chaperon, as Grandfather was so sick. He moved away shortly after that anyway.

Charlotte leaned back and shut her eyes, resigned to a life without love.

Frank noticed Charlotte's eyes close and hoped she could rest. She was pretty; her blond curls danced from under the wide-brimmed hat. He found himself wishing she'd take it off, wanting to see her hair loose and flying as the breeze came in through a partially opened window. She was probably too young to think of settling down, and he was suddenly thinking seriously about it. He was twenty-seven, after all. Yes, there comes a time when a man should start thinking about a wife, a home. Yes, even doctors needed to be married.

His father had been a pastor, and Grandfather a circuit rider in Arkansas before that, yet Frank had never felt the calling to preach. After his little sister died, he knew he wanted to be a doctor. His father had continued to argue, but he died before Frank entered medical school.

He'd practiced in two towns in Ohio simultaneously and then answered the call from McCook. He wasn't expected for a full month but had felt the need to leave early. His tentative plans were to take the train west, go on to Oregon, and then return to Nebraska. This might allow him enough time to heal from the tragedy back in Ohio. He'd done everything he could, but a young mother had died in childbirth, and he had not been able to save the baby. He could still see the father's face, the anguish in his eyes when Frank told him they were both gone. If only he had been called to the home sooner. If only he had done something different. Try as he might, he had not been able to get that face out of his mind. Perhaps he should have gone into the ministry.

"Frank." Robert tugged on his sleeve. "I like sitting with you."

"And I like having a traveling companion."

"Lottie is sleeping, I think."

"And we need to see that she gets her rest." He put a finger to his mouth. "It's been a hard thing for her to do, moving away like that and going to a new place."

"You mean all that packing and stuff, trying to decide what we had to take and what we *had* to leave behind?"

"Yes, that." *And much more,* Frank wanted to add. More responsibility too. He couldn't explain his sudden desire to care for and protect the young woman and her brother.

"Will you send me a letter when you get to Oregon?" Robert asked, leaning forward. His feet didn't quite reach the floor so he had to lean up, which made them barely touch the wooden floorboards.

"I'm not sure of an exact location."

"I hope it's Oregon. And you can follow the Oregon Trail and the covered wagons. I wish I could go in one of them."

"Trains are the main means of transportation these days," Frank said. "I doubt that many go by way of a covered wagon now."

"Do Indians still attack?"

"No, not now. Indians live on reservations and are more peaceful."

And so began a story of a family who had lost everything and eventually their lives except for one child who then had to ride with another family.

"Sorta like me," Robert said. "I only have Lottie and if something should happen—"

Charlotte sat up at the sound of her name and scolded Robert. "You are being a pest. Now come back here and sit with me."

"He's fine," Frank said, his hand touching the boy's shoulder. "I'd like him for a seat mate, if you don't mind."

Robert's chest puffed out as he beamed.

"If you're sure—"

"Quite sure."

And as the train chugged over the miles, Frank told another story, one his father had told him countless times. It was the story of the lost sheep and about how farmers felt when they lost a sheep.

Soon Robert's head was nodding, and Frank put his coat over Robert's legs. Trains were drafty, and though it was the beginning of summer, the late afternoon breeze could turn chilly. It wouldn't do for the lad to catch cold.

Taking one more glance in Charlotte's direction, Frank was satisfied that she was okay as her head leaned against the dark green cushion. She clutched something and then he saw it was a Bible. He swallowed hard, remembering his own precious Bible in the bag he'd carried on the train. Did cowboys carry Bibles? He pondered that. If they didn't, they should. Maybe he could be the first, he thought as he allowed the train to lull him to sleep.

Chapter 3

Frank felt something touch him and jerked awake. It was Robert's head, resting against his shoulder. The coat had slipped to the floor, yet the little boy slept on. Frank's fatherly instincts gave him a warm, good feeling. Had God entrusted them to his care?

Moving slightly, so as not to disturb Robert, Frank turned to see if Charlotte was still sleeping. Her eyes were closed, and he couldn't help noticing she looked like an angel with the sun streaming in the window, casting shadows on her flushed cheeks. He was glad now he'd accepted the position in McCook. He'd be close to the small school across the border in the growing town of Traer. If she was willing, and the Lord already knew how willing Frank was, he would visit often.

He thought back to his youth and the problems he'd had in school. "Preacher's son," his classmates called him.

"Preacher's son can do no wrong." He bristled at remembering how the words stung. He'd come up fighting with both fists, and that always got him into trouble.

"Troublemaker," one teacher had labeled him. Once a

kid had a name, that was it; he was stuck with it.

He thought again of his Bible tucked in the bottom of his bag. The well-worn leather volume had been a gift the Christmas he was eight. He'd carried it ever since. He also thought about how it was assumed he would be a preacher; the last thing his grandfather had said to him was: "Carry on with the message to God's people, Son. There are lots of souls to be saved."

Frank had the last sermon his grandfather had given. There were times he wished he'd carried on with the tradition, but there was also a need for doctors. How would he ever go back to that profession? Would he be able to deliver a child without remembering that last time? For now his major concern was how he was going to reveal the truth to Charlotte and Robert.

The whistle blew three long blasts; the train braked suddenly then lurched to a grinding halt, causing their belongings to slide to the floor.

"Oh, my," Charlotte cried out, her eyes wide in a too white face. "What happened?"

Robert had wakened too, lurching to his feet while others scampered out of seats and looked around. Rubbing his eyes, he glanced over at his sister. "Lottie?"

"It's okay, Robert," Frank said. "I think there was something on the track. Probably a cow or a horse." He noted with amusement that Charlotte's hat was askew, and he longed to reach over and straighten it for her.

"Trains don't make smooth stops; it's something they're hoping to change."

Wisps of dirty air floated through the train car, landing

on the seats and floor. Charlotte coughed.

"Some day they may have it so it's not so sooty. It helps to cover your mouth," Frank said, covering his face with his hand.

"Are we almost there?" Robert asked, putting his hat back on. "I do hope so."

"Oh, no, Lad. It'll be several hours before you reach your destination."

One of the passengers had hopped off the train and had come back to report that a hay wagon had overturned on the track. "They said we'd be ready to move in ten minutes or so."

"Hay wagon?" Robert asked. "But what was a hay wagon doing on the track?"

"Might have been pulled by mules," Frank said as he winked at the boy, "and you know how cantankerous an old mule can get."

"But, wouldn't they know they were going to get hit?" Robert persisted.

"Mules don't much care, Robert."

Two people walked through the car: a lady toting a small bag and a gentleman carrying a large box. They sat toward the back of the car.

"Sorry about the unexpected stop," the man said, glancing over at Frank, then Charlotte. "That's Pa's wagon that overturned and caused all the problem."

"Can't be helped sometimes," Frank said. "At least no one was hurt."

The train lurched twice, blew its whistle, and they chugged down the track, trying to pick up steam again.

This time Charlotte was prepared as she held the hanky over her nose and mouth. The smoke didn't seem as thick, or smell quite as bad, but maybe she was getting used to it. Robert chattered, asking Frank another question. How that boy could talk.

"How long does it take to get to the West?" he asked.

Frank felt a sudden knot lodge in his throat. "I can't rightly say. Probably another four or five days."

"Oh, my, that long?" Charlotte looked serious.

"At least."

"I sure wish you were going with us, Frank," Robert broke in. "Are you sure you can't?"

"Robert, mind your manners," Charlotte chided him. "One must not assume, and what a body's got to do, they've got to do."

The trip to Oregon no longer held an interest to Frank. He could arrive at his new office a few weeks early. It was acceptable, as people would think he couldn't wait to get started.

"Do you think I could learn to be a cowboy?" Robert asked, turning in his seat. "I think that's what I'd like to do too."

"Now, Robert, let's hear no more of this nonsense." And this time Charlotte had a formidable look on her face. "You are going to Kansas with me, and that's that."

"You'll change your mind a hundred times before you grow up," Frank said. "At least I did."

"Did you ever want to be just a plain old farmer?"

"Oh, my yes. I *was* a farmer at your age."

"You were?" Robert bounced up and down in the seat.

"And now you're gonna be a cowboy."

"Oh?" The young man who had just boarded the train turned in his seat. "A cowboy?"

Frank's face reddened. "I entertained the idea once, yes." He hoped this discussion would end, as he didn't want to talk about it.

"And he can make sounds that make you think it's someone else talking."

"Oh, one of those ventri—"

"Ventriloquist," Frank finished the word.

Soon Frank was singing a song, making it sound like the voice was Charlotte's. They all laughed and asked him to do it again. Embarrassed, Frank told a story about a young boy and his sister on their first train ride and how much the boy liked it.

The young man shook his head. "Anyone who can throw their voice like that doesn't need to be a farmer or a cowboy."

Robert asked more questions while Frank gave yes or no answers.

Charlotte wondered if all boys Robert's age asked so many questions. She hoped she'd be able to answer them. She knew she would have children of various ages in a one-room schoolhouse, teaching in a place where she knew no one. If she taught in Iowa, she would have known the neighbor children, and it would have been less frightening.

She also pondered about the man who seemed to have all the answers. She gazed out the window, not wanting

Frank to see her face. It was embarrassing, but in a dream she'd seen a small child with a toothless grin beaming at her, and his hair was the very color of Frank's. The smile he wore made his dark eyes twinkle. Yet she knew school-teachers could not marry so she put the idea out of her mind immediately.

Besides, it was wrong to think about some cowboy who probably had never stepped foot in a church. Then it was as if God was chastising her, whispering to her heart, saying it was that very sort of person He loved the most.

"Oh, dear," she said aloud, suddenly realizing how terribly warm it had become inside the car. She undid the carpetbag and looked to see if the trumpet vine was okay. The shreds of paper she'd so carefully wrapped around it that morning were completely dry.

"Is something wrong?" Frank had stood and was bending over her. She nearly jumped.

"It's just that, well, I need some water."

"You're thirsty, of course. I believe I can fetch some for you."

"But it isn't me—it's for my vine."

"Vine?" Frank looked puzzled.

"Yes," Robert answered then. "Lottie brought some of the vine that grows alongside our house. She's got it in that bag."

Charlotte, feeling a bit silly, lifted out the small green slip. It drooped, and she wondered if it really would last until it was once more planted.

"What a wonderful idea. You brought part of your

farm with you. So now let's go get some water, what do you say, Robert?"

Charlotte nodded at her brother and watched as the two went up the aisle, the tall man's arm draped around Robert as if he were his own. She swallowed hard. She had to stop thinking about Frank, how she liked it when he looked at her, the way his eyes seemed to smolder. . . *What is wrong with me anyway?*

Her fingers went into the bag, touching the wrapped cookies, but it wasn't food she wanted. Not that kind. She wanted to read her Bible. She needed comforting words about now. She opened her Bible to Matthew 28:20 and read. "And, lo, I am with you always, *even* unto the end of the world. Amen."

She began humming, ever so lowly, one of her favorite hymns, "Wonderful Words of Life."

"Sing them over again to me, wonderful words of life."

Frank was back, his deep bass voice joining in, singing the words with gusto. Startled, Charlotte looked up into those eyes and trembled. "You know that song?"

"Yep. Sang it in my mother's arms at the little church we attended."

Charlotte took the water to pour around the limp slip of trumpet vine. It was a comforting thought to know that Frank knew hymns and had gone to church.

"Were you just a baby?" Robert asked, always wanting complete details.

"No, not a baby. I couldn't remember from when I was a baby, now could I? No, I was closer to six, maybe seven."

Charlotte had wonderful memories of sitting on her mother's lap; Robert did not. He often asked about his mother. All Charlotte had was one picture in a safe place in the huge trunk and her own recollections to pass on.

"Sing it again," Robert urged. "I like your voice."

I do too, Charlotte wanted to say, *oh, I do too,* but she said nothing as Frank's voice filled the car, then another voice joined in and yet another. Last was Charlotte in her high soprano singing the beloved song:

Let me more of their beauty see,
*   Wonderful words of life*
Words of life and beauty,
*   Teach me faith and duty,*
Beautiful words, wonderful words,
*   Wonderful words of life*

The singing was so wonderful, and soon tears rolled down Charlotte's cheeks. Other than one or two slipping out of her eyes, she'd held her head high, putting up a brave front—but she could do so no longer. Then Robert was there, putting his arm around her, only making her cry more.

"It's okay, Lottie. We have God who loves us, and it's going to be all right. Just you wait and see."

If only he were right. If only I could be sure. Yet a feeling of fear, of insecurity filled her.

Again, Frank wanted to take Charlotte into his arms to console her, to reassure her that he would take care of her the rest of his life, but he knew it would startle her, make her back away. She needed to regain her composure, so it was better if he looked the other way. He would let her manage it.

"Mr. Hill, it was so kind of you to fetch the water for my trumpet vine."

"You're certainly welcome. And it's Frank, all right?"

"Frank," she murmured, lowering her gaze.

"I know what!" Robert was all smiles again. "When you get back from the West, you can stop by to see us and see just how good this here trumpet vine's a doing."

Charlotte laughed. It was the second time he'd heard her laugh, and he knew more than anything he wanted to hear that laugh again and again.

God, he prayed, *You've given me quite a task to do. Guess I'd better look in Your Word and get some guidance.*

And as Robert swung his feet out into the middle of the aisle, Frank dug into his satchel for two things: another stick of candy, a lemon one this time, and a worn, loved songbook. It had been his grandmother's. She loved to sing, not only hymns, but also folks songs and especially "I've been Working on the Railroad." Somewhere from deep within, he was back home, gathered around the warmth of the fire in the living room as his mother played the piano. He'd held onto Mama's hand tight as they sang one song after another. He began humming the tune under his breath again, and then Robert joined in with his lusty, off-key voice.

I've been working on the railroad,

all the livelong day,
I've been working on the railroad,
just to while the time away,
Don't you hear the whistle blowing?
Rise up so early in the morn,
Don't you hear the whistle blowing,
Dinah blow your horn.

After three more songs, Charlotte brought out the basket of lunch, and they had the crusty bread and ham and cheese. A songfest was the perfect way to end the afternoon.

Chapter 4

The train was quite different from a buggy or hay wagon. The motion kept lulling Charlotte to a sleepy state, but she couldn't quite still the fear in her heart.

They would arrive in McCook soon. As trees and small rolling hills passed by, she thought of how she and Robert would adjust to their new surroundings. What would Cousin Lily's home be like? Did Lily believe in God? Would Charlotte learn to love her new life? And what about Robert? He needed a father. Before he'd had Grandfather, now, no one. He admired Frank. Her heart pounded. She liked Frank too. He was a nice person, a caring one. Singing the old hymns and songs had been enjoyable. Charlotte could hear his deep bass voice now. Had her father liked singing? She remembered mother playing the piano and singing along. A tight knot filled her throat. How she missed her!

Charlotte knew she must trust God to take care of any problem should it arise. Maybe she could locate work in a hotel or a boardinghouse. She was a good cook. At least

Grandfather had always said so. Other than teaching, it was the only thing she felt comfortable doing. She had tried sewing, but it didn't come easy, and Grandmother had said once that it took a special knack. She wasn't sure about the teaching. What if she failed? Yet, God had promised He cared for her. She opened her Bible to the verse in Matthew: "Behold the fowls of the air: for they sow not, neither do they reap, nor gather into barns; yet your heavenly Father feedeth them. Are ye not much better than they?"

Charlotte's eyes closed, her hand holding her Bible tight.

Frank was using his ventriloquist trick again, pretending it was Robert talking. Robert also had another candy stick. She couldn't believe he could eat three sticks of candy. She'd wanted to accept when Frank first offered her a candy, but it would not be polite. How could she ever pay him back for all his kindnesses? Maybe he would come through Traer when he returned. *If* he returned. She found herself hoping so.

"Lottie, are you sure we can't go west with Frank?"

She couldn't believe he'd even ask such a thing.

"Young man, maybe you'd better come over here and sit with me."

"Oh, Lottie, I won't ask again." Robert looked crestfallen.

Frank leaned in her direction. "The boy has a natural curiosity."

"I know," she murmured. "I think he needs to sit with me for now."

Robert came over and put his hat over his eyes. He said nothing.

Frank leaned back, thinking about Ohio and how his grandfather had ridden on horseback from town to town, preaching one time in Arkansas, another time in Missouri, and how he had not been there when his child, Frank's father, was born. He also knew his grandmother had been a midwife, bringing hundreds of babies into the world. Another tale he'd heard was that Uncle Peter had fought for the Union while his twin, Paul, had become a Rebel. When both her sons died, Grandma took to her bed, never to get up again.

Frank's life had been uncomplicated by contrast. He had never considered marriage until he laid eyes on Charlotte. Something about the stubborn thrust of her chin and the softness behind the fear in her blue, blue eyes had made him care and feel concern. He wanted to protect her. Robert was a bonus. He loved the lad as if he'd known him forever.

He thought about his past community and those patients he'd brought to health. Such stalwart souls! People in Nebraska would be the same. They were farmers with big hearts. He already knew that.

Charlotte relaxed. Robert had to understand that Frank was just passing through. He was a good person, even if he was a cowboy. Not that Charlotte thought that a cowboy was all bad. Probably there were good cowboys. She wished he wasn't going out west. It would be nice to know someone nearby in town, someone she could visit. But he was leaving on the next train, or she assumed so.

If only she could calm her fears and just lean on God and His everlasting arms.

She decided to read again. It might help keep her awake.

She fumbled inside the bag on the floor. The trumpet vine was in one corner and looked fine. A lump came to her throat. The vine must live; it had to make it. She opened her Bible again. It was the one treasure she could count on when she felt so bereft. God's Word helped her over the rough spots. It had been hard when Mama was sick, and Charlotte did all she could do to help out. Robert had been her sole charge, and since her mother could not nurse him, Charlotte fed him from a bottle. He reminded her of a little calf with his mouth open and greedy. It had been such a hard time, but she felt empathy for her baby brother since he would never know Mama's sweet face, her endearing smile, or the way it felt when Mama pulled her onto her lap and smoothed the hair back from her hot cheeks. Then Papa left; Charlotte felt a tightness in her now, one that had not been there before. Try as she might, she could not forgive him for leaving like that.

Grandmother died of heart failure, the doctor said, and later Grandpa died. Charlotte knew he was good and strong, but after contracting the influenza, he had died of a broken heart. He missed Grandma too much.

Charlotte had never been alone before. Neighbors and people from church brought food and offered to stay. Charlotte had lifted her chin and said they would manage just fine.

She and Robert had fended for themselves. Then the sky fell in with the news that the farm was no longer theirs. Now she was responsible for getting settled in a new home, finding a church, and attending on a regular basis. She would teach, and Robert would enroll in the third grade. He had not gone to school much the year everyone was ill so he had fallen behind in his studies. She wished she could have helped him, but there was too much to do and too little time for any of it.

The train whistle blew as it passed through a small town. Robert woke up and asked for permission to sit with Frank again.

Charlotte nodded. "Try not to be a pest."

Soon they were chatting away. Charlotte tried not to listen, then heard Robert's question about Frank's family.

"You didn't have any brothers?" Robert's voice went from low to high-pitched excitement.

"No. I had a sister but no brothers." Frank's smile faded for a moment as he looked away from the searching eyes of the young boy beside him.

"But, what happened to her?" Robert probed.

"She's in heaven now, with God. I've never been more sure of anything."

Charlotte's heart skipped a beat. In heaven? Had she heard right? She put a bookmark in her Bible and leaned over to hear better.

"I can be your brother," Robert said, "especially since I don't have a brother. And Lottie can be your sister."

Charlotte's cheeks flamed at the thought.

"Yes, that you could. And I'd be proud to be a big

brother to you both."

"Hear that, Lottie?" Robert bounded across the aisle and plopped down beside Charlotte. "Frank's going to be our brother. That means we get to see him again—that is if he comes back from out west." He turned back to Frank. "Isn't that right?" He ran back and stuck his hand out. "I think we need to shake on it."

Charlotte couldn't stifle the giggle that rose inside her. Robert was so funny at times, and Frank was trying hard not to smirk.

"Yes, we can shake on it." His gaze met Charlotte's over the top of Robert's head. "I'm right proud to be part of your family."

"But you have to shake Lottie's hand too, or it won't work."

Frank smiled as he clasped her hand.

Charlotte removed her hand, her cheeks flushing a bright red as she looked down at her Bible, then back at Frank. "It's a nice thing you've done for my brother."

Frank's gaze never wavered. "It's all my pleasure, Miss Lansing."

"Lottie," Robert said. "You get to call her Lottie now because we're family."

Charlotte smiled. "Yes, we're family now."

"Holdrege is coming up," Frank said, looking at a train schedule he had pulled from his pocket. "We could get out and stretch a bit. I understand we'll be there long enough to get supper."

The picnic lunch eaten earlier had filled the empty space, but Charlotte felt hungry again.

"A lady cooks meals for train passengers so we could get a bite to eat, or we might buy ice cream at the emporium."

"What's an empor-yum?" Robert asked.

"It's a store that sell lots of items, but the main ones for now are the root beer, a very much sought-after soda pop, and ice cream, which I know you will enjoy."

"It's all right to get off the train?" Charlotte asked. She secretly feared it might leave without them.

"It's fine," Frank said. "The conductor said earlier that there would be several head of cattle to load. It will take at least a half hour."

Robert had grabbed his hat and pushed it down on his head. "I'm for getting off this train; that's for certain. And I want to get one of those root drinks you just talked about."

"Now, Robert, we still have cookies left in the basket from Mrs. Farnsworth." They didn't have money for such tomfoolery, but her mouth watered as she wondered what the treat would taste like. It sounded wonderful.

"But, Lottie, I ain't ever had—"

"Have never had," Charlotte corrected, interrupting him. "That is why you must be enrolled in school, young man. You have much to learn."

"I know." He hung his head just a little. It was a way he had, a sort of pout that made her heart soften. But not this time.

"I'd be happy to buy you both a root beer," Frank said. "It's my gift to my new family."

Charlotte felt the twinge again under her breastbone. Frank was her new "brother," but she didn't want him to be her brother. She felt something different and wondered if it might be this feeling that Mama felt for Papa, lo those twenty years ago. She'd caught Frank looking at her more than once and had trembled when their gazes met.

"We couldn't possibly accept such a gift."

Frank shook his head and stated firmly, "If I can't buy a root beer for my family and friend, then my name isn't Frank Hill."

The whistle blew as the train chugged to a halt. Frank jumped to his feet.

"You have one hour," the conductor said, appearing on the platform as people got off.

"See? We have more time than I thought," Frank said.

Robert bounded down the steps the second the train came to a complete stop. Charlotte started down next, but Frank stepped in front of her and held his arm out to help her down.

"Thank you so much, Mr. Hill." She thought of him as Frank, but it didn't seem proper to call him Frank to his face.

The emporium, already crowded, captivated Charlotte. There were barrels with pickles swimming in brine, glass cases full of goodies, colorful bolts of yardage, and racks of shoes of all sizes.

"Come this way," Frank said, taking her elbow and leading her through the throng of passengers. "I know where we can sit and order our root beers."

Soon each had a tall glass of root beer and a scoop of ice cream in a small dish and were sharing a piece of chocolate cake.

"This is just too much," Charlotte said. "You must save money for your trip to Oregon."

Frank shrugged. "Don't you worry one minute about my trip out west. I have money tucked away in a safe place."

Robert licked his ice cream spoon repeatedly until Charlotte ordered him to stop. His manners were lacking, and she knew it was something else she had failed in. There were so many things she failed at. How could one be a mother and know everything when there was no one to set an example?

"I could buy more ice cream—"

"Absolutely not!" Charlotte's voice shrilled.

"Lottie, can I go look around?" Robert gave his little pouty look that melted her heart once again. She looked at Frank. It was almost as if it was expected that she would rely on him for an answer.

"Do you think it would be all right?"

Frank's eyes twinkled. "I say it would be something a boy needs to do to get the kinks out of his legs."

"You stay right out front then," Charlotte said. "Do you hear me?"

"Yes, Lottie."

Charlotte's ice cream was a melted pool at the bottom of her dish. She had wanted the treat to last forever. It was the first time she'd tasted the cold confection, and here it had melted, but she ate it anyway.

"I think you two were more impressed with the ice cream than the root beer," Frank said, his gaze meeting hers. "I'm glad there was time to get off the train."

Charlotte nodded, taking the last spoonful and letting it stay on the back of her tongue for a long moment.

"I wonder where my little brother went," Frank said.

Alarmed, Charlotte jumped up. "Oh, dear, he isn't where I told him to stay, is he?"

"No, but I can well imagine where he might be. One block over is the livery stable. Don't you think he went to see the horses?"

Just as the word "horses" was out of his mouth, the whistle blew, signaling everyone to get back on the train.

"Oh, no! Robert! What am I going to do?" Charlotte ran out the door, holding her skirts high to avoid a mud puddle in the front of the emporium. "I shouldn't have let him go. He just doesn't listen, and now we'll get left behind—"

"We have five minutes," Frank said. "Enough time for me to find him." He put his bowler hat on and commanded Charlotte to board the train in a sharp, no-nonsense tone. "The conductor probably can't hold up the train, but I'll be back as soon as possible. Maybe they can wait for a few minutes."

"Oh, I pray they can!"

Charlotte clutched her reticule and prayed her heart would stop pounding so fiercely as she kept looking down the street. There was no sign yet of Robert or Frank. She hadn't been this scared since the time she'd fallen in the duck pond before she'd learned to swim. "Dear, heavenly Father, please help Frank find Robert, and let the train wait for them," she murmured.

Her knuckles were white as she climbed the steps and

went to her seat. "My brother and his, uh, his companion are not here yet," she told the conductor who came through the car.

"We are leaving in three minutes. We cannot wait, Ma'am; we must stick to a schedule." His tone was icy, and fear hit her. If they couldn't wait, perhaps she'd better get off. To leave Robert was unthinkable.

Charlotte headed for the door. "I must get off then."

"Ma'am, they can catch the next train."

"Oh, my goodness, no. That won't do at all." She started to push past him just as the train began to roll. Charlotte had forgotten her bag with her Bible, the trumpet vine, and her toiletry items. She couldn't leave them, but she couldn't stay on the train either.

A shout sounded, and she saw Frank running with Robert haphazardly carried under one arm as if he were a small pig.

"We're coming! Here!" He half tossed Robert to the conductor who grabbed the small boy and set him on his feet. Robert's hat fell, and Frank stopped to get it, but it went under the wheels.

"Frank!" wailed Robert. "We can't leave Frank!"

"Here!" The conductor held out his hand as Frank ran alongside the slow-moving train. He grabbed the conductor's hand and jumped aboard. Perspiration poured down his face as he breathed in long gulps of air and slumped over onto the first seat by the door. Charlotte, who intended to give Robert a thorough tongue-lashing, stood mute, too scared to speak or scold. Robert flew into her arms, and she held him tight. She caught Frank's glance over the top of her brother's head.

"Are you all right, Mr. Hill? Oh, I do hope so." She turned back to Robert and with no forewarning burst into tears.

"Lottie, I'm sorry." A grimy hand reached up and touched her face. "I had to see the horses, and I didn't mean to be bad."

"Robert, you scared me so!" Her crying, instead of subsiding as she hugged the small body close, became loud, jerking sobs.

Recovered from his frantic race with the train, Frank was at her side, his arms wrapping around her as he pulled both of them close. He felt as if God was telling him: *This is what matters, my son. Not anything else but the lives of people. Think of what you can do, how you can touch someone with your care and concern.*

"You're going to be all right," Frank said. "Sit down. Take long, deep breaths." He finally stepped aside, yet still felt the young woman's warmth, the fragrance from her hair, the face that had been so close he could have kissed her. . .

"I'm fine." Charlotte straightened her dress, looking away, not meeting Frank's gaze again. "I was so frightened."

"I know."

"And I'm sorry," Robert repeated. "I won't do anything like that again, Lottie, I promise."

Charlotte nodded. "Yes, but just the same, I think you'd better sit beside me, and we'll read some Scriptures."

Robert didn't argue.

Frank leaned back against the cushioned seat. His heart hadn't slowed down, though he knew it wasn't beating now from the race to catch the train—it was racing from something far more meaningful. He had never felt this way about a woman before, though a young widow from his practice had shown more than a casual interest in him back in Ohio. At one time he proclaimed he would never marry. Some people were meant to marry, but he didn't feel he was one of them. Now his heart was telling him differently. Now he reckoned he knew what people talked about, why they set their feelings to song. He liked the thought of Charlotte in the kitchen preparing breakfast, flashing him one of her warm smiles and taking his hand. How his mind raced on, his thoughts tumbling over one another.

"Frank." A small hand tugged at his arm. "I'm sorry."

"I know you are, and it's okay."

"Lottie says it's not—and perhaps you won't be my brother now."

"I'll be your brother, always. A promise is a promise, and one doesn't stop being a brother because of some little problem." He reached out and ruffled Robert's hair. "The very first thing we'll buy in McCook is a new hat. It can be the same color and style as the one you lost."

"You will do that?"

"What are brothers for, anyway?"

"How far now until we get off the train?" Robert asked, clearly eager for another excursion.

Frank looked at his watch. "I'd say a little after daybreak."

"You mean we sleep on the train too?"

140

Frank now wished they were on one of the larger trains with a sleeping car so he could offer it to Lottie, but the small trains didn't offer sleeping quarters.

"Lottie, how can I pay for my hat?"

Charlotte had wondered the same thing. She knew one wasn't to be concerned about owing people, that God sent people to help. It was His way of answering prayers. And one especially did not wonder if the person belonged to God, but did Frank belong to God? She wanted to ask but somehow couldn't bring herself to do it.

"Don't you worry now. Having the two of you for friends is all I want. I might come by for a home-cooked supper one night. How does that sound?"

"Oh, Lottie, you can make chicken and dumplings and maybe a fresh gooseberry pie."

"But, Mr. Hill, you are going on to Oregon, isn't that correct?" She felt her cheeks flame as she looked at Frank, hoping they did not betray her.

Frank smiled. "I'll return though. Of this I am sure."

"Oh, that's such good news, isn't it, Lottie?" Robert tugged on her sleeve, but all she could do was nod yes.

Chapter 5

The windows were closed as the sun set and passengers settled in for the night. Frank wondered if one day people might cross the countryside in a matter of hours. The train was much faster than covered wagons had been, so only on rare occasions would someone travel that way now. There had been talk of a vehicle people would drive; a horseless buggy they called it. He just might see one before he died.

Robert sat next to his sister, and the two huddled close to each other. Frank had an extra blanket he often took on the train. He didn't need it. He'd rather give his friends extra cover. The train could be quite drafty at night, even in the summer.

His family. His charges. "Thank You, God, for using me in this way," he murmured as he spread the blanket over them.

While Frank wondered about the cousin the two expected to be waiting at the train station, he thought about the lady at the boardinghouse where he would stay temporarily. She was not expecting him this early. He had planned the side trip to Oregon but knew he could not go now. He would not rest a bit until he knew Charlotte and Robert were in safe surroundings.

He had no idea how late it was when the conductor came through the car, carrying a lantern. "Is there a doctor aboard?"

Frank bolted to attention.

"A woman in the next car is in terrible pain. I wondered if someone might help."

Charlotte sat up, but Robert slumped over, his head in her lap. This was one adventure he'd miss out on.

"Is something wrong?" she asked.

In the pale light of the lantern, Frank saw the concern in her eyes. She had faced a lot of sickness and much death for her young years. He explained while the conductor went to the next car.

Frank grabbed his coat and got to his feet.

"Mr. Hill, are you going somewhere?"

"I want to see if she needs my coat. It could be she got a chill from the damp night air."

"You would give her your coat?" Charlotte sounded impressed.

He leaned over and whispered, "Yes, I would." He liked the admiration in her eyes.

Frank walked to the front of the car and opened the door. The night wind rushed through before he could close it. He waited on the platform for the conductor to come back through.

"Alas, there are no doctors aboard."

"I'm a doctor," Frank replied. "I don't have my medicine

bag with me, but I'll take a look."

"A doctor?"

Frank nodded. "I had an office in Ohio but haven't practiced for the last few months."

"But I thought you said you were a cowboy. I overheard part of that conversation with the young boy there."

"I know. It was a silly thing to say, and the young lad picked up on it so fast I couldn't get out of it."

"Well, come with me. I hope you can help."

The woman was writhing while her husband held her hand.

Frank bent over her, his insides recoiling as he recognized the problem. How could he do this? "Are you pregnant?" he finally asked.

"She is only into her sixth month," her husband answered as the woman arched again. He lovingly leaned over to kiss her forehead. Frank swallowed. Such tenderness. What a joy it must be to find a loving mate, one who would put his wife's care above his own.

"I'm afraid she's gone into labor."

"But, it's too soon—"

"I know." Frank shuddered, thinking about another mother and child. He knew now that he probably couldn't save the premature baby, but he had to do everything to save the young woman. He didn't want to be here, but there was no choice.

Frank turned to the conductor. "I'll need your lantern—and another one if you have it—boiling water, and some clean towels."

"Oh, Lizzie, did you hear that? This doctor is going to help us."

The contractions intensified as she cried out and gripped the sides of the seat cushion. A makeshift curtain had been set up to allow privacy.

Ten minutes later the baby came. It never took a breath and lay still in the palm of Frank's hand. He wrapped it in a washcloth, put it in his coat, and turned back to the woman.

"My baby?"

He leaned over and wiped her forehead. "He didn't make it. I'm so very sorry."

She cried openly as her husband held her close. Frank's concern was to stop the hemorrhaging and to make a bed for her to rest. They were close to McCook, and he prayed that she would survive until then. If the bleeding stopped, she'd be fine.

The husband crooned to his wife, his gaze not leaving her face except for an occasional glance at the coat holding his dead son.

"These things happen, and we have no way to stop a contraction once it begins," Frank explained.

"I've never had anything like this happen on my train," the conductor said.

"And I pray it never happens again."

"We'll have a proper burial in McCook," the young father said.

After checking his patient again, Frank asked the Lord to take care of Lizzie, then made his way back to his car and found his seat in the semidarkness.

"Is she going to be all right?" A soft voice came from across the aisle. Charlotte. He had hoped she might be asleep.

"She is going to be fine because God is with her."

Charlotte leaned closer. "God was part of my grandparents' lives and my mother's, but He didn't heal them."

"He answers prayers always, but perhaps not in the way we had hoped."

"How would you know? You being a cowboy and all?"

"And you think cowboys don't know or worship God?"

She sighed. "No, you're right. Of course some probably do. And I guess you're one of them."

Frank pulled his hat over his eyes and hunched up. At least he now knew he could doctor again. The loss of the baby was something that couldn't be helped. He shivered and slunk lower in the seat in an attempt to ward off the early morning chill. What he wouldn't give for a good night's rest in a bed with blankets and a quilt. Grandmother Julia's patchwork would have worked fine.

Charlotte said no more, and Frank was thankful. He slept fitfully for the next hour, slipping down the aisle once to check on the woman. She was asleep, and the bleeding had all but stopped. He was glad to see the first rays of dawn filling the train car.

When Frank reached his seat, Robert jumped up like a spring. "I slept, didn't I?" He grinned as he made his way to the end of the car where the water closet was located.

"Yes, you certainly did," Charlotte said.

She noticed Frank's blanket spread across her legs. She clearly hadn't realized it until now.

"Oh, my, you needed this."

"No, I'm fine. Really."

"That was a noble thing to do, giving up your coat and all."

"Yes, well—"

"And you gave me your blanket."

Charlotte put a hand to her hair. "I must look a fright." She took a small mirror from her reticule and gasped. "Oh, I do hope you aren't laughing at me."

Her hat was askew, and he nearly laughed at the sight, but he knew that no gentleman ever laughed at a lady who had not had the benefit of a mirror.

Frank grinned. "Never." He stuck his hat on his head. "I do believe we're all in the same situation."

Robert reappeared, adjusting his coat. "Lottie, do we have any of those cookies left?"

"Of course. Did you wash your hands?"

"Yes."

He grabbed a cookie and began munching. Charlotte offered Frank a cookie, but he shook his head.

"I'd say about two more hours, and we will be into McCook."

Robert raised his hands as if to shout for joy that the journey was nearly over, but Charlotte covered his mouth. "No noise, young man. Some people are still sleeping."

The conductor came down the aisle, stopping in front of Frank. "That was a special thing you did for that woman last night. And the prayer helped also. Too bad about the baby though."

Charlotte held her breath. *Praying? Did he say Frank*

prayed for her? And what about a baby? He didn't mention that. Maybe he is a preaching cowboy; I suppose they have such. Then he has a special calling. Frank has been called from God, and I am more than a bit fortunate to have met him.

"She was relieved that we had a doctor aboard even if the baby couldn't be saved."

Frank rose. "I'd better go check on her."

A baby died? Charlotte wondered if she'd heard right. *Had the conductor said "doctor"? But how could that be?*

Robert looked puzzled. "I thought you were a cowboy, Frank."

"Oh, he may be one of those too, but he's going to have a practice in McCook, isn't that right, Sir?" the conductor asked.

Frank nodded. Yes, he was a doctor, and, yes, he had prayed, but it was God who brought wellness to a fellow passenger. But to Charlotte, he was a bold-faced liar. He could not bear to look in her direction, nor did he want to hear what she might say, though he knew he would hear soon enough.

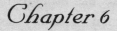

Chapter 6

Y ou're a *doctor?*" Charlotte said it as if it were a forbidden word.

Frank nodded. Robert stared, looking at the pointy end of his lemon stick.

"Why didn't you tell us?" Charlotte asked.

"I was going to."

"When?"

"When the train pulled out of the station and left me behind—with you and Robert."

Her face flushed at the comment. "So you never *were* a cowboy?"

"Only in my heart. Everyone has wishes, and mine was to go west and be a cowboy. I was considering giving up being a doctor, due to an incident that happened where I blamed myself for the death of a mother and her child."

"Oh, my," Charlotte began, but Frank continued.

"I know it was stretching the truth."

Charlotte stared and finally spoke. "But why would you say you were a cowboy? That's the most unlikely part."

"I know what you must think." Frank withdrew his Bible from the valise and brought it over to Charlotte. Psalm 44, verse 21 may plead my case: 'For he knoweth the secrets of the heart.'

"We all dream and wish. You hope for a new life in Kansas as a schoolteacher. I thought of going west because I have a touch of wanderlust. Robert dreams about riding trains and going to a new school."

Robert made a face. "I'm not looking forward to school."

"I understand." Frank ruffled his hair. "I felt that way too, when I was your age. All I thought about was my dog and riding my horse out into the hills behind my house."

Robert's ears perked up. "What was your horse's name?"

"Cinnamon, because he was the color of a cinnamon stick."

"I like that name."

"And it's okay for you to wish for a new horse one day."

"Is it, Frank?"

Charlotte looked out the window, staying out of the conversation. Frank hoped she might at least look their way. Anything was better than silence.

"Frank, are you really not going to Oregon?" Robert asked.

"That's right."

"Well, we are going to Traer," Charlotte said.

The train began slowing down, and Charlotte put the small carpetbag on the seat. Robert held the empty picnic basket, and Frank picked up his new, shiny black valise. It had been a gift from a former patient.

Charlotte didn't know what to think. What reasons did Frank have for hiding the fact that he was a doctor? Could she believe what he was saying now? She knew how she felt about him in her heart, yet there was the fact that she had begun falling in love with a man who was a charlatan.

She sat, hands folded in her lap, knowing she could not accept help from Frank. How could she tell Robert to be truthful when someone he admired so much had lied?

Robert, bless his heart, had washed his face earlier, but somehow he had found something sooty and had black smudges on both cheeks. She reached over and rubbed at it with a handkerchief she'd dampened with spittle.

"Lottie, don't." He pulled away.

"Don't you want to look presentable for your cousin, Lily?"

"She doesn't care about my face. She'll hug you and talk to you."

"And here you don't even have a hat."

"Frank said he'd buy one for me."

"I'm afraid we cannot accept his gift."

"But, Lottie—"

She reached over, shushing his words, making him swallow them. "We'll have no more of that."

The train came to a full stop, and just as Charlotte rose, it gave one more lurch and she went flying across the aisle, almost into Frank's lap. He caught her, steadied her, and looked into her face. She saw regret in his eyes but chose to ignore it.

Wagons pulled up as workers began unloading trunks and boxes from the baggage area. Charlotte quickly ascended, holding onto Robert. She wasn't about to let him out of her sight. Not ever again. Not even once.

Frank was talking to Lizzie, who had been carried from the train and lifted onto a wagon. Her face looked pale, but it was the bundle in the coat that wrenched his heart.

Her husband shook Frank's hand. "I can never repay you for what you've done. I'll see that your coat is returned."

"Are you from McCook?" Frank asked.

"No. We've come to visit my parents," the young man said.

Frank smiled. "I'll be seeing you around here again. I'd like to check up on your wife in a day or so. I'll be putting my shingle out in a few weeks."

Charlotte stood, forlorn, as if lost. Shadowing her face with her hand, she looked down the tracks and by the station, searching the crowd.

"Robert, I do hope the top of your head doesn't get sunburned, what with losing that hat and all. Maybe you better go over there in the shade of the station."

"Do you know what your cousin looks like?" asked Frank.

"I have a picture," Charlotte said. "She's blond with a round, plump face."

"She's probably been detained for whatever reason."

He wanted to shelter her, to make things better, but he knew she had lost any feeling she might have had toward him. He waved at one of the boys who had a loaded wagon and was ready to take it to the local hotel.

"Can you get any more on there?"

"Of course, Sir."

"The lady, boy, and I will walk; it's not that far. We'll have the bags taken to the boardinghouse." Charlotte started to protest, but Frank wouldn't hear of it.

"I would not be doing you any favor if I left you and Robert out here in the hot sun with no food or water. You must come with me."

Thankfully, Frank had visited McCook earlier to meet the people who were eager to have a town doctor and thus knew his way around the growing town. Charlotte had no choice but to let him help her.

Robert, who had been unusually quiet, suddenly shot ahead of them.

"Really, Mr. Hill, we can fend for ourselves."

Frank was firm. "I'm afraid I can't allow that. A young woman and small boy cannot be left alone on an empty train platform with no people and no place to go."

Robert came back. "Are you going to take us to our cousin's house?"

"Robert! How impertinent of you!"

Frank laughed. "He's saying what's on his mind, and there's nothing wrong with that, no sirree."

"Let's go over to the boardinghouse where travelers stay and a few of the local people live," Frank suggested.

"I cannot pay—"

Frank held up a hand. "I realize that, Charlotte. What I'm thinking is that you can help earn your keep.

Mrs. Collins—I met her last time I was here—is a kind woman and seemed shorthanded before."

Charlotte nodded. "Yes, I suppose that is acceptable. I wouldn't have been working right off anyway since school starts in the fall."

The huge, three-story house needed a coat of paint, but the garden of petunias and marigolds out front made Charlotte smile.

Mrs. Collins hugged Charlotte and Robert and insisted they sit right off while she finished cooking breakfast. In a matter of seconds, Frank had explained the situation, then left to attend to business.

"I wish I could have gone with Frank," Robert said, after downing his glass of orange juice.

Charlotte gave him a cross look, and he sat back down. "You just stay with me. I told you I'm not letting you out of my sight ever again."

He wrinkled his nose. "Not ever?"

"Well, maybe when you're eighteen."

"Ah, Lottie, I won't do that again. 'Sides, we'll never go on a train again."

"And how do you know that? Maybe Lily isn't coming after all, and we may have to go on the next train coming through and head back to Creston."

"We couldn't do that." He raised his eyebrows, his expression stricken.

Charlotte sighed. "I have no idea what we'll do. But in the meantime, we'll accept the food and possibly a place for the night."

Mrs. Collins had brought in coffee for Charlotte, milk for Robert, and a large stack of pancakes when Frank sauntered back in.

"I have unfortunate news," he said, meeting Charlotte's anxious gaze.

"Does it have to do with Lily?"

He nodded. "She sent a wire; it was at the telegraph office."

"What happened?" Charlotte's insides were knotting up. "I must know."

Frank sat across the table and looked back at the two scared faces. "She said she couldn't get away after all to fetch you. Her children are sick, and she can't leave them."

"But, she *will* come?"

"She couldn't promise when."

"Then it's settled. I'll work wherever I can."

"I can help that man with the luggage at the train station," Robert said, puffing his chest out. "I watched, and it's a job I can do."

"Of course you can," Frank said. "I have a better idea. Why don't you two come west with me? We can look it over, and if we don't like it, we'll just head back." His face held no expression.

"Mr. Hill, surely you aren't serious."

Robert stood, his mouth hanging open. When he finally found his voice, he let out a loud whoop, causing others to turn and stare. "That's the best idea yet!"

"It's absurd." Charlotte set her cup down.

"I thought it was a good solution." Frank reached over and took her hand. Charlotte's lips twitched in disdain.

"Don't worry. I was not serious, but what I *am* serious about is getting rooms right here for the night and then worrying about tomorrow when it comes. You need rest. After freshening up, you'll feel like facing the problem."

"I cannot—"

Frank put a hand up. "I know what you're going to say but please don't. Allow me this one thing. You both have made my trip pleasant, and I want to do this because of the second commandment Jesus gave us: 'Unto one of the least of these my brethren, ye have done it unto me.'"

Charlotte sighed. There was no other answer. She had to accept Frank's offer.

"Can I help out?" Charlotte asked, dabbing at her wet cheeks.

"Mrs. Collins said her other helper left to be with her daughter's family, so she needs someone to do the wash and change the linens."

Charlotte's face brightened. "I can do that." She was proud and did not want to take from someone she didn't know.

A young girl set heaping platters of scrambled eggs and slabs of ham next to the stack of pancakes. "Are you hungry?" she asked.

"Like bears," Frank said. He reached across the table and took both Charlotte's and Robert's hands. "Let's ask the Lord to bless this food."

Frank's loud voice filled the room, and Charlotte suddenly felt safe. Maybe he really had wanted to be a cowboy and had truly intended to go west. Maybe it wasn't an intentional lie to deceive her and Robert. Should she forgive him? Isn't that what God would expect? While she was mulling that over, Robert ate five pancakes, two slices of ham, and a large serving of eggs. Now he was ready to explore. Charlotte relented and let him go with Frank to the stables. She stayed and finished her food, thinking she might as well start right off by washing their dishes.

Mrs. Collins was happy with her work, and after the kitchen was cleaned, she showed Charlotte the room at the top of the stairs.

"From what you've told me about your love for flowers, I think you'll like my new wallpaper."

Charlotte clasped her hands at her throat. Sunshine poured in through a white-curtained window and danced on the pattern of violets and daisies on the walls. A nightstand and large chest filled one corner. It was perfect.

"It's surely God's provision," she murmured.

Mrs. Collins nodded. "Sometimes He sends someone to help."

"Like Frank."

They went back downstairs and found Frank and Robert playing checkers. The sight warmed her heart. Frank looked up, and as their gazes met, she held out her hand. "I've judged you harshly; forgive me."

He took her hand and held it an extra moment. "There is nothing to forgive."

Robert smiled but said nothing. It was as if he had a secret, one he didn't want to share with anyone, at least not yet.

"C'mon, Lottie, show me the room."

Charlotte took her little brother's hand, then nodded at Frank as grateful tears filled her eyes. God was making sure she was taken care of. He was fulfilling His promises.

"Mrs. Collins said your room is on the top floor."

As the two went up the stairs, Charlotte began singing: " 'Standing, standing, standing on the promises of God, our Savior. Standing, standing, we're standing on the promises of God.' "

"I love it when you sing," Robert said. "It makes me happy."

"And that's why I sing; it's from a grateful heart."

She imagined God must have looked down and smiled at His children. There was nothing better than voices rejoicing with song.

Chapter 7

Frank was glad to have Robert stay with him for the night. They were not far away should the boy need his sister.

The timing had been perfect. A new church was being built in McCook, and the crew needed helpers. Besides meeting the train, Robert would be the fetch-all kid, bringing water, iced tea, and lemonade to the workers. The first service would be in two weeks, and Frank was looking forward to it. That meant he would get to know the townspeople better. The inside would not be completed for awhile, but fancy floors weren't necessary.

"The people are the church," Frank's father had said more than once. "What they meet in to worship is not the most important thing. Coming with a ready heart to serve and praise God is."

God's provision was so evident. When the train came in each morning, Robert would meet and give the passengers directions to the boardinghouse where they would be served a substantial meal. If someone needed help carrying luggage, he would help with that too.

"I can hardly wait to start," Robert said shortly after they'd come to the room.

"You'll do a fine job," Frank replied. "Charlotte will help Mrs. Collins who definitely needs an extra pair of hands and steady feet to carry food to the table."

"Will Charlotte still teach school?" Robert asked as he stretched out on the bed. He had changed into his nightshirt and looked up at Frank.

"It depends on whether they still need her in Traer."

"I want to stay here," Robert said. "I like it here."

"And you don't know what to expect in Kansas." Frank finished Robert's thought.

The young boy looked pensive. "I guess I have to go with Charlotte."

Long after the child had fallen asleep, Frank sat with his Bible in hand. He welcomed having a family to care for. He was more than ready for the responsibility of having a wife. If a child came too, it was an even bigger blessing. If Frank made the decision, Charlotte would become a doctor's wife, not a schoolmarm. He knew, now, he wanted that more than anything. His strong feelings had bloomed instantaneously, but he knew that nothing was coincidental, that the Lord had a definite hand in the timing and making sure His children were guided in the right direction.

Frank lowered his head. "Lord God, You have blessed me in so many ways, and I thank You for this town, my friends, and for Charlotte and young Robert. You already know my heart's dream; it's in Your hands now."

Though extremely tired and thankful for a nice room in the boardinghouse, that first night was fitful for Charlotte. Nightmares caused her to break into a cold sweat. She'd fall asleep, only to dream that Robert was falling from the train. She'd reach out for him, but he'd slip from her grasp. When she woke, her cheeks were wet from tears.

She rose before dawn. Surely Mrs. Collins needed help with breakfast preparations.

Pulling a slightly wrinkled but clean muslin from the trunk, Charlotte dressed and went downstairs.

Mrs. Collins was up and had a huge pot of coffee perking on the old woodstove.

"My goodness, Child, I didn't hear you on the stairs." She smiled warmly. "I don't need you yet—"

"I couldn't sleep."

"Was the bed uncomfortable?"

Charlotte shook her head, fighting back tears that suddenly threatened. She'd had no idea that tears were close to the surface. "The bed was what I needed, but my thoughts and fears would not let me sleep."

An arm went around Charlotte's shoulder as the older woman pulled her close. "There, now, you are among friends, and there is to be no fear in your heart. God, in His infinite wisdom, has provided—as He always does, I might add. Ah, Lass, you had no way of knowing that I prayed for someone to come off the train yesterday that could help."

Charlotte wiped her tears away with the apron. "You did?"

"I certainly did. And we prayed that our doctor might come early as so many of us are needing medical care."

Charlotte thought back to the train and how Frank had delivered a premature infant and saved the young mother's life. The conversation about Frank going west to be a cowboy seemed unimportant. Would he stay here and be the doctor the town needed, or would he still have the desire to go out west?

"We have a fine young man in Dr. Frank Hill. I knew that the minute I laid eyes on him. And he's certainly what this town needs."

"Yes, he is a fine person."

"He took you and your brother under his wing, and I daresay you two might be the reason he's not continuing on with his trip west."

Charlotte gasped. "You knew about this?"

The older woman nodded. "Told me about it while you did last night's dishes. Said he'd had a change of plans."

Charlotte didn't know what to say, and whenever that happened, she found it worked if she busied herself at some task.

"What can I do first to help?"

"Can you make baking powder biscuits?"

"That I can. My grandmother made the best ones, and I learned from watching her."

Soon biscuits were in the oven and the eggs were scrambled and waiting to be cooked, while thick slabs of ham were frying in two large skillets. A noise from the dining room made Charlotte turn.

"Robert!" she cried, running to her little brother. "You have a hat, I see, and must be ready to go meet the train."

"Yes, Lottie. Frank bought the hat and gave it to me this morning." His freckled face was scrubbed clean; his eyes looked rested. He hugged Charlotte around the middle.

Charlotte looked beyond the boy, hoping to see Frank in the room. It was empty and a sudden chill went through her. She hadn't realized until that moment how much she wanted to see him and had hoped he might be there with Robert.

As if reading her mind, Robert answered, "Frank's gone to buy a newspaper."

"Oh."

"Said he'd be back to eat breakfast with us though."

Mrs. Collins pointed to the door. "You've done more than enough, Miss Charlotte. Go with Robert to the train station. Train should be in around seven. Welcome the people who get off, then come back to help serve the food."

"Are you sure you don't mind my leaving?"

"Absolutely."

The morning sun hailed from a full blue sky as the two, arm in arm, trudged down the dusty dirt road to the station.

"I think I can hear it," Robert said, tilting his head toward the east.

"You cannot. I hear nothing but the wind blowing."

"It's coming. We better hurry!" Holding his new straw hat on his head with his hand, Robert took off running. Charlotte, laughing, ran after him.

This time when the train rolled into town, stopping with a huff and puff of noise and steam, Charlotte wasn't frightened. She rather liked this steel monster after all.

Faces peered from the windows, and soon people were lighting, waiting for their baggage. Had it only been a day since she and Robert had stood on this platform waiting for Cousin Lily?

Robert went from person to person and found a couple that needed his assistance.

As they went down the street to the boardinghouse where a good meal waited, Charlotte looked up again, thanking God for bringing her here. She had no idea how long she might stay, but she found herself thinking more and more like this was home. This was the place God had destined for her to be. She liked seeing Frank each day, and Robert had blossomed under Frank's tutelage.

She would take it a day at a time, as His answer would be forthcoming.

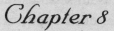

Chapter 8

I t had been a week since Charlotte, Robert, and Frank arrived in the Nebraska town. The office where Frank would practice had been furnished with medical supplies, and people were stopping by to chat.

Each day Robert and Charlotte met the train, and each morning was a flurry of excitement while she helped Mrs. Collins with the meals.

On a Saturday, a man lighted from the train, saying he was looking for a Miss Charlotte Lansing and her brother, Robert.

Charlotte froze.

"I'm Robert, and this is Lottie," her brother said.

The man with craggy eyebrows and a determined look was dressed in pants and a shirt that needed laundering. He stepped forward and held out his hand.

"Lily sent me. Name's Jack Slater."

Charlotte stood, hands at her sides, ignoring his hand. A chill swept over her, and she wanted to turn and run.

He stepped closer. "You really need to come with me. Lily's eager to see you again."

Robert's face blanched.

"I am afraid that is impossible," Charlotte finally said. "My brother and I are quite happy here now, and we both have gainful employment."

Jack scowled, reaching out to take her arm. "I didn't come all this way to be turned aside. . . ."

Charlotte moved back again. "I am terribly sorry, but Mrs. Collins is expecting me back at the boardinghouse to help with the meals. I can perhaps come later."

"Why did you come from that way when Kansas is that way?" Robert had found his voice and stood pointing south.

"I was unavoidably detained on a business trip to Omaha; I insist that you both come with me now."

Charlotte's insides twisted. She didn't want to go to Kansas now. She wanted to stay here and knew Robert did too. What could she do to convince this horrid man?

Murmuring a prayer under her breath, she started off in the direction of the boardinghouse.

"You *will* come with me." Jack gripped her shoulder, spinning her around. She started to scream, but a hand clamped over her mouth.

Robert yelled and began hitting the man, but he was no match, and Jack shoved him aside. "You can stay here," he said. "It's Charlotte I want."

Charlotte felt faint, and her knees buckled. Her vision blurred, and she feared she might lose consciousness.

Robert bent over his sister, begging her to get up. Jack scooped her into his arms and started to board the train. Nausea gripped her as she struggled to regain her footing and clear her vision.

"Wait a minute!" Robert yelled. "You can't be going to Kansas because this here train goes out west—that's what Frank said."

"Is that so?"

He pushed past Robert and turned to climb the steps where Charlotte caught a glimpse of a young man standing with his arms folded. And was that the conductor behind him?

Thank You, God, for sending help to my brave little brother. Another wave of nausea assailed Charlotte.

"I know *her*," she heard the conductor say. "She came through with the lad here and a doctor fellow. The good doctor saved a woman's life."

"That's Frank," Robert said proudly, "and he wouldn't want Lottie to go anywhere without his knowing. Besides, we like it here in McCook."

She was half standing, and someone was fanning Charlotte's face, their putrid breath assaulting her nose. She opened her eyes wide and screamed—directly into Jack's filthy face.

"Offhand, I'd say the young lady doesn't want to go with you," the conductor said.

"Well, she must. We're all the family she has."

"I have family," Charlotte said, pushing away from the grimy man. His grip held, and she landed on a small crate. The nausea was subsiding, and her head was beginning to clear at last. "I have friends from church and people in this town. They are all the family I need. Let go of me."

Releasing her, Jack scowled and muttered loud enough for her to hear. "We'll see about this. Lily will not be too happy, I can guarantee you."

"Lily's kids are sick," Robert challenged. "She sent a wire, and Frank read it." He moved protectively to Charlotte's side.

"Sick? Kids?" Jack adjusted his hat and laughed. "Lily just couldn't get away from her job at the bordello."

Charlotte knew she had heard that term before, and if it meant what she thought it did, she was more than happy that Lily had not been able to come.

The train started pulling away from the station. Jack did not get back on but walked toward town. She knew Robert wanted to get Frank, but he was afraid to leave Charlotte alone.

"I need to get back to help serve breakfast." She held onto Robert and reached out to a nearby bench for support, but her legs gave way again.

Once again Frank's mind went to Charlotte as he wondered if he dare say what was in his heart, if he could ask her to come courting. He loved her with all his heart. It had become more apparent with each day since he'd first laid eyes on her. Sometimes he caught her looking at him, and he wondered if she could feel just a smidgeon of the love he felt.

He put his hat on and walked outside as a young man ran up, breathless, and nearly knocked Frank over. "You gotta come quick, Dr. Hill. Miss Charlotte needs help. An awful man tried to force her on the train."

Frank's insides churned. *"Help* Charlotte?"

"Her brother is with her down at the station. She

can't seem to move."

Frank took off running, afraid of what he'd find. Charlotte always went with Robert in the morning to greet the train. Sometimes he went along, but not this morning. Now he wished he had.

Charlotte sat on one of the wagons as it headed for town. Robert sat with her, propping her up.

The wagon driver stopped, and Frank jumped aboard. He bent down and pulled Charlotte into his arms. "What happened?"

Robert started to explain, but Frank cut him off halfway. Frank knew about Jack Slater. He'd seen the man once before on a train in Ohio. A professional gambler and thief, he had hoped Slater and his kind would never come to McCook.

"Charlotte, please answer me." He so hoped she wasn't in shock, but it was likely. She'd had a good scare, and if Robert hadn't been there, who knew what might have happened. He checked the pupils of her eyes. They were fine.

"I did not like that man," Robert said, hovering over his sister. "He said he was taking us to Lily. He was going the wrong way, huh, Frank?"

Frank pulled the boy close. "Yes, you're correct. He was going the wrong way."

"The conductor wouldn't let him on the train with Lottie," Robert added.

"Thank goodness for that."

Charlotte opened her eyes and smiled. "You came."

"Of course. Did you ever doubt it?" Concern pulled at Frank's face as he realized more fully what might have happened. "Are you feeling better now?"

"I am now that you're here."

"Let's get you home." He nodded to the young man driving the wagon. "I'm much obliged, Jacob," he said before turning back to Charlotte. "No helping Mrs. Collins today. As your doctor, I insist on complete bed rest."

"I'll be fine. Really, I will."

Robert still hovered. "I can clear the table, Frank, and help with the dishes too."

Frank nodded. "I know you can. And it's mighty nice of you to offer, but one of the women can also help. I'll see what I can do once I get Charlotte settled."

Charlotte was not at supper that night. Robert waited on the long table, an apron over his pants and shirt. He looked proud to be helping out.

"Is Lottie okay?" Frank asked, as he grabbed a carrot stick. He'd been back several times already, and each time Mrs. Collins shook her head. "Says she has a headache."

Frank went up the stairs. He tapped on the door, knowing he dare not go into Charlotte's room, as it wouldn't be proper.

Her voice sounded, then the door opened. If ever there had been a doubt, it vanished the minute their gazes met. "Charlotte," he said, putting an arm around her, "I've been so worried about you."

"I'm going to be fine, Frank." Sudden tears filled her eyes. "He was awful. He wanted us to go and insisted we do so. I just couldn't go with someone I had never met before."

"Jack Slater's up to no good, I'm sure. He left town this afternoon. You're safe now." He wanted to hold her close, to reassure her he would always be there for her. He also wanted to ask her to be his wife and to take Robert as his own son. Yet the time wasn't right.

"Let me fix up a bit, and I'll come down."

"Have you eaten at all today?"

"Just some soup."

"I could have Robert bring you some of Mrs. Collins' bread pudding."

"No, I want to come down. I'm fine. Having you here has given me strength."

"I'll wait outside the door then."

That evening after the dishes had been cleared and the table set for morning, Mrs. Collins thanked Robert—making a big show of it in Charlotte and Frank's presence—causing the boy to beam with pride. "You worked hard today, Lad. I'll do the washing now. Go on and be with your sister and Frank."

"Charlotte, I don't want you to go to Traer now or ever," Frank said when they walked into the parlor.

"Frank, what are you saying?"

Frank took the handkerchief out of his pocket and formed it into a figure. "Miss Charlotte Lansing, will you be my wife?"

Robert laughed as Charlotte gasped, unable to speak.

"She says 'yes!' " Robert answered, tossing his hat into the air.

Charlotte's face turned crimson, but her eyes gave the

answer to Frank's question.

"How soon can you get married?" Mrs. Collins asked from the doorway.

"As soon as a preacher can come," Frank said.

"But the lady hasn't said yes, yet."

Frank looked at Charlotte with hope in his eyes. "I have asked our Lord for His blessing and believe He has said yes. Now it's your turn to pray about it."

"Charlotte's prayed about it, and I know what the answer is," Robert said, hugging his sister hard. "It is yes!"

"I have no dowry," Charlotte said.

Frank took her hand and held it tight. "A dowry is not important to me. Don't give it another thought. I just hope you can grow to love me."

"She loves you already," Robert said.

Charlotte looked into Frank's eyes and murmured, "Yes, I do, and that's a fact."

"I'll stand in as a proxy mother," Mrs. Collins said. "And I'll even bake the cake."

Charlotte looked at Frank incredulously and burst into laughter. "Yes, Franklin Hill, I will be honored to marry you."

Epilogue

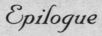

July 8, 1900

Charlotte wore a simple, white lawn dress and new white gloves, a wide-brimmed straw hat for her "something old," and her "something borrowed and something blue" being the borrowed shoes gracing her feet. She was radiant, and Frank never wanted to forget this moment. At his request, she had worn her hair down, letting her loose, blond curls flow from beneath her hat and dance in the gentle breeze.

To please his bride, Frank wore a dark, pinstripe suit with a navy blue tie. Now they stood at the train station, before the preacher who had arrived on the morning train.

They repeated their marriage vows, gazing into each other's eyes, while Robert, wearing his straw hat and a new pair of trousers, beamed up at them.

When the train chugged out of the station, making its way west, Frank cast a quick glance its way, thinking of when he had wanted to go on an adventure. He no longer needed that adventure, for he had found the wife he needed on the very train that brought him to his new position as the town's only doctor. God had indeed answered more than one prayer in providing Charlotte, his heart's desire. Robert was an added bonus.

Alongside the home that would soon be theirs, the trumpet vine had been transplanted; Frank hoped it would bring a smile to his young bride's face each day as she watered it.

BIRDIE L. ETCHISON

Birdie lives in Washington State and knows much about
the Pacific Northwest, the setting for the majority of her
books. She loves to research the colorful history of the
United States and uses her research along with family stories to create wonderful novels.

The Tender Branch

by Jane LaMunyon

Dedication

To librarian Bill Purdy of the Mojave Branch library.
He went out of his way to get books
on the Union Pacific Railroad,
even loaning me one from his own personal library.
Thank you.

Chapter 1

Kimberly, Massachusetts
March 15, 1874

Journal entry:

This has been the best day of my life! I was so nervous when I opened the letter from the Boston school board. Thank You, God, for Winston Heights Academy accepting me! I will be the best teacher they've ever had. I'll miss Eugenia, Lolly, and Mrs. Palmer, who have been more than family to me.

This afternoon, just before the mail came, I saw the first robin of the year and. . .

The next morning Mary Sherwood stood on a two-foot-high stool, holding an open book in front of her face. Strains of Bach from the piano in the parlor filled the house, and the citrus smell of lemon cake just out of the oven drifted through the high-ceilinged rooms. She felt a tug on the hem of her skirt and looked down.

Eugenia, her friend and former nanny, on her knees, frowned up at her. "Stand up straight, Girl. You want your hem to look wig-waggy?" Mary straightened, holding the book higher. Eugenia carefully marked the hem on the peach-colored skirt. "I declare, you gonna cross your eyes with all that readin'."

Holding the book close to her chest and remembering to hold very still, Mary said, "Oh, Genie, this is the story of a teacher who risked her life to rescue one of her little students."

"Girl, you may find that school teachin' is just plain work." She stood and walked around Mary, pausing to move the hem marking on the back left, and circled again.

A loud knocking at the door silenced the piano music. Mary and Eugenia walked through the hallway, Eugenia muttering, "Who's come knocking?" Lolly, Eugenia's sixteen-year-old daughter, joined them from the parlor, and they opened the door.

The three women eyed the man who stood on their front porch. Dark, wavy hair crowned a friendly face. Mary had never seen such eyes, a cross between gray and deep blue, fringed with long black lashes. His skin was tanned; his clothes, though of the latest fashion, looked casual on him.

A faint smile curved his lips, and he said, "I'm looking for Mary Sherwood."

Of all the heroes in the books she'd read, this man personified them. He definitely had the look of a prince seeking his princess, of a knight coming to the rescue of his lady.

"What you want with her?"

Eugenia's question brought Mary from her daydream. "I'm Mary Sherwood," she said.

The man's smile broadened. "My name is Jesse Harcourt. Your father sent me."

A cold ripple of distress went through Mary. Fighting down her shock, she met his eyes, attempting a confidence she did not feel. "My father?" Mary hadn't seen her father in thirteen years. Her last memory was of him walking away from her. She clutched her book to her chest, too stunned to move.

Eugenia hugged Mary's shoulders, saying, "Mr. Sherwood? He's alive? Glory to God! Girl, where's your manners? Come inside, young man, and tell us why Mr. Sherwood hisself isn't on our porch!"

"He wants to see you." The man looked into Mary's eyes, a question in his own. She turned abruptly, not wanting him to see her confusion. He followed them into the house, and she escaped to the kitchen. She set the book on the cutting table and leaned on it with both palms, squeezing her eyes to shut out old memories. She'd made very sure her life was well ordered, and everything had gone exactly as she'd planned it, with no surprises. Now this visitor, sent by her father, was a threat to her schedule.

Eugenia entered the kitchen, her soft shoes making little noise. "Honey-Girl?" She put her hand on Mary's shoulder. "What's wrong?"

Mary took a deep breath, then stood and clenched

her fists. "I don't *want* to see my father!"

"Why, Child? What's this all about?"

"He left us! He just walked away and left us defenseless!" She tried to push down the memory of her mother looking back at her, pleading with her to be silent, as she was dragged away by Union soldiers to her death. The memory faded, to be replaced by their home consumed in flames.

Eugenia pulled Mary into her arms. "Hush, now. He didn't know they'd get that far south. None of them knew."

Mary stiffened. "He shouldn't have gone."

Eugenia dropped her hands from Mary's arms. "We'll talk about this later. Now, the young man in our parlor had nothing to do with that. The good Book tells us to be hospitable."

She lit the fire beneath the kettle and got plates from the cupboard. "Cut the lemon cake and save a piece for Miz Palmer. She'll be home soon."

Mary blinked back tears. She thought she'd gotten over the trauma of feeling abandoned by her father, losing her mother and her home, and making the long trip north with Eugenia and Lolly on the Underground Railroad. She simply had refused to think about it. But she was unprepared for the memory to come up unexpectedly and strike her.

Determined not to let the man see her confusion, she forced herself to maintain her composure, which came to her so easily now after years of practice. She sliced the cake, gathering the familiar defenses that never failed her. By the time she had the last piece of cake on its plate, her control was in place.

Jesse sat on the edge of the settee in the parlor, waiting. The room was homey but tastefully decorated. The high ceiling was rimmed with ten-inch crown molding, the walls papered in a small flower design. Three wing chairs faced each other near the front windows, where the housekeeper's daughter sat waiting for her mother and Miss Sherwood to return, and the side pieces and inlaid tables flanked the walls.

He heard murmuring in the kitchen. Jesse hadn't known what to expect when he finally met Mary Sherwood, but he had never imagined such a petite, auburn-haired beauty existed. Her ivory skin contrasted with the rosy bloom on her lips. But he'd never forget her eyes. Pale blue, large, and so expressive.

He'd expected her to be thrilled to hear that her father was alive and wanted to see her. Instead, her face grew stiff and pale, her body rigid. She had tried to hide her reaction by quickly turning away.

The women were justifiably surprised by his news, and clearly the housekeeper was elated. But Miss Sherwood looked shocked. Did she think her father was dead? Perhaps he shouldn't have been so direct, but he never imagined there'd be a problem.

The housekeeper, Eugenia, came in carrying a tray with a silver service on it; Lolly stood to help her mother. Mary Sherwood followed, looking cool and confident, carrying a tray with four servings of lemon cake. He stifled a grin as he caught sight of pins at the hem of her skirt, winking in the light. He concentrated on his piece of cake to avoid embarrassing her.

Jesse was trying to think of a way to broach the subject he'd come to discuss when the front door opened and a tall, elegant lady with gray strands in her blond hair strode in. "Another letter for you, Mary!" she called, unpinning her hat. She stopped abruptly when she saw Jesse. "What a surprise! We have company."

This must be Thelma Palmer. The Pinkerton detectives told him Mary had been living with her for many years. He liked her instantly. She had a no-nonsense way about her, coupled with intelligent, wide blue eyes.

Jesse needed to talk with Miss Sherwood alone, but her standoffish attitude told him she'd not welcome his request. He should have written first, to give her a chance to think about it. But he was there, and he was sure that coming in person was the right thing to do.

Their small talk turned to his home, which brought up many questions. What was California like? Were there wild Indians? Not in Eureka, he told them. He talked of his work in the logging business and glanced at Mary as he said he worked for a fine man who was good at managing the camp. She maintained her aloof appearance.

"So, what brings you to Massachusetts?" asked Mrs. Palmer.

"I had business in New York for the outfit I work for," he replied. He smiled at Mary; she looked down at her hands in her lap. "I came to Massachusetts to see Miss Sherwood."

Mrs. Palmer, Eugenia, and Lolly all turned to Mary. She raised her head and looked at him with courage and confidence. "You can say whatever it is you have to say here, in front of my family." She glanced from one to the other and repeated "my family."

That was fine. They'll probably discuss it between themselves anyway, so I'll avoid being misunderstood by stating it in front of them all. Jesse leaned forward, his forearms on his knees. "As I said, I'm here representing Mr. Sherwood."

A glimmer of anxiety shimmered in Mary's eyes but vanished almost instantly. "He had no idea you had survived the traumatic events in Tennessee, and when he found that you were alive, he was thrilled. He sent me to bring you to him in California."

Mary sank back into her chair. He wondered why she wasn't as happy as her father had been when he heard she was alive. "He's an honorable man and wants to see you."

The silence lengthened as he watched Mary struggle to compose herself. Finally Mrs. Palmer spoke. "Perhaps we should give Mary time to think this over. It is shocking news to find that her father is alive after all these years."

"I agree." He started to get up. "Maybe later—"

"I won't go." Mary leveled an obstinate look at him. "I don't want to see him, and I'm sorry you came all this way for nothing."

Caught off guard by her vehement refusal to see her father, Jesse stared at her. As their gazes met, his clung to hers, watching the play of emotions on her face until she turned her head. But not before he saw an unguarded instant of anguish in her eyes.

Eugenia, seated beside Mary, reached over and patted

her hand. "Honey, don't be rash; we'll pray about it, hmm?" She glanced at Jesse. "You understand?"

"I understand."

"No you don't! I'm not going to see a man who abandoned me and left my mother to die. I'm not that child anymore, and I've gotten my life just the way I want it. I don't need him."

Jesse stood. Now was not the time to tell her the rest of the story. "I'll come back tomorrow morning, if that's all right."

Mrs. Palmer walked him to the door. "I'm sorry it turned out this way."

"Thank you for your hospitality," Jesse said and walked away, wondering what he could have done to make his case without upsetting Mary. But one thing he knew: Mary Sherwood could be the woman he had been waiting for all his life, and she was going with him whether she liked it or not.

Chapter 2

March 17, 1874

So much has happened since yesterday! My father is alive! I don't know what to think. I should be over-joyed, but I feel so. . .empty and angry. It's hard to explain. He sent someone to take me to him, but I refused to go. I prayed for guidance and still wasn't sure what to do. Later, Eugenia and I had a long talk, and although I still feel the same, I agreed to make the trip. She reminded me that when God said to "honor your father and mother," He didn't mean only if you want to. So I'm going simply because it's the right thing to do. I will honor my father by meeting him. I'll say hello, then leave to come home. And I'll be back in time to prepare lessons for my new position.

Eugenia was so excited, telling me that I'll be going out west where I'll see all sorts of wonderful things to teach. I'm taking a world geography book along so I can study. I won't have time for sightseeing.

187

I'll be on that trip for only one reason, and I won't be sidetracked.

I am so tired—couldn't sleep last night wondering lots of things. Where has he been? Why didn't he come back before the soldiers came? Why doesn't he come himself? Oh, God, why now?

I must quit for now. I'm leaving soon. . .

Union Pacific Station, New York City

Mary sat on the wooden bench, her nose in her geography textbook, the same one she'd used to keep Mr. Jesse Harcourt from talking to her all morning.

He sat beside her. "You were so adamantly against going with me yesterday; I was surprised that you had your bags packed when I arrived."

"Yes." She turned a page in her book. She'd said her good-byes to Mrs. Palmer, Lolly, and Eugenia, then simply pulled her gloves on and said, "I'm ready." He put her bags in the carriage, and even when they turned off her lane onto the road, she didn't look back.

"I didn't want to take you to California against your will, but I can't imagine what you're thinking. I'd like this to be a comfortable and pleasant trip for you, Miss Sherwood."

She ignored him, focusing her attention on her book as if it held the secrets of life itself.

Out of the corner of her eye she could tell he was

looking closely at her. At the shout of the stationmaster calling their destination, she slapped her book shut. Standing, she picked up her smaller suitcases, and he picked up the other. He followed her to the track, where she stood, dazedly looking up and down the length of the train.

As people surged past, a page from a newspaper at her feet fluttered in the turbulence of their rushing feet. Mr. Harcourt set his bag down and pulled the tickets from his pocket.

She kept a firm grip on her intent to make it through the next few days in one emotional piece, and with God's help she'd succeed.

Gazing at the huge, iron train before her she felt a tremor. Like a beast pawing the ground, it roared and hissed. A sooty smell assailed her nostrils, wrinkling her nose.

A gentle tap on the shoulder jarred Mary from her thoughts and back to the present. Jesse Harcourt stood before her, his expression gentle and contemplative. "Miss Sherwood?" He held up two tickets and nodded toward the train. "It's time to board."

The crowd had thinned, and a man in the blue Union Pacific uniform stood watching them. She felt as if she were about to step off a precipice.

Regaining a firm grip on her emotions, she started forward. "Let's go, then," she said more brightly than she intended.

He handed their tickets to the uniformed man who then smiled and pointed. "Car Number Six."

Mr. Harcourt handed her up into the railcar, and she paused, looking down the aisle for a vacant seat. The ceiling looked higher than she'd imagined, and the car roomier than she'd expected. The wide, wooden bench seats each had a cushion and a pillar holding up large storage spaces above. A child was in one of them, and Mary realized they could also be used as sleeping areas.

The conductor approached, crisp and businesslike in his uniform and round, white cap.

Mr. Harcourt held out their tickets. "There must be some mistake," he said. "We reserved space in a parlor car."

The conductor looked at their tickets. "I see." He smiled apologetically. "This sometimes happens. Those spaces were given to last-minute travelers who had high priority."

"No. We paid for that service, and it's important for the lady's comfort. I intend to see that we get it."

"I'm sorry, Sir. You will be refunded the extra fare. If you'd like to step off the train, you can speak to the stationmaster and try for a parlor car on the next train."

He stared at the conductor for a moment, then Mary said, "We can make do here."

The conductor gave her a thankful smile. "As you wish." He punched their tickets and gave them back. "There is a seat halfway back on your left," he said.

They moved forward in the wide aisle, past families, businessmen, children, and two elderly ladies traveling together. They found the empty seat behind a balding scarecrow of a man sitting beside a blond boy about nine years old.

Mary pulled out her new trip journal, a gift from Mrs. Palmer, and a small, blue velvet bag from her valise before Jesse stowed it in the space over their heads. He offered her the seat beside the window, and she slid in. A feeling of adventure crept in for a moment, making her feel like the heroine of *The Girl in White,* a book she'd read last winter. She shook off the idea; that heroine had been kidnapped. She was on this train of her own free will.

Jesse leaned forward and looked out the window. "I wonder where that train will be going."

Beside them a row of tracks separated their train from a series of railcars with no windows. He sat back. "Someone once called the completed Pacific Railroads 'the grand highway of all nations.' "

"I read about it," said Mary. "The newspapers said because of the railroad, the treasures of the Orient that come into San Francisco are now available to Boston and New York." A loud noise, the crashing of metal, ripped through the air accompanied by shrill screeching. The cars on the freight train shuddered forward.

"Have you ever ridden on a train?" he asked.

"No."

"It's a wonderful time we're living in, Miss Sherwood. You're going on a grand adventure."

Mary glanced up at him and found it impossible not to return his disarming smile. She was reminded of his surprise appearance at her front door. It was that same smile.

She opened the travel journal, took the bottle of ink from its velvet bag, and wrote a description of their accommodations. Outside the conductor shouted, "All aboard! Last call."

In a moment the train lurched forward, jerking her back against her seat. The steam engine hissed, and as each railcar was pulled taut, it sounded another crash. The passengers sat tight and held on. She looked over at her traveling companion.

Mr. Harcourt leaned forward and smiled. "The trains always jolt forward when they start moving. I'm sure you'll enjoy the ride when we're out in the countryside."

The freight train looked as if it were moving, but as the wheels clacked over the tracks and they emerged from the station into the afternoon sunlight, Mary realized it was only they who were moving. In the seat in front of them the boy's head bobbed up and down as he bounced on his seat. The man beside the boy sat ramrod straight, his head forward. Smoke wafted through the car from an open window. Somewhere behind them a baby wailed.

Through the smoke flying past, Mary saw more tracks, commercial buildings, then small homes with thin, yellow lawns in front. A girl, with long red braids flying behind her, ran beside the train for a short while, waving at them.

They picked up speed and, finally leaving the New York suburbs, passed through the countryside. She sat back with her new journal on her lap, relaxing her grip on it as the ride smoothed out.

"It's eight hundred miles to Chicago," said Mr. Harcourt. "Our longest distance between major stops."

"Interesting." Mary avoided looking at him. Every time

she did, she liked him because he seemed so friendly. She concentrated on pressing her hand to an already flat page in the journal.

He touched her hand. "Relax, Miss Sherwood. I'm here to help you. Your father—"

"I don't want to talk about my father." Mary yanked her hand back.

"He's a good man! He just—"

"Am I not speaking plainly, Mr. Harcourt?"

"Call me Jesse. You are indeed speaking plainly. We'll talk of other things." He clasped his hands on his knees. "For now."

Mary gave him a look which she hoped was firm, but his serene gaze cooled her anger, and that confused her. It had been a long time since she felt flustered. She'd overcome that long ago as a schoolgirl dealing with giggling, tightly knit groups of girls whose mysterious requirements for entrance eluded her. She lifted her chin and turned her head toward the view outside.

"We can talk of other things," said Jesse.

She was tempted to turn to see if he had a smirk on his face but resolutely kept looking at the farms and pastures passing by. She didn't want anything from Jesse Harcourt, especially his eager friendliness.

"See those white cows? They are called Charolais." His deep-timbred voice sounded too good.

She didn't answer, realizing she was being testy but feeling perversely justified. After all, she was being big-hearted by consenting to make this trip. She touched her forehead to the window and once again, in her heart, complained to God. *You're asking too much of me! I don't want to do this.*

"They come from France," Jesse added.

It wasn't his fault she felt out of sorts. He'd been kind to her from the first, and she hadn't been agreeable to him. She should apologize, but she wouldn't. "We have many of them on the farms near Kimberly," she said flatly.

"Oh. Of course." In the window, Jesse's reflection winked at the boy in the seat ahead who'd turned to face them.

The train clacked along the tracks, rounding a curve, and Mary saw the engine, with black smoke billowing up and flattening out over the cars behind.

A child screeched, and a boy about five years old ran past them, followed by a woman's voice calling, "Nate! Stop! Grandma wants to talk to you."

The child yanked at the door handle at the end of the car but was unable to open it. He ran back, then dived under the seat in front of Mary and looked up at her with mischief dancing in his eyes.

"May I borrow this?" Jesse pointed to the bag in Mary's lap. She handed it to him.

The boy's grandmother bent down in the aisle beside Jesse, peering under the seat. "Nate, darling boy, come out." She reached for his feet, and as soon as she had hold of one, he kicked wildly. The man in the seat turned and said, "Madam, take care of your hooligan, or I'll call the conductor."

She smiled coyly at him. "He's a sweet boy. Really."

The boy gazed at Jesse, who had Mary's small velvet

bag and was tying the cord in intricate knots. Jesse leaned forward with his forearms on his knees and arms outstretched. The boy in front of Mary also had his focus locked on Jesse's nimble fingers until the man beside him ordered him to turn around.

Nate's grandmother reached under the seat again, and the boy kicked her away, as a horse flicks his tail at a pesky fly.

"Na—a—ate!"

Her nasally voiced plea grated on Mary's nerves. The man in front of them turned and glared.

Jesse spoke before the man had a chance to. "Nate, if you come out for your grandmother now, I'll teach you how to tie this knot."

He gave Jesse a narrow look. "When?"

Jesse looked at the woman, who was now standing. "When your grandmother says so." The boy wriggled backward into his grandmother's plump embrace. She held her hands firmly on his shoulders. She looked so relieved and grateful she almost pushed the boy at Jesse. "Now would be fine." She lumbered back to her seat.

Jesse handed Mary her bag and stood. "Let's go find us something to practice with." He and the boy walked to the front of the car. Jesse opened the door, and they left.

Chapter 3

March 17, 1874

I'm on the train, somewhere in Pennsylvania. I feel awful. I've been unkind to Mr. Harcourt, but he has been nothing but nice to me. I have this urge to thrash around in my own annoyance. I don't want to be sulky, but it bothers me to have everything in my life go off in a wild direction. I'm feeling off kilter. I'm embarrassed to admit it, even here, but Mr. H. makes me think unladylike thoughts.

We didn't get the privacy my father paid for, so we're in a crowded car. Mr. H. put our bags on the floor in front of the seat and has climbed up above to sleep. I write this beneath a blanket as I lean with my head holding a pillow against the cold window. In the silvery moonlight I can see a few outlines of trees, but it's mostly pitch-black out there. I'll write descriptions of the scenery in the journal Mrs. Palmer gave me, so there won't be many here.

> *I promise to be more pleasant to Mr. H. tomorrow. But I still won't talk about my father.*
>
> *Last night we stopped for a tasty but quick dinner about eight o'clock and. . .*

Mary awoke with a start, not sure where she was. A baby was crying, and she felt a gentle rocking motion. Then she remembered. The movement of the train had lulled her to sleep. Outside, rosy crests of the hills glowed in the dawn's first light. The train's *k-nick k-nock, k-nick k-nock* kept a steady rhythm as they moved through the countryside.

She turned away from the window and saw Jesse. He stood in the aisle, his hand on the back of the seat, looking down at her. With his hair still slightly damp from being combed and with a fresh shirt on, he was entirely too good-looking. She tried to look away but couldn't. Instead, she stared at the buttons on his shirt so she couldn't be distracted by his smile.

She quickly put her hand to her hair and sat up straighter, though she couldn't put her feet on the floor.

He smiled, laying a small, black Bible on the seat. "Good morning. I hope I didn't wake you." He spoke softly, even though the man in the seat in front of them was stirring.

"Oh, no. I was admiring the scenery." She pulled her blanket into a knot in her lap.

"Before we get to San Francisco, you're going to see the most spectacular scenery on earth." He quickly stowed their

197

bags overhead and stepped aside for her to go freshen up.

She returned and, trying to be more agreeable, considered a congenial topic of conversation. How would she start? The Bible he held in his hand? Ask him if that's his Bible? No, it obviously was. Ask him if he read it every day? Ask him what he'd read? Every question seemed nosey.

She decided to open with the obvious. "I see you have a—"

"We'll be stopping for—"

They both spoke at once. Mary felt the long-forgotten heat of a blush creep up her neck.

"Pardon me, go ahead," he said.

"No," she stammered. "You."

He gazed at her for a moment, then said, "I was just going to say that we'll be stopping for breakfast soon." His eyes, a deep shade of blue, were full of adventure. "Our next stop is a small eating house. Delicious food. But they only give us a few minutes."

The pungent smell of fruit floated over to Mary. Across the aisle, a woman carefully peeled an orange. Her daughter sat on her father's leg while he jostled her up and down, quietly singing, "All around the mulberry bush the monkey chased the weasel. . . ."

A memory so strong it shocked her came to Mary. Her father was singing that same song, holding her hands and turning her in a circle as they danced together. They were in his study. He was smiling as he lifted her high. Across the aisle the little girl sang out "Pop! Goes the weasel" and giggled.

Jesse said something, but Mary's mind failed to register what it was. She closed the door on those sudden memories. "I'm sorry. You were saying?"

"Nothing important. The buckwheat griddle cakes with Vermont syrup were the best I've had since I left California." He peered closely at her. "Are you all right, Miss Sherwood?"

Something about the mother daintily wiping her fingertips on a napkin captivated Mary. Her own mother had long, tapered fingers like those. She looked away. "I'll return in a moment," she said, standing.

Jesse moved into the aisle. She hurried away, avoiding three lively children running races up and down the aisle. Jesse's young friend, Nate, was in the lead.

Back in the tiny, curtained-off areas allotted for washing and grooming, she gripped the metal bar beneath the open window. She longed to feel the cool air on her hands, but black ashes from the engine spiraled past the window. She picked up one of the thin cloths lying on the narrow ledge beneath a mirror and dipped it into the water basin. Even though the basin was anchored to the wooden counter, the water rippled with the movement of the train.

Dabbing the wet cloth to her temples, she struggled to gain her composure. She reasoned that it was natural for a memory of her father to surface now that she was on her way to him. Those memories, somewhere inside, lay hidden beneath her refusal to recognize them. Someone wanted in so Mary took a deep breath and dropped the cloth in the hamper.

Weaving through passengers in the aisles, some reaching up into their overhead spaces, others simply standing because they were tired of sitting, so many smells assailed her. Food, perfumes, unwashed feet, and smoke coming in an open window. She got back to find the young boy, Nate, sitting cross-legged in her seat. He jumped up and climbed onto the seat back perching close to Jesse. Jesse dusted her side of the cushion, and she eased in past Nate's legs. He and Jesse busily twisted and tied lengths of twine in multiple knots.

Glad of this opportunity for reflection, she gazed at the bold sweep of the mountains with great expanses of pine trees and an occasional log cabin. Soon the *k-nick k-nock* of the wheels slowed as they passed a scattering of horses and cows browsing on the cold hillside.

Nate climbed down and ran back to his grandmother. "Nimble little fellow." Jesse shook his head, smiling. "He's a fast learner."

He turned his attention to Mary. "So, what brought you to Massachusetts?"

She was going to answer his question and keep her past out of the conversation. But he was so easy to talk to, she found herself telling him how she, Eugenia, and Lolly made their way north on the Underground Railroad. "We were headed for Canada, as far away as we could get, but found a home in Kimberly with Mrs. Palmer."

"She seems like a good woman."

"Yes. She's a teacher, retired now. She helped Lolly and me through school." She smiled, remembering. "And filled in the gaps in social graces we all lacked.

"My mother wasn't there to instruct us." She spoke so softly she wasn't aware he'd heard her. But his eyes filled with tenderness.

Neither one said a word for a few seconds, then Jesse asked, "How did your mother die?"

Just thinking of it upset her stomach. She didn't know if she could talk about it.

He touched her hand lightly. "You don't have to talk about it."

She wanted to, but it had been so long since she'd thought about it, she wasn't sure where to begin. "I haven't thought of it for years. Until two days ago," she said, pushing a strand of hair away from her face. "I suppose I've been numb."

He nodded, his eyes searching her face.

"She died when the house was burning." Her voice broke. "Genie, Lolly, and I were hiding in a secret place in our woodshed when the Yankee soldiers. . .when they—"

Jesse gently pushed back a strand of hair that had fallen over her eyebrow again. "How old were you?"

"I was six, and Lolly was three." She shuddered and hugged her arms close.

"You're fortunate to have had Eugenia take you under her wing."

Mary was surprised at how easily she told him personal things she'd never tell an outsider. But Jesse didn't seem like an outsider. He was somehow different. Still, she thought they should keep their conversation on lighter topics.

The train ground to a stop, the wheels screeching. A bell clanged outside, and the conductor opened the door. "Thirty minutes for breakfast!" he cried.

They hurried to the restaurant. Many passengers ate on the train as enterprising young boys came through the cars selling boiled eggs, milk, strong tea, and other foods. Jesse and Mary rushed through a stack of buckwheat pancakes with Vermont syrup as delicious as he'd said. Outside, the train lurched and slammed as it was being rearranged.

They got on just in time as the front of their divided train went south, while they were whisked toward Buffalo. They passed through more beautiful mountains and miles of dark pine and spruce. In one area narrow pavements of lengthwise peeled logs streaked down the hill amidst little streams of water. Huge trunks, stripped of bark, came shooting down like lightning to gray sawmills and shining ponds below. There were more undisturbed forests, then sloping, cleared fields with white stumps waist high, some lying roots upward.

The man in front of them bowed forward, moaning. Mary leaned between him and the boy with him. "Sir, is there anything I can do for you? Shall I call for the conductor?"

The man shook his head, took a gasping breath, and sat up. "Tommy, get my bottle of stomach bitters." The boy rummaged around in the suitcase on the floor and brought out a small bottle of dark liquid. He chewed on his lower lip and glanced at Mary. The man glared at her, and she sank back into her own seat.

He took a long drink of the elixir and leaned back with a sigh.

Several passengers rushed to the windows, pointing and exclaiming. Mary looked out on a huge chasm and a river leaping at least seventy feet over rock walls, a glittering sheet of snow, diamonds, and topaz. Jesse and Nate arrived, and Nate slipped in beside Mary.

"We're going over the highest wooden bridge on the continent!" said Nate. "The conductor said so."

Jesse agreed. "That's the Genesee River."

"Beautiful!" breathed Mary.

Jesse gazed down at the man in the seat in front of him, a look of concern on his face. "Are you all right, Sir?" he asked.

The man cursed, scowled, then slumped sideways. The boy with him scrambled from his window seat and stared down at his companion.

Jesse quickly knelt beside the man, loosening his collar. He held his hand out to the frightened young lad. "Come here, Boy." He shyly approached Jesse, glancing down. "What's your name, Son?"

"Tommy." The boy put his hand in Jesse's and looked up at him.

"Is this your father, Tommy?" Jesse felt the man's wrist for his pulse.

"No, Sir. He's my uncle, Wilfred Taylor."

"Has he been sick like this before?"

"Yes, Sir."

Jesse glanced at Mary, a touch of concern and question around his eyes and mouth. "Nate, I'd like you to find the conductor and bring him here. Mary, would you take Tommy to the dining car and get him a glass of milk?" Jesse reached into his pocket and brought out some coins.

The boy squeezed Jesse's hand and gave Mary an uneasy look. Mary approached him with a smile. "It's all right, Tommy. I'm a teacher, and I like children."

The dining car had only two people in it—a young couple who leaned close to each other over their hot cups and ignored Mary and Tommy. Between sips of his milk, the lad told her he was traveling with his uncle to Omaha where his grandparents awaited them.

Her heart ached with sympathy for this boy's dilemma. His mother died of the fever, and in great grief his father had gone to sea on business, leaving his uncle to accompany Tommy to his grandparents. He spoke quietly, becoming more withdrawn as they talked.

Saying a quick prayer for the right words, she asked Tommy if he knew Jesus. He shook his head. She covered his small hand with hers. "Tommy, I know what it's like to lose your mother. But even more important, God knows. He loves you very much."

"My mother used to tell me that."

"She was right." Mary took a deep breath. "God loves you so much He sent Jesus to live in your heart and carry your troubles for you."

For the first time, she saw a glimmer of hope in Tommy's eyes, then he looked away in despair. "My heart hurts. He won't want to come in."

They talked for a few more minutes and prayed together. When they returned, Jesse was in Tommy's seat with Mr. Taylor's head in his lap. The man looked asleep.

Jesse offered her a small smile, then shook his head. "Tommy will sit with you for awhile. Is that all right?"

Mary squeezed Tommy's hand. "Perfectly. We've become friends." She let Tommy slide in first so he had the window seat. Outside, low hills covered with orchards dotted with apple and cherry blossoms glided past.

Tommy sat quietly beside her, and Jesse gazed out the window most of the time, looking back at her occasionally.

Soon Mr. Taylor was sitting up, talking with Jesse. He ordered Tommy to behave, and Mary assured him he was being good. She gave him her trip journal and watched him draw a picture on the last page.

When they got to Buffalo, Jesse drew her away from the press of people leaving to transfer to other trains. "Thanks for being such a good sport about Tommy."

Mary smiled. "It was nothing. He's a delightful child."

"They need our help." Jesse drew her farther away from the hissing of the steam engine. "The conductor wants to put them off here, but I convinced him to let them ride to Chicago."

"What's the matter with Mr. Taylor?"

"It's a stomach problem, similar to," he paused, raised his eyebrows, then continued, "to that of another older gentleman I know. They both contracted the illness in prison camps. In the case of the other man, I helped him through it, so I'm familiar with the ailment."

"Are you a doctor, Mr. Ha—" As his dark eyebrows momentarily slanted in a frown, she paused before saying his name softly, as if testing it. "I mean, Jesse?"

"No, just an assistant." He looked as if he wanted to say something more. Instead he looked away, watching the family that had been across from them departing. "I'm going to go into the restaurant and get a meal for all of us."

He took a few steps, then turned, and said, "It would be a hardship for Tommy to be left here all alone with his ill uncle. I don't think he's old enough for the responsibility. As I said, I've had experience with this ailment and can help Mr. Taylor at least as far as Chicago."

He looked down at his feet for a second, then back up to her face. "If this is all right with you, that is."

"Of course it's all right. I don't mind Tommy's company; in fact, I like him very much." She told him the sad tale Tommy told her.

He nodded. "Yes, Mr. Taylor told me a little of it. I'm going to see about that parlor car for the four of us. It will be much more comfortable for Taylor and you too."

Mary inclined her head in a small gesture of understanding. "Of course it will be more comfortable for him, but I'm all right where we are."

Jesse grinned. "You're a lot like. . .a certain gentleman I know." Before she could say anything he looked toward the eating house. "I'll be back as soon as I can."

Mary went back to her seat beside Tommy.

Jesse hurried to the food line, pondering an emotion that flitted across Mary's face when she'd told him of her travel from her home. Her sudden tension when he mentioned her father again worried him. He'd have to find a way to help her face the truth before they got to San Francisco. It would break Mr. Sherwood's heart to see her so hurt and angry. He wanted a better reunion for them than Mary's stiffly acknowledged greeting, then her turning away to leave. And he knew that was what she intended to do. Yes, he had to help her change her mind. Whether she liked it or not.

Chapter 4

March 18, 1874

Some memories are beginning to surface. It's probably because I'm going to see my father. I don't want those memories and will try to think of other things when they arise. J. still wants to talk about my father. I don't, but I have found him easy to talk to and did share a few things.

He is a kind man though, giving aid to a fellow traveler. He wants to secure a larger accommodation for us, in order to help the sick man. I too felt sorry for them, especially the young boy traveling with him. Concern for his fellowman seems to be J.'s way of life.

I n Chicago the next day, the train had a three-hour wait, so Jesse and Mary took an omnibus to the hotel for sightseeing. The elegant hotel's great halls and parlors were filled with people, walking arm in arm through the high front doors, seated on plush chairs and sofas, and standing in line at the registration desk.

They walked a few blocks, admiring store window displays of Indian items. A replica of an Indian village with miniature teepees caught Mary's attention. "I've read of them, but this makes it seem so real!"

Jesse pointed to a figurine of a brave on horseback. "One time at the village near our home, your father and I—"

"I told you, we are not going to talk about him." Mary turned on her heel and indignantly walked away. *Thick-headed man.* She ignored him calling her. He probably wanted to recite another anecdote about her father. Well, she wouldn't hear it!

"Miss Sherwood! You're walking the wrong way." She stopped and glanced back. "The hotel is back this way." He stood, relaxed, smiling at her. *Arrogant too.*

Back at the hotel she stood on tiptoe, concentrating on the view outside the large window, hoping to see the omnibus. She settled back on her feet and turned to him. "Mr. Harcourt, I have something to say to you."

"Oh, now you're being formal again."

"I think that's best. After all, we'll never see each other after this trip, so even a friendship would be superfluous. I suggest you keep your stories to yourself, or I will ride in another car." If he thought she was crazy or rude, she didn't care. She didn't have time for Jesse Harcourt or tales of her father. Her goal was to get to San Francisco, pay her respects, then return to her life in Boston.

"You can't do that. I have your ticket." His voice was firm and final.

"You yourself said it. It's *my* ticket. And I will decide where I sit." She lifted her face, glared at him, and put her hands on her hips.

He smiled that mischievous, charming smile and linked his arm through hers. "The omnibus is here." She wrenched her arm away and fumed all the way to the omnibus. She found a vacant seat between two gentlemen and took it, studiously avoiding Jesse.

Back at the station, Mary stayed with the Taylors while Jesse visited the ticket window. He returned with parlor car tickets for the four of them as the conductor called "All aboard!" Jesse assisted Mr. Taylor as the four of them found their car near the end of the train.

Mary was caught off guard by the difference from the coach they'd traveled in so far. She entered a small, square room, the whole width of the car, with a narrow passageway on one side. The carpeted room had a long sofa, two arm chairs, two shining spittoons, plenty of mirrors, and a floor-to-ceiling bookshelf. *The quiet and privacy must have cost a lot of money.* But she wouldn't miss the press of people, the smells, the cigar and pipe smoke, unruly children, and general chaos of a small area full of people.

"What is the meaning of this?" Mr. Taylor leaned his gaunt frame in the parlor doorway scowling, refusing to enter. "Tommy, come back here." The boy ran to his uncle's side. The station outside slid by as the train moved forward.

Jesse grinned at Mary and swept his arm around the

room. "This is a parlor car."

"Harcourt! We ain't staying here." Taylor swayed as the train lurched forward.

Jesse took his arm and helped him to the sofa. "The young lady and I have reserved this room. You can call yourselves our chaperons. Your fare to Omaha is covered."

Taylor grumbled. "Too fancy." He closed his eyes wearily, then snapped them open to glare at Tommy. "Mind your manners, Boy!"

"Yes, Sir."

Mary opened one of the two doors, and to break the tension she said, "Look, Tommy! A little room."

The boy walked into the tiny closet. He wasn't tall enough to see himself in the mirror over the washstand basin. "What's the other door for?"

"I don't know."

Jesse answered, "It's the door to the other drawing room. We share the water closet."

Mr. Taylor's voice behind him said, "Highfalutin iron horse twiddle, if you ask me."

Mary thought the poor man couldn't be as bad as that bristly shell he showed them. "Just think how comfortable you'll be until you get to your dear family," she said.

"Dear family!" He snorted, waving her away. "Don't need 'em." He grimaced and arched his back. "Feels like a mule kicked me in the gut."

Jesse was instantly at his side, telling him to lie on his stomach. Taylor refused, with an oath. "Boy! Get my bitters."

Tommy ran to their valise and drew out the bottle, his eyes downcast.

Jesse put his hand on Tommy's shoulder. "Mr. Taylor, for the sake of the boy and the lady, I ask that you refine your language."

Taylor glared at Mary as if she were at fault. "I'm not staying here." He started to rise, then doubled over as pain gripped him.

Jesse eased him back onto the sofa. "Rest now. We can talk later."

His concern is real. There was something about Jesse that held her attention. As if he knew she watched him, Jesse glanced up at her. She turned away and walked to the window. This land was strange, not like the hills in Tennessee, nor the mountains on the horizon back in Kimberly. The farther she traveled away from home, the more her footing seemed unsure and disconnected.

Jesse had said he'd been in prison camp with an older gentleman. Would that have been her father? She was almost sure of it but refused to ask him, angry that he'd played the game of raising her curiosity so she would ask.

She couldn't imagine her father in pain. She remembered him riding up the road to their house, calling her name. Standing on the verandah where she'd been waiting, she stretched her arms up as high as she could and called "Papa!" She ran down the steps as he drew near and reined his horse to a halt a few feet away. He dismounted, swept her up into his arms, then swung her into the saddle and mounted behind her. Together they'd ride Hero to the stables.

She put her fists together beneath her chin, annoyed. She'd successfully banished good memories of him. But did she really want the familiar memory that had surrounded her heart with bitterness? The one of him leaving, promising to come back? The one which always followed it? Her mother's eyes pleading to her and Eugenia to stay in hiding and keep quiet while she was dragged away by Union soldiers. Those memories had constricted her heart for years, but they were habitual, easy reminders. They bound the broken pieces of her young heart, keeping it in one piece and keeping her from being too soft, too trusting.

"He's resting easy now." Jesse's voice, close by, startled her. She ignored him, annoyed that she'd been thinking about things that were over and done. Some things were settled, and it was too late for forgiveness.

Forgive, as I have forgiven you.

Startled, she turned quickly to see if Jesse had murmured the words. He stood nearby, braced by his arms on the silver curtain track overhead. A question was in his eyes. Suddenly feeling a need to get away, she said, "I'm going for a walk," and she slipped out behind him before he could say anything.

Outside, in the breeze, she watched the ground up close as rocks and gravel sped by beneath the train. On the very edges of the crumbling, dusty banks beside the tracks, pink, blue, and yellow flowers stood undisturbed. If only she felt as serene as they appeared.

Jesse watched Mary leave, noticing she was troubled about something. That only reinforced his decision to have none of her petulance and use all the persuasiveness he could to get her to talk. He'd do it. Even if he had to fill up the quiet times with his own stories.

She needed to know some things about her father, especially what an exceptional man he was, and for both their sakes, she needed to let go of her anger.

Chapter 5

March 19, 1874

We arrived in Chicago today. I thought J. was an agreeable person, but he's been bossy. He won't quit referring to my father, although I distinctly told him I wouldn't hear it. I told him politely, ignored him, and walked away, but he won't let up. If he continues, I'll have to resort to rudeness, and that could make the trip unbearable. Maybe I shouldn't have talked of personal things yesterday.

I'm writing this in the luxury and privacy of our own drawing room. Wilfred Taylor and his nephew, Tommy, are sharing the room as far as Omaha. Although I didn't mind the crowded car, it's nice to relax and simply enjoy the countryside sliding by. And oh, what countryside it is! Leaving Chicago we passed through miles and miles of rich prairie land with houses in the distance and trees surrounding them like green walls.

The coachman came in, his brown face shining

*as he asked us if we were ready for him to make our
beds. We were all curious and watched in fascination
as he pulled the armchair seats in to meet in the
middle, and the backs pulled out to lie level with the
seats—a bed! The sofa pulled out and opened into a
bed too. Tommy's eyes almost popped out as he pulled
down another bedstead from the ceiling! From overhead, he drew out mattresses, pillows, blankets, and
curtains for the windows. When he left and locked
the door, I felt as if I were in a castle on wheels.*

*I do wish Mr. H. would be content to escort me
across the country without trying to be a friend. Last
night I had to call him to task again. He and crotchety
old Mr. Taylor were both in the war, so he talked of
those experiences to keep Mr. T. awake and his attention off his pain. I finally became exasperated by stories
of my father's war experiences and told him to quit.*

Within her curtained-off bed space, Mary's
eyes opened at the first light. Outside was
more prairie, unfenced now, undivided,
unmeasured, and unmarked. Awed by the enormity of
miles and miles of land stretched out toward the horizon, she thought, *this is what the word "West" means.*
Great spaces, droves of cattle in the distance, now and
then a shapeless, lonely village. She stared, trying to fix
it in her mind so she could describe it in her journal for
Mrs. Palmer. In the pearly new light, the different colors
of grass or grain dappled the ground.

She opened her Bible and read Proverbs, chapter ten. She closed it with a sigh, satisfied that she was doing right by making this trip. Nevertheless, one verse stayed with her: Verse eleven, "The mouth of a righteous man is a well of life. . ."

She said a quick prayer, then peeked out her curtain. Jesse lay on one of the armchair beds, his back to her. On the other, Tommy slept on his stomach, only his blond head visible on the pillow. Sitting on the sofa was Mr. Taylor, glaring back at her. Mary snapped her curtain shut. If only she could feel as kindly toward him as Jesse did. But she saw Tommy's fear and uncertainty and wondered why Mr. Taylor didn't. Or if he did, why wasn't the older man more kind to the boy? *Lord, help me watch what I say.*

Enjoying the gentle sway of the train, she dressed and put her journal on the shelf. When she heard sounds of the men stirring, she pulled the curtains back to the wall.

Jesse and Tommy were sitting on Jesse's bed with their heads bowed over a book.

"Good morning, Miss Mary!" Tommy looked up and grinned at her.

With a quick, shy glance at Jesse she answered, "Good morning to both of you. Tommy, want to take a look outside?" He rushed to the window and pressed his nose to it. This far back from the engine, sparks and soot were almost nonexistent.

Mr. Taylor emerged from the small water closet, a towel in his hands. He saw Mary and quickly pulled his suspenders over his shoulders.

"Good morning, Mr. Taylor." She smiled tentatively, then looked down as she passed him on her way to the tiny room to freshen herself.

"Humph." He shuffled past her.

She shut the door, wondering if the man ever smiled. When she emerged a few minutes later, the coachman was turning the beds back into sofas and easy chairs. He smiled as he left and told them the train would be stopping for breakfast in forty-five minutes. Jesse took Tommy to the platform for the cool morning air.

The moment the door clicked shut Mr. Taylor peered closely at her. "What have you got against your father? He sounds like a brave man."

She stiffened her back and stared at him. A tense silence filled the small room.

"I beg your pardon, Mr. Taylor, but I prefer not to discuss my family."

Taylor snorted. "You were willing to discuss *mine* last night. Prattling on about how I should look forward to meeting my *dear* family."

"I did *not* prattle! I merely—"

"Told me how I should feel." He didn't smile, but his eyes gleamed. "You don't know them, and you don't know me nor what they done to me. Yet you gave me advice."

Baffled, Mary stared at him, not knowing what to say.

Taylor continued. "Your father sounds better than my stinkin' family, and I think you should look forward to seeing *him*. There. How do you like that advice, Miss?" His eyebrows shot up, and he scrutinized her. "You got somethin' against him?"

"I—he—" She couldn't turn away from his fierce gaze. The train swayed, its rocking motion breaking the spell. She yanked her gaze away, toward the passageway windows.

"Looking for a way out? Do you always run from trouble?"

She looked back at him. He waited, challenging her to respond. He was enjoying this! His thin-lipped animosity goaded her to reply, "Mr. Taylor, I don't wish to be rude, but neither will I discuss my personal life. If you refuse to speak of more pleasant matters, I must leave."

He chuckled. "Let's talk about that Bible on your shelf."

She glanced at her Bible. "Are you seriously interested in discussing Scriptures?"

"I am." He leaned forward. "Do you believe that tons of water in the Red Sea just stood up, leaving a wide road which miraculously dried up in an instant for more than a million people to walk across?"

She wasn't sure if the eyes looking up beneath his bushy gray eyebrows were sincere or mocking. "Of course I believe it. God spoke and created it all. He could just as easily speak and change it." She tossed the question back at him. "Do you believe it, Mr. Taylor?"

He laced his fingers together, staring down at his hands. "Well, I haven't made up my mind about that one." He was silent for a minute, then said, "You probably believe there really was a Tower of Babel."

"Of course." Mary relaxed somewhat, wondering where he was going with this comment.

"Then you believe that men got so smart they built a tower almost all the way up to heaven, scared God 'cause He thought they'd walk right in on Him sometime, so He put a stop to it by scrambling their language. That right?"

"Nothing scares God. He did what He thought was best. He always does." Was he sneering? Was he serious? She couldn't tell. He simply looked down at his clasped hands. Was this old curmudgeon softening?

She sat in the armchair across from him. "Mr. Taylor," she said softly, "those topics are interesting, but what matters is whether you believe what the Bible says about Jesus. When you decide He is who the Bible says He is and accept Him in your heart, these other things become more clear to you."

He continued to sit stone still, his hands clasped together between his knees. *Father, soften his heart and give me the right words.* Mary leaned forward. "Let's talk about Jesus."

Taylor jerked upright, his back stiffly away from the chair and scowled at her. "You're preaching at me?" Indignation shone in his eyes. "Harcourt already tried that. At least he doesn't hide ill feelings toward none of his kin."

Mary shot up out of the chair. She swallowed hard, trying not to reveal the anger which almost choked her. The old crosspatch was toying with her, and she refused to play his game. "I bid you good morning," she said and opened the passageway door. Before she shut it she added, "I intend to pray for you, Sir." She left with his mocking laughter ringing in her ears.

She fled through the train, across the platforms, and

through crowded cars. Nearing the front of the train, she opened the door to people harmonizing to "The Man on the Flying Trapeze." Some stood in the aisles, others sat sideways, singing along. Someone squeezed a concertina, and those who didn't know the words kept time by clapping.

Halfway down on the left, she saw a young pregnant woman, her feet propped up on a valise. She beckoned to Mary. "I saw you when I boarded in Chicago. My name is Elizabeth."

Mary knelt beside her. "I'm pleased to meet you. My name is Mary."

"Sing along, if you know the song. I can't carry a tune, but I do love the singing." The woman beside her leaned forward, belting out the end of the chorus, "my heart he has stolen away!"

A man across from Elizabeth got up, gaily continuing to sing, and with a flourish offered Mary his seat. She happily took it and spent the next twenty minutes away from Jesse's hard questions and Mr. Taylor's scowls. The train slowed as the singers launched into "Little Brown Jug," and Mary reluctantly left her new friend to make her way back to the parlor car.

Jesse and Tommy had returned, and Mr. Taylor ignored her as though nothing had happened. She thought she saw the hint of a smile on his face but decided it was most likely a grimace. She'd never seen the man smile. They all exited the train for another hasty breakfast.

They'd had no more personal discussions all morning. Mary studied her geography book, making notes. Jesse spent time teaching Tommy to make knots. Mr. Taylor reclined on the sofa, resting.

About noon the train slowed to a crawl. Mary peered out and saw nothing but a line of tracks heading away from them like a thin thread lying across the prairie. The brakes squealed, and they stopped. "Look, Tommy! Another train!" It puffed its way down the tracks, its passengers gaily waving handkerchiefs. She gave Tommy one, Jesse opened the windows, and they waved back. Leaning her head out the window, Mary saw a line of white handkerchiefs fluttering from their own train. After the other train cleared their tracks, they moved on.

"They're probably going to Denver," said Jesse as the other train disappeared into the distant horizon.

Mary snapped her head around, surprised to find him so close. She was so caught up in the handkerchief greetings she hadn't heard him approach. His knee was on the ledge near her, and he was so close their noses almost touched. She felt consumed by his alert gaze.

She was glad he straightened at that moment because she felt a rush of heat climb up her neck to her cheeks. *What is happening to me? I feel flustered.* She grabbed her geography book and held on tightly as she looked out at a grove of trees in the distance.

Alone again, the way she liked it, Mary opened the geography book but found it difficult to concentrate. She kept thinking about Jesse, and that irritated her. With a shrug, she yanked her concentration back to the book. *Hungary. Borders on Romania to the east, Austria to the west.* . . Eugenia's placid brown face smiled in her mind.

Finally Mary could no longer pull her wandering mind back to Baltic Europe. She lay the book down on her lap and gazed out the window, thinking of Eugenia's last words to her. The four of them prayed together before she left, Eugenia reminding her that until she forgave her father she'd have a hurting place that would not heal, and unless she gave it up to God, it would cast a shadow on her life for years.

The prairie, which had been perfectly flat out of Chicago, had grown more and more rolling, now broken by deep ravines and sweeping hills. A dark belt of forest lined the western horizon.

Jesse and Tommy joined her at the window. Jesse held out a hand to Mary. "Want to go out to the platform and get a wider view? That green strip is trees along the Missouri River."

Tommy's eyes widened. "Are we almost there?"

Mary smiled at him. What a sweet boy. She put her hand on his soft, blond curls. "I think we are." Buoyed by his excitement, she took Jesse's hand, and they went out.

On the platform, Mary leaned out the opposite side and saw in the distance a town on a hill—a lovely view. Crowned at the top was a large white building overlooking the city.

Jesse lifted Tommy and held him tightly. "Omaha," he declared. Tommy stared hard, as if trying to see his family waiting for him.

Mary touched his arm. "God has a good plan for you, Tommy." The boy's gaze held hers, looking for reassurance. He smiled absently, then looked back at his new home. She drew a deep breath, thinking how far she was from home and yet not even halfway across the continent.

The train slowed, and soon, in Council Bluffs, at the foot of the hills, all passengers boarded mammoth omnibuses, and with mail wagons, express and baggage wagons piled high, were ferried across the river to Omaha. "Wow!" Tommy breathed in awe, unable to take his eyes off a steamer puffing away from the Omaha landing on its way downriver.

Jesse watched Mary, unable to forget the spark of something in her eyes. Was it a trace of sadness? Need? For a moment it seemed like deep loneliness; then the look was gone, replaced by her mask of calm control.

He wondered if she allowed anyone to really know her, to share her thoughts and dreams. He saw a lovely, sweet woman with a hurt too deep to face. *It's not easy being surrounded by people but having no one to trust, no one in whom to confide. Lord, she needs to talk to You about this and trust You to take the pain away. And I know You do all things in Your time, but I think Mary should come to forgiveness for her father before we get to San Francisco. Help me to reassure her it's the right thing to do.*

Chapter 6

March 20, 1874

I can hardly write all the things that happened yesterday. We truly crossed from our comfortable, familiar East and into the West. Oh, what that word means! Wide-open spaces, a world so very different it is difficult to imagine, even from the literature I've read. And J. tells me this is only the beginning.

I've described the landscape in the trip journal, but I continue to marvel. From the flat prairies to the hills of Council Bluffs, across the Missouri River with steamers heading for places with exotic names, to the shrieking locomotives, and the crowds! In Omaha I heard at least six different languages spoken by people holding checks, clamoring for their luggage, which sat behind a high wooden wall. One poor woman knelt beside her chest, which had broken open during the journey, crying and speaking Norwegian to the kind souls who helped stuff her belongings back inside and tied the chest with ropes.

It's hard to believe what happened when Mr. Taylor and Tommy met their family. The grandparents rejoiced with tears. They ran to Tommy with open arms. Taylor nodded slightly to his mother, stood back, then coldly turned to walk away! The mother reached out and called his name, but he didn't look back. His father glared at his retreating back while comforting his wife. Mr. Taylor lost himself in the crowd; we never saw him again.

It should have been a tender scene. I'll never forget the look in Tommy's eyes as he watched his uncle leave. J. went after Taylor, but he was unable to convince him to reconcile with his family. So sad.

I had to laugh at J., frowning at a fierce but jolly-looking miner who tipped his hat at me. There were many of them, all boots and beards, striding about, watching their rifles or guns and strapped rolls of muddy blankets. . . .

Mary awoke, prayed, and watched a herd in the distance. She couldn't get the horrid memory of the Taylor family from her mind. What could have happened to make Mr. Taylor so unforgiving and angry? He could at least have been polite before he walked away. *Like I'm going to do? Can I walk away if my father comes to meet me with open arms as they did?*

A sudden movement among the herd startled her. At first they had seemed like ordinary goats, but when they began to leap she knew they were antelopes. Jesse dropped something in the room outside her curtain. He'd made his bed near the door, as far from her as he could get, to be proper. "Consider me a bodyguard," he'd said.

Seated on the edge of her bed, she angled her mirror on a narrow ridge in the window frame so she could pin up her hair. Jesse's footsteps softly sounded on the rug. *He's a nice man,* she thought, remembering all his kindnesses. Maybe they *could* be friends just for this trip.

With one last look in the mirror, she pinched her cheeks to pinken them, then pulled the curtain open.

Jesse smiled up at her from where he sat. "Good morning."

"Good morning," she answered, her heart hammering. He seemed to strike a vibrant chord, which she desperately tried to quell. She stepped out, trying to be dignified. But she couldn't keep her rebellious hands from pulling her jacket down and smoothing out imaginary wrinkles. Blushing at this unnecessary fussing over her appearance, she lifted her head and went to the wash room.

In a moment the coachman came in to make the beds back into furniture, announcing, "Thirty minutes to breakfast!" She and Jesse went out to the platform to watch the country roll by. They laughed at the antics of small animals that looked like puppies peering out of holes in the ground, first defiantly barking at the train, then darting back underground in fright.

They stopped laughing at the same instant, and their gazes locked. Their smiles died away as Jesse brushed her arm. It tingled where he touched her. He caressed her with a look that made her feel a strange yearning, then he slowly kissed her. Just a brief touch of the lips, but it changed everything.

She reminded herself that he was on her father's side. Flustered, she said, "Oh, look! There's that half-mile bridge the guide book told about."

"We're crossing the North Platte River."

On their way back from their hurried breakfast, Jesse stopped and pressed a coin into the hand of a thin Indian woman wrapped in brown canvas-type material. Mary was fascinated by the papoose strapped on her back. Beneath the arch of his basket, his wide, placid eyes shone in his soft, brown baby face. They shared a brief, but sweet, confiding look.

Back in their parlor car, she resisted the urge to check her appearance in the mirror. Jesse had been quiet in the restaurant, and she sensed he had a lot on his mind. She prayed for herself and for reconciliation of little Tommy Taylor and his family.

"Miss Sherwood." Jesse watched her closely. "Mary. We really need to talk. We'll be arriving in San Francisco in three days. There are some things you need to know."

"Oh, please, Mr. Harcourt, not now." She rounded her shoulders and gripped her upper arms, as if protecting her heart.

"It has to be now. There isn't much time."

"I am going to San Francisco, Mr. Harcourt, and that should be enough for you."

"It's not. If you have any faith in the God of that Bible you brought, you'll know that unforgiveness is not an option. Your father is a good man. You may think he let you down, but you don't know the whole story."

"He left and wasn't there when we needed him. That's what I know." She closed her eyes, hearing the cry she'd wailed when Eugenia took her and Lolly from the blackened, smoking shell of their burned home. *He said he'd come back! I want my daddy!*

"You are simply looking at it from your own selfish perspective." He held his hands up in surrender. "I know it was hard for you. But can you imagine how hard it was for him?"

Mary opened her mouth to interrupt.

"No, I have more to say. I like you, Mary, and would make it all better for you, if I could, so your hurt would be gone and you'd come to your father with a loving heart. He loves you very much, and that's what counts. If you'll sit down, I'll tell you about him."

"All right. But you can't erase the years I've spent trying to forget him and learning to live my life without him." She sat stiffly in the armchair facing him.

"I know I can't erase your pain. But have you asked God to help you forgive him? How can you have peace while you're holding this anger inside? You've made an altar of your right to be angry."

"What more do you want? I'm making the trip."

"I want you to look at this from your father's point of view, then ask God what your response should be."

"And what is his point of view?"

Jesse looked down for a few seconds, then lifted his gaze to hers. He spoke softly at first. "Imagine this. A man loves his country, his family, and goes off to fight for his land. He's captured by the enemy and injured on the way to prison camp. Your father stayed alive by sheer willpower to keep his promise to return to you and your mother. When I was thrown in the barracks with him, I was impressed with his courage and determination to get back home to his family.

"I'd joined the army as a cocky young man, but I was plenty scared when they marched me and my fellow soldiers to that camp. I was only fifteen. I'd had little medical training, as I was merely the assistant to the medic in our unit, but enough to know that your father needed to drink as much liquid as he could and that the bandage on his chest and leg needed frequent cleansing."

He clasped his hands. "He was old enough to be my father. But we formed a close bond and soon were depending on each other for our very survival. Even when he was weak, he watched out for me. He gave me water when I thought I'd die of thirst and watched over me when I almost *did* die."

Jesse's eyes had the faraway look of someone in another place. Mary gasped as they focused on her, piercing her heart. "Are you understanding what I'm saying?"

"Yes," she breathed, her imagination bringing his story to life.

He looked away, but Mary saw the flicker of pain in his eyes.

Jesse's hands closed into fists. His voice tight with control, he continued. "We found nothing but a burned-out shell where your home had been. We. . .walked about the area and found a grave with your mother's name on it. Neither he nor I moved or said anything for a long time. We stood there, trying to understand the enormity of what we were seeing. I walked away to give him some privacy to grieve. Then he sank to his knees and sobbed."

A tear slid down Mary's cheeks. The scene he described was as bad as her last memory of her home.

Jesse took a deep breath. "After that, we—"

"No!" Mary put her hand up to stop him. "I can't. Give me a minute to think." She tore herself away, choking back a sob. Her thoughts churning, she stood at the window, seeing Jesse's description of her father lying sick somewhere. This picture didn't mesh with the one of his confident farewell as he left for the battle.

Neither said a word for several minutes. Only the swaying and *k-knick k-nock* of the train punctuated their thoughts.

"Mary." Jesse's voice held so much emotion she couldn't look at him. "He loves you so much, and your coming to see him. . .I can't describe how much it means to him just to glimpse your dear face. I can't because the depth of his love for you and sorrow at the years he's missed are more than I can imagine." He touched her arm. "I don't mean to preach, but it is important for you to get your heart right toward your father—if only for your own sake."

"I–I don't know. It's. . ." She put her hand over her mouth and looked out, seeing nothing. She thought she'd dealt with it, but the wound in her young heart had grown, not healed. "Please understand. You've given me a lot to think about. I need to take a walk."

"I understand." Jesse spoke gently. He walked to the door. "I'll give you time alone." He turned to her and added, "Or would you like some company?"

Although she needed to think, she didn't want to be alone now. "We can walk together."

As they stepped onto the platform, a buffalo was running alongside. She backed away from the huge beast. Jesse laughed and opened the door for her. In the next car she saw the passengers' faces pressed against the window, watching the buffalo running alongside, but unable to keep up.

Suddenly, she heard a shot. A man leaned out the window pointing his pistol at the running buffalo and shot again.

"No!" Mary ran and pulled his arm back, and his next shot went into the air.

The man uttered an oath and glared at her.

Mary's frightened heart beat in her throat. "You can't do that!" she cried, thinking of the poor animal's lifeblood pouring out on the ground after the train had gone. She wanted to ask why he wanted to kill the harmless creature, but his hostile scowl told her the question would be futile.

"Get out of my way, Girlie. I'll do what I want." He slammed his hat down on his head and leaned out the window. There were no more buffalo. The shots had apparently frightened them away.

Jesse hurried Mary away from the angry man. Elizabeth, the pregnant woman they'd seen in the Chicago station sat in the next car, two seats away from a card game in full play. She welcomed Mary and Jesse and scooted over so Mary could sit beside her. Jesse hunkered down in the aisle. Elizabeth rubbed her back, saying she was fine, although a little tired and stiff.

They visited a few minutes, then headed back to their car.

Mary managed to avoid Jesse for most of the day, reading, writing in her trip journal, and thinking about her father, herself, and relationships in general.

Standing on the platform late that afternoon, she watched lonely houses and spacious ranches. *It's like make-believe. The farther I get from home, the more unreal everything seems.* She felt disconnected from the stability of her home.

As the sun lowered, she tired of looking out over miles of wastes of sand, the desolation broken by slow-moving immigrants, their white-covered wagons and herds of cattle all half-hidden in clouds of dust. The wind began kicking up and blowing sand into her eyes, stinging her cheeks. She shook the sand from her dress and went back to her room.

Jesse, at the window, turned to her when she entered. "Hello, Stranger." He faced her with his air of friendly self-confidence.

"Hello," she replied breezily. He regarded her with a serious look. Since he seemed determined to continue their discussion, she took the initiative. "I appreciate your kind portrayal of my father. I'll remember that when we reach San Francisco."

"I hope you do more than remember. I had hoped you'd

see that he loves you, and it hurt him to know you were alone and in trouble, and he couldn't do anything to help."

"If he hadn't gone in the first place—"

"Mary! Will you stop thinking of yourself and see it from his point of view?" His jaw tensed, and one eyebrow shot up.

She felt her temper rise. "How else does a six-year-old child see a situation?"

"You're not six anymore," he said patiently.

"No, but I've had to live with it." She clutched the back of the chair. "Oh, I've told you all this before. What's the use?"

Jesse held his hand out to her, pleading for understanding. "Please don't meet him with an unforgiving attitude, like old Mr. Taylor did to his family."

She winced at the memory of the pain in their eyes at his rejection. "I'd never do that!"

"Wouldn't you?" He moved closer to her. "He's not stupid, Mary. He'd know."

"I can't pretend."

"That won't do. Just think about forgiving. Remember that if you don't forgive others, God cannot forgive you."

"I'm not the one who was in the wrong," she said peevishly.

Jesse shook his head. "Just think about it." He shook his head. "Don't hurt him."

"Oh, for goodness' sake!" Mary stormed into the water closet and slammed the door.

She leaned over the wash basin, the images Jesse had told her filling her mind. Her father, in ragged clothes, lying on a cot somewhere in a steamy, humid Carolina prison. In pain, alone, eating moldy bread to survive. Was she with Eugenia on her way north, or was she already cozy in Mrs. Palmer's home?

Fighting the impulse to cry, she yanked the door open. Jesse was gone. Taking a deep, unsteady breath, she began to pace. Nothing made sense. Some things she couldn't talk about, but she knew a way to bring out her thoughts. She picked up her journal and turned on the gaslight. She stared at the starry sky outside her window. *God, I need to be completely honest here. Help me understand.*

Something happened. Memories and feelings tumbled over one another. She grabbed her pen and ink and began writing. Something deep inside her had come uncapped, and it flowed out through her pen. She filled page after page, her hand barely able to match the speed with which the words flowed as emotions overtook her.

Hours later, she sagged against the cushion with tears streaming down her cheeks. The sun touched the nearby mountaintops with a lavender blush. The words she had written came from a deep, honest place she hadn't known existed. Exhausted, she closed the journal and put away the ink and pen. She realized that she'd been very angry at her father and ultimately at God. She had to admit that if it hadn't been for Jesse's persistence, she wouldn't have known all this.

In his bed near the door, Jesse lay, lulled by the swaying train and the feel of the wheels turning beneath. He saw the light on behind Mary's curtain late into the night. *Did*

I push her too hard? He could see it hurt her to remember, but like a boil that must come to a head, it was necessary to bring it all up in the open and deal with it. And it had to be done before they met her father. With his hands laced behind his head, he stared up at the ceiling, hoping she was talking to God about it. She'd need that strength because there was more she needed to know.

Chapter 7

Wyoming

March 21, 1874

I feel wrung out. After writing all the hurt last night, I have no more emotion left. I'm empty. I couldn't sleep after reading what I purged on these pages last night.

I have a headache. It's almost noon, and I'm so tired. I just want this trip to be over. I wonder if I can ever go back to my old life. I feel I'm a different person. I didn't know what lay hidden beneath my competent, well-ordered behavior. I'm ashamed of the fury I bottled up over the years.

I don't blame my father anymore. Blame is a feeling, and I feel nothing. I'm like an empty slate waiting for God to write the answers.

J. kissed me! But I can't even think about that. Actually, it's the only thing on my mind, but I'm trying not to think of it. It was just a light kiss, but

I felt my soul begin to melt. I'm not going to think about it though.

Jesse opened the door to find Mary reclining on the sofa, her eyes closed and a cloth over her forehead. He tiptoed closer and stood a moment, looking down at her. She was truly lovely, the delicate features of her face finally relaxed. She had no idea she was pretty; he'd never seen such expressive eyes, the color of a summer blue sky. Large and sad, they were the eyes of a girl who had been abandoned and worried about it happening again.

A wave of protection welled up in him, its intensity startling him. His gaze moved slowly over her face, taking in each detail with warmth. He wanted to wrap her in his arms, kiss her again, and tell her he'd never leave her; he'd always be there and love her. He stumbled back a step. Love? What was he thinking?

At that moment her eyes opened, and she looked up at him. The soft glow in her eyes and the sweet reddening of her cheeks snared him again. For one heart-stopping moment their gazes gently held, then the lost look was there again.

She pulled the cloth from her forehead and sat up. "What time is it?"

"Twelve-thirty. You must be hungry."

She shaded her eyes with her hand and looked down. "Are you feeling well?"

"I didn't get much sleep last night." She looked up at him with a half smile. "It's nothing, really. But perhaps you're right. A cup of tea would be welcome right now."

Glad to be able to do something for her, Jesse hurried to find a cup of strong tea. By the time he returned to their parlor, Mary had washed and tamed her soft, auburn curls. "Here's your tea. We'll be stopping for midday meal in Cheyenne City in a few minutes."

"Thank you, Jesse."

The brakes hissed, and he braced himself as they began to take hold. Mary went to the window and leaned forward to watch Cheyenne City come into view.

He joined her. Pointing at a huge sandstone building, he said, "That's a locomotive house. And the buildings beside it are the railway's machine shops."

"It's as if the city rose up out of the bare desert. There's not a tree in sight." Mary glanced at him. "But the mountains! They're magnificent!"

Jagged peaks rose into the sky, white with snow. "That's the Great Divide, the Rocky Mountains." Jesse cupped her elbow. "Come. You'll get a better view outside. We don't have to hurry through our meal. They give us two hours here."

She's different. Something has changed. She was more quiet, almost subdued. Maybe she still had a headache. He asked her, and she smiled that half smile and told him no. He decided to distract her and show her the beginning of the West he had come to love.

They stepped off the train and heard a shrill, furiously ringing bell, rung by a boy shouting "Meals for fifty cents!" They walked past a one-story wooden building full of brightly painted signs advertising Billiard Saloon,

Sample Room, and Fresh Fruit. A young girl in a Gypsy costume stood by a small mule, selling tickets to the circus to be held that night.

"We're going to the Union Pacific's hotel to dine on the most tender steak you've ever eaten," said Jesse. "Unless, of course, you'd like to dine here." Many people stood eating full plates of food set on a long board. Aromas of bread, meat, fish, pickles, and spices filled the air.

Mary shook her head. "It looks interesting, but no thanks."

"The West! It lures the adventurous." He gestured to a lively woman who presided over her stall serving bread, cheese, and pickles. "There's a valiant pioneer woman who lived through Indian fights, one which killed her husband. But it couldn't shake her love for the West. No, Ma'am." She looked up as they passed and smiled at them.

Mary looked back at the woman. "Is nobody a stranger to you, Mr. Harcourt?"

He laughed, noticing that she'd used his last name again. "I find people fascinating. Each one is a story as complex as the knots I taught little Nate."

"And Tommy." Mary's gaze softened, and she raised an eyebrow, the same way as her father. He realized there were several unconscious mannerisms that mirrored her father's.

"Here we are." The sign on the hotel said they could dine four hundred people and lodge fifty. They were quickly seated and served.

Jesse leaned toward her. "You're very quiet, Mary Sherwood."

She blushed prettily. "You win. I'll call you Jesse if you'll call me Mary."

He smiled, thinking about how proud George Sherwood would be of his intelligent, kind, sweet daughter. He wished she could come north with them from San Francisco to see their logging business. She picked at her dinner when it was first brought to her, but after a few bites, she said, "This *is* the most delicious, tender steak I've ever eaten!"

After their meal they strolled through the town. They passed low, flat-roofed wooden shops full of goods and saw a scattering of tents and shanties on a side street. Across the street were two gambling and dance houses.

In one of the shop windows, Mary's eyes were drawn to a tray of agates. Jesse pointed to a large gray one. "They're called moss agates. See how nature set the design in and through the solid stone."

Mary leaned closer. "Look, that one has dainty ferns and feathery seaweeds in it."

"And there's one with tassels of pines." He was glad to see her perk up a little.

"Where do they come from?" She looked at him with a glint of wonder in her eyes.

He had to force his gaze away from her. "They are gathered in Colorado. Each one must have taken centuries to make."

She sighed. "They are exquisite! That one has rippling water lines of ancient tides."

"Let's go in. You can pick one out to take with you."

"Oh, no! I couldn't." She drew back, looking longingly at the gems.

"Your father would want you to have them. He—"

"Maybe some other time." That sadness in her eyes was quickly replaced with calmness.

Back at the station, passengers milled about, waiting for the "All aboard" call. Jesse introduced Mary to the colorful woman who ran the eatery stall and bought two large dill pickles and some crackers and cheese for later.

As they boarded, he looked back. Elizabeth sat on a bench, leaning forward with her head down. A uniformed railway man stood beside her, looking flustered. Something was wrong. "I'll be right back," he told Mary.

He hurried to Elizabeth. "Are you all right?" he asked.

She looked up at him with misery in her eyes. "I had a stomach pain, and they won't let me on the train!" She squeezed her eyes tightly, and he wondered if she were having a pain now. "I *have* to get there! Only two more days to California!"

"All aboard!" came the loud cry. Jesse looked back. The train hadn't moved.

Another railroad man approached. "Madam, you cannot board the train in your condition. There is no doctor aboard. Please listen to reason!" He signaled someone near the station.

"I have been on your train since Chicago in this condition, and I am *not* having the baby today." She stood and reached for Jesse's arm. "Let me on that train!"

The station guard came toward them. "Is there trouble here?"

While the men told him about Elizabeth's condition,

Jesse leaned close to her and asked, "Are you sure it's not time?"

She whispered furiously, "Of course I'm sure! Do you think I'd jeopardize my baby by giving birth on the train?"

Behind him Jesse heard the hiss of steam and banging of couplers, along with the shrill whistle from the engine. The train was moving. He faced the three men. "I'm not a doctor but have assisted one. I believe this woman when she says she's not having the baby. Sometimes women in her condition have stomachaches, just like the rest of us." He tried to hurry her toward the slowly moving train. "I'll be responsible for her."

"You're too late," said the guard. "The train is in motion. No one is allowed to board."

Shock at being left gave way to fury. "You kept us from boarding! I know you can stop the train. We hold tickets to San Francisco, and I intend to get there." He pointed to the train, still passing. The last car had not left the station. "Stop this train. Now."

All three men shook their heads, and Jesse watched the last car roll down the tracks away from them. He yearned to run after it but wouldn't leave Elizabeth. Feeling strangely desolate, he shoved his hands into his pockets. What would happen to Mary? *God, please take care of her.*

Chapter 8

March 22, 1874

I read the last part of what I wrote last night and winced at the force of my emotions. I have repented for being angry at God. I know now that it wasn't just my father I was angry with; it was God. And I'm very sorry about that. He didn't make the tragedy, but He was there with protection and guidance for me all the time. And from what J. says, I have to believe that He was there for my father too.

Yesterday J. left for a moment and never came back. I worried and fretted, wondering why. I can't help feeling that I've been left alone again. The same old desolate feeling taunts me. I miss J., even though I've done enough to drive him away. I can't blame him if he decided he doesn't want to escort me to San Francisco. I thought of searching the train to see if he simply decided to ride elsewhere but thought better of it. What if I found him sitting with a congenial group of people? What could he say? What would I say?

I've asked God to give me strength if I have to face my father alone. How will I recognize him? If J. is not on the train, then I'll need God to show me what to do. I don't expect a fairy-tale ending, with my father and I falling tearfully into each other's arms, but I don't know what will happen, and it unnerves me.

Mary spent her afternoon studying the geography book and paging through the trip guidebook. After leaving Cheyenne City they traveled steadily up, the throbbing puffs of the hard-at-work engine moving them slowly. Passing stretches of snow and clumps of firs and pines, the fantastically shaped rocks were the only things to break the land's desolate loneliness.

Sherman is the highest railway point in the world, the guidebook said. Over eight thousand feet above the sea. Outside, cattle stood in a fenced space beside a boulder fifty feet high, and Mary wondered about the rancher and his family who chose to live in this isolated place.

The train was so high above the tops of many mountains that they themselves blended and became a wide field of hills, but at the horizon rose higher peaks, white with snow. A pang of loneliness for Eugenia, Lolly, and Mrs. Palmer swept through her. She longed for Jesse's steady, positive company.

As the train continued to climb, she had to walk uphill to the forward cars. She wondered if she'd see Jesse enjoying himself with a group of cheerful travelers. Outside, grotesque stunted and bent trees and more large rocks stood like hillside sentinels watching them pass.

She'd just stepped into a car full of people when the train shuddered to a stop. A mother had laid her tired baby on the seat as the conductor strolled through calling, "Sherman. Half-hour stop." Mary went back for her coat. Outside the chill air cooled her cheeks, and her breath came out in puffs. If she thought Cheyenne City was small, it looked like a metropolis compared to Sherman. With only a half-dozen dwellings, most of the passengers milled around aimlessly, some fleeing the cold inside the small Black Hills Tavern.

Hearing the bang and crunch of the trains, Mary noticed that they were uncoupling one of the engines.

A gentleman in a brown three-piece suit approached. "I noticed you earlier. Is this your first trip west?"

"Yes." Mary tucked her hands into her pockets to keep them warm. The huge couplers undid themselves like unclasping a necklace.

"We won't be needing that extra engine we added back at Cheyenne," he said. "It's mostly downhill to Laramie."

Although she didn't know him, Mary was glad for the company. "Do you work for the railroad?"

"Indeed I do," he replied, his pecan brown eyes smiling down at her. "I manage the car, machine, and repair shops in Omaha."

The extra engine chugged away, leaving the train with its original engine. "It's just amazing," she said, "that the railroad has laid tracks all across our great country."

"There's not much a man can't do if he puts his mind to it," he said, lifting his brows. "Would you like to go inside the engine?"

Mary hesitated, wondering if she should.

"Pardon my manners, Miss. Permit me to introduce myself. I am Jared McNulty." He removed his hat and swept it before him in a deep bow. "At your service."

Mary smiled at his overacting. "Mary Sherwood. And I'd be happy to see the engine."

"Capital!" He offered his arm, and they climbed aboard.

He introduced her to the engineer who was standing, making notes in a logbook. Mr. McNulty showed her the great breastplate door behind which burned the heart of fire that kept the train moving. She looked ahead at the glistening black double road. A workman jumped inside, tipped his hat to her, and poured oil into various joints of shiny knobs and rods and handles, then jumped back out for more maintenance work.

The engineer looked up from his logbook, lovingly patted a shiny handle and smiled at Mary, lifting his wide mustache to show even, white teeth. "Well, Miss, what do you think of her?"

Mary took a deep breath, looking at the array of knobs. She wanted to think of something intelligent to ask, so she said, "Which one of those levers steers it?"

Laughing, he said, "Oh! I don't steer her. She steers herself. Put her on the track," he said pointing ahead, "and feed her." He pointed at the boiler. "That's all."

Mary felt her cheeks grow hot. "Oh," she said in a small voice.

He shook his head. "Don't feel embarrassed, Miss. It was a good question."

Another trainman jumped on board and handed the engineer a note. His fist tightened, crumpling it. "What? Why those—pardon me, Miss. McNulty, it looks like we'll be here for awhile. I hope your men can take care of this quickly."

He handed the crumpled note to McNulty, who escorted Mary off the engine. "Indians have torn up the tracks a few miles up the road. We'll have to fix them before we can go on."

Mary pulled her coat collar up in the cold breeze. "Indians? Why?"

"Yes, Indians. Don't want us crossing their territory, you see. We've stopped most of them, but there are still a few who think they can stop us if there are no tracks for the train to run on."

"How long will we be here?"

"Oh, I expect a couple of hours, depending on how bad the damage is." He gestured toward the tavern. "Would you like to go inside and have a hot cup of tea or something?"

Mary eyed the tavern but hesitated. She didn't frequent such places and had misgivings about it. She glanced back at the train, thinking of her lonely room. She'd begun to depend on Jesse and missed his company more than she could have imagined. The cold from the planks seeped into the soles of her feet.

"I would be happy to see you to the entryway," said McNulty, chafing his hands to warm them.

Jesse's face invaded her thoughts, and she suddenly

felt an acute sense of loss. "I don't think so." She shivered as the dusk deepened. The train sat like a huge beast at rest. "I think I'll go back to my seat. Thank you for showing me the engine and for the company."

"I enjoyed every minute." He touched his hat and took her elbow. Handing her up the steps, he held her hand a moment longer than necessary. "You are one special woman, Mary Sherwood. I'll see you in Laramie." He turned and walked away.

Mary couldn't stop thinking about Jesse's words, *"Love one another. That's what counts."* The words echoed in her brain as she boarded the train. They filled the empty places left from her angry outpouring into her journal the night before.

Back in her room Mary sank on her knees beside the sofa. *Please bring Jesse back, and help me, Lord, to have the love in my heart You want me to have. Father, I am sorry for doubting You, and I ask You to forgive me.*

In her mind's eye, she saw her father, not as he left her, going off to war; now it was as if he were in a misty place waiting for her. She laid her head on her arms and stayed that way quietly for some minutes, unable to continue praying. So she stood and paced the room, wondering why she felt God wanted something more from her. She stared out the window, her mind a blank. Then her gaze landed on her journal. She cringed at the shameful venom she'd poured onto its pages.

But it had to be done. In that one night of feverish writing she had purged her heart of years of anger, and for once she felt swept clean of it. "Thank You, God," she breathed. She thought of her father again.

Pushing the memory aside, she wondered where Jesse was. She ached with loneliness, missing him. *Take care of him, Lord.* It wasn't just that she felt alone. She had the company of a gentleman this afternoon and knew she could spend more time with Mr. McNulty, but she missed Jesse. She missed his ready smile, his friendship, and steady company.

Something happened at Cheyenne City to keep him from getting on the train. She would have seen him here in the delay and milling passengers. His belongings were still in their car. His valises stood near the bookcase.

She perched on the chair for a moment. Tense, she jumped up and began pacing again. The windows were black with night. She'd been gone from home not even a week, and so much had happened. Jesse had broken through her safe barriers, forcing her to examine the sorrow and anger she'd held for so many years. He had been in terrible circumstances but hadn't let them pull him down. He faced life with an open heart, ready to help, to give when he saw a need. He'd shown her that by faith a believer can walk in peace, with no weights from the past.

As she paced and thought, she found herself drawn to the freedom which beckoned, but which had the terrible price of forgiving her father. If she did, how would she make sense of her life? If there was no one to blame, then was no one in charge of anything? Not even God? She ground her teeth and pushed back the hair that had fallen over her forehead. If there was no reason for her family being violently torn apart, then nothing made sense.

No. It was her father's fault. If he hadn't gone, if he hadn't left them. . . *Oh, God, help me see from Your perspective.* She went to the window and gazed out at the tracks shining in the darkness. Remembering parts of a Scripture she'd read somewhere, she picked up her Bible to find it. Something about God caring for a tender branch. From the concordance in the back, she found the words in Job, chapter 14. "For there is hope of a tree, if it be cut down, that it will sprout again, and that the tender branch thereof will not cease."

She read the verses before and after, but verse 7 made her heart beat faster. She thought of how Jesse said love was what mattered. Although other interpretations may apply, she linked the thoughts of love and the tree cut down. Somewhere on the way from Tennessee to the safety of Mrs. Palmer's house, she had let bitterness and anger come in and wrap their thorns around her heart. Love had been squeezed out. Like the tree in the verse, it had been cut down.

But, Father, I always loved You. Biting her lip, staring at the open Bible, she wondered if that were true, then realized that she did and that God knew it. Even though she'd been angry with Him, she'd never stopped loving Him. But the anger had cut down her love, leaving a tender branch struggling to survive. All these years, trying to be safe from harm, she'd gotten by with nine parts self-control and one part trust in God. The thought shamed her.

Mary fell on her knees. *Oh, God, I've been so willful and controlling over my life. I felt I had justifiable resentment because of the injustice of my problems.* She gave Him the anger, hurt, and bitterness and asked Him to forgive her and to help her forgive her father and restore love between them. She thanked Him that he was alive and that she was not alone; she had real family.

She talked with God a long time, until she felt clean, as though her soul had been washed. And a deep peace filled her heart. It was as if her life had stopped that day the soldiers burned her home and killed her mother. It began again the day Jesse appeared on the doorstep with the news that her father was alive and wanted to see her.

As though heralding the change in her, the engine's whistle screeched. Wondering what time it was, she wiped away the tears. In the water closet she splashed cold water on her face, then went to see what was happening outside. Holding on to the bar she leaned out. Just as the conductor shouted "All aboard!" a carriage drew up, the horses skidding to a stop. A man jumped out.

"Jesse!" Mary's heart turned over, and the heat of joy flooded her.

Jesse reached up to help the other passenger from the carriage. A woman. Her joy faded, and she felt herself fading with it.

As the engine's whistle blew, Jesse thanked God that they'd arrived in time. "We made it!" He helped Elizabeth down and thanked the driver for making haste.

They hurried to Elizabeth's car, and a conductor helped her board. "I can never thank you enough, Mr. Harcourt," she said, smiling down at him.

"I needed to get back too." He tipped his hat and ran to the rear of the train. He saw a familiar face as he got closer to the parlor car. Mary! His heart skipped, and he ran faster. The train had started moving when he jumped on the step and into the car. Laughing in triumph he wrapped her in a big hug and gaily swung her around.

All his concentration had been to get back to her, and he'd done it! He lowered her to the floor and gazed into her eyes. She, too, was smiling, and there was something else. The sadness that flickered sometimes in her eyes was gone.

Chapter 9

Wyoming

March 23, 1874

*J. is back! He stayed in Cheyenne City to help
Elizabeth. Yesterday I got to visit the engine,
escorted by a very nice man. I was lonely and didn't
realize how much I'd miss J. I couldn't get him out of
my thoughts all day, and when I thought I was
thoroughly distracted, he was there at the edge of my
mind, ready to snap back in.*

*I was almost resigned to meeting my father
without him. Then he arrived, just as the train was
leaving. He was so happy he hugged me, as if he
really cared. I'm ashamed of how I reacted. Like
coming home, like a child who has received a present
she's been waiting for all year. I can't explain, except
that "overjoyed" barely describes my elation that he'd
returned to me. My reaction shocked me so much I
had to go to my chamber and close myself off for the*

rest of the evening and think.

I'm beginning to like him too much. I thought our relationship would be barely friends, but I found out yesterday being with him is almost a need, and that scares me. Nothing can come of any feelings I have for him or any he'd have for me because I'm going to return to the East Coast, and he lives on the West Coast. To keep my heart safe, I must stay away from him. Leaving as quickly as I can after I greet my father is imperative.

Last night I decided to enjoy the awesome scenery. I saw canyons thousands of feet deep, so narrow that a river could barely make its way through by shrinking and twisting and leaping in a silver line. The tracks seemed to be hung on the side of the canyon wall, and we crept along a narrow shelf, viewing the strange, shadowed world by starlight. In the morning we'll be in Utah.

Mary put the pen down and flexed her fingers. There was so much to see and record. The sun was now fully risen. They were near a field of boulders, pale yellow, red, and brown that rose massive and solid amid others that were piled and strewn in a majestic, wild confusion.

On the other side of the curtain she heard the swish of a page turning, probably Jesse reading his Bible. She kept her curtain closed and reached for her own Bible. She read another chapter in Proverbs, savoring each verse as she gazed out, watching the canyon walls close them in under a blue belt of sky. She was awed by the majesty of God who'd fashioned the spectacular scene yet saw into her heart and cared enough to comfort and help her.

She dressed and patted her hair into a subdued control with combs holding it up. With one last glance at the mirror, she opened the curtain.

Seated in the easy chair, Jesse looked up at her. His long legs stretched out before him, and he leaned forward with his elbows on his thighs, hands clasped. "Good morning." The warmth of that devastating smile echoed in his voice.

How was she going to go on without him? Leaning against the wall for a moment, she tried to gather strength. "Good morning," she answered and stepped into the room. According to schedule, they'd be in San Francisco tomorrow. She must keep Jesse at a distance until then. She stood awkwardly in the room, trying to pretend he wasn't there.

"Mary."

The way he said her name was soothing, like a prayer, yet sent a ripple of awareness that drew her to his gaze.

His dark eyes studied her. "I must apologize for taking liberties with you yesterday."

She pulled her gaze away to hide her confusion.

"I don't apologize for the joy I felt at seeing you leaning out of the train when I arrived. I don't apologize for the affection that drove me to action."

He paused, and she couldn't resist another glimpse of his dear face.

His eyes were gentle, calm as they looked back at her.

"But I owe you an apology for hugging you and twirling you around. It was wrong, and I hope you forgive me."

Mary shrugged, glancing at the bookshelf behind him. "Forgiven?"

"Yes, of course." She said it over her shoulder, not trusting herself to look into his dark eyes, full of emotions that drew her like tacks to a magnet. That hug was a turning point in their relationship. She reveled in the feel of being in his arms, of being cherished and almost loved. She'd never forget it. Never. Frightened of where her thoughts were taking her, she reminded herself that keeping a distance between them was the only way to remain unscathed and have her heart in one piece as she returned to Massachusetts.

When she finished freshening up, the coachman came in to tidy up their parlor. "Echo City and Ogden coming up," he said, picking up towels from the water closet and throwing them on the heap near the door. "Breakfast in Promontory. Union Pacific, last stop." He gave them a toothy smile and left with the bundle under his arm.

Jesse grinned. "A man of few words."

"He said all that needed to be said," agreed Mary. She grabbed the sofa back as the train lurched around a sharp corner. The canyon's arms were gone, and they had come out on a broad plain. She approached the window, with Jesse behind her. The sight of the jagged snow-topped mountains took her breath away. Jesse standing so close didn't help.

He pointed to a hillside threaded with green where

streams ran down into the plain. "I'd like to meet some of those folks in the houses on the hill. What is life like up there, I wonder."

Mary imagined charming woods, picnics beneath shaded trees, a family, children playing.

"See the cows. They probably supply milk for their neighbors." Jesse's attention shifted to her. "You're going to be a teacher, aren't you? Do you wonder who teaches the children in those houses?" His soft gaze melted her again.

She steeled herself against his charm. His eyes were normal eyes, nothing special. Forcing herself to settle down, she said, "That's right. I have a position in Boston when I return."

"Mary, before we meet your father, there's more I need to tell you." His eyes narrowed warily, as if expecting her to refuse the subject.

She moved away from him—it was safer—and sat on the sofa. "It's all right. I've talked with God about this, and. . .well, it's all right to talk."

Jesse stood behind the chair. "He's a good man, your father. I told you how in prison camp he took me under his care and treated me like his son."

Mary sighed. "I knew him as a little girl knows her father. I saw the "daddy" side of him."

"He still loves you; he always did," said Jesse. He came around the chair and sat, leaning his forearms on his knees. He looked at her with pain in his eyes. "When we were released and went back to your home, I thought the pain would break him. We asked around, but no one knew anything about what had happened to you."

The thought of her father returning to such a bleak scene was almost more than Mary could bear, and she shuddered inwardly. *Oh, God, all I thought of was myself and how I'd been stranded. I'm so ashamed of my selfishness. Forgive me!*

After a pause, Jesse continued, his voice filled with anguish. "He was so distraught I led him to a home we'd seen a mile or so before and got us a room. He walked in a daze and seemed overcome by defeat."

Mary sighed, her heart heavy with pain.

Jesse knelt before her and covered her hands with his. "I'm sorry to be the one to tell you this, but you must know."

His warm hands comforted her, and she nodded mutely. "I know. But it's hard to hear."

"I prayed with him that night, and after a long time and much weeping, we put everything in God's hands. Neither one of us had a home to go back to, so we joined forces and headed west. Many people from the South had to start all over again."

"All the way to the West Coast?" Mary wondered if they just struck out for the farthest place away from the tragedy as they could.

"There were no opportunities in the South. A man in your father's regiment had relocated near Eureka, California. That's where we went. He straightened out their financial books, and I worked at logging. Soon your father became a partner, and—"

The coachman came through the parlor car calling, "Promontory. Breakfast. End of the line."

"I'll tell you more later about how we found you." His face radiated strength and peace. "Meanwhile, we've got to have our bags ready because we change trains here."

Welcoming the interruption in the tale of her father and Jesse's sad journey west, she thought of what he said about having no family to return to. She imagined Jesse as young, lost, and lonely, just as she had been. God had provided a family for each of them.

She longed to comfort him, then realized that perhaps her desire to comfort him wasn't all that innocent. She took a deep breath. Keeping him at a distance was going to be tricky since she wanted to learn more of her father. She'd just have to keep her emotions in check and concentrate on her father's story. That shouldn't be too difficult.

Promontory, neither a city nor a camp, was merely a few ramshackle buildings and tents on the alkali dust beneath the scorching sun. The exodus of passengers from the Union Pacific to the Central Pacific trains was accomplished quickly and with little fuss.

Mary and Jesse found themselves in a small, enclosed, double-seated room with thinly padded, dark blue bench seats. They stowed their belongings in the overhead cupboards and went out in search of their breakfast.

Seated at a table with two other passengers, conversation was scant. She couldn't stop thinking of the changes that had come over her in the last two days. The old resentments were gone, swept clean out of her soul. When a familiar, bitter thought beckoned, it was as if an intruder had knocked on the door of her heart. She could let it in or turn it away and keep the peace that had filled her that night. Never before had anything that wonderful happened to her.

Jesse watched Mary carefully after they left the restaurant and boarded the train again. He was glad she had agreed to let him talk of her father, but she was withdrawn. As though she were with him but not really there. She even seemed to be avoiding him. He searched his memory for anything that he could have said or done to offend her but could think of nothing.

As they began passing the Great Salt Lake, people rushed to the windows to see it. The view went on for hours, so they tired of it after a few minutes. After awhile there were only glimpses of its deep blue waters and snow-topped mountains through breaks in the hills. Mary was back to putting her nose in her book.

"What are you reading?"

Mary pulled her book closer. "Geography. I'm trying to catch up for when I teach it next fall."

A sadness stirred inside Jesse, missing her already. "You've experienced a lot of geography already, and there's a lot more to come. And you're going to love California!"

"That's what Eugenia said—that I'd see some geography firsthand." She looked at him oddly. "But there's nothing but desert out there. It looks like a dreary waste that stretches on and on forever."

"Some things go on forever but not the desert. And if you were on the ground, you'd see little plants and animals eking out a life amid the sandy dunes. It's not a wasteland at all."

She shot him an unconvinced glance and went back to her book.

In the late afternoon they walked to the back platform. They had climbed higher, and the desert bloomed with sagebrush and bunchgrass. Various tints of dusty green and yellow plants glowed in the cool promise of evening. Jessie edged closer to Mary. If only she'd come north with him. He could show her so much love and adventure.

Chapter 10

March 24, 1874

I can't get over the change! Last night we were in the desert, and now we're in the midst of a beautiful forest in the Sierras. We're probably in California already! I am a little nervous and excited about seeing my father again. I dreamed of him last night, a good dream. We were walking together in an old European castle looking over the walls to the water swirling below.

So, although I'm ready to meet him, I'm filled with sadness because when I come back to Boston I won't ever see Jesse again. I'll never forget him. I love him, but we will always live on opposite sides of the continent. I hurt to think of it. I'm through writing....

Mary picked up her guidebook and turned to the California page. They had passed through a forest of dark green pines, firs, and spruces with yellow moss on their trunks and were headed down the western slopes. According to the book, they would pass through sixteen tunnels and twenty miles of snowsheds.

Needing to compose herself, she sat on the edge of her bed and opened her Bible. Psalm 148 spoke eloquently for the splendor of the view outside. An eagle soared up over the treetops in a breathless display of the joy of flight.

After a few minutes, she opened the curtains. Jesse's Bible was closed and on the table beside his chair. His dark hair tumbled over his forehead as he looked down, meditating. She thought she should memorize every little thing about him so she'd have something for the cold, lonely days ahead.

"Good morning," she said, pulling the curtains back. "Look at that view!" He came by her side as the train moved onto a bridge. It was as if they were in flight over a valley at least two thousand feet below.

"Lovely," said Jesse, looking intently into her eyes. She felt a blush creep up her neck. In a husky voice he said, "On the other side is a view of the mountain, straight up to its snowy summit." They stood in silent companionship, awed by the majestic scenery.

"Wait here. I have something for you. I think it's time." He went to his valise and pulled something small from an inside pocket.

He approached, his gaze locked with hers. "We found this in the ashes. . . . Your father told me that if I found you, and if you'd come to him, I was to give it to you." He held out a scorched square of blue silk with a ribbon attached.

Mary felt the color drain from her face and her mouth go dry. "Oh," she said in a small voice. He set the silk on her open palm, then gently dropped a coin on it. She gasped as memories flooded her. It was a coin, minted in 1855, the year she was born. It was her special coin—a gift from her father, sewn into the blue silk pocket by her mother. One of the two ribbons used to tie it around her neck was gone, the other, burned to a stub. "I don't understand! I cried and cried when it was lost. How. . . ?"

"Your father said it was a miracle. He thought the Lord preserved it to give him hope."

Tears welled up in her eyes as they went through the darkness of a snowshed. "I have been so unfair to him." In a hoarse whisper she added, "May God forgive me."

Jesse put his arm around her, and she leaned into his embrace. "He has forgiven you, Mary. You know that, don't you?"

She shuddered a deep sigh. "I know. But I don't deserve it."

"No one does." They stood close, Mary clutching silk and the coin. She gulped hard, trying to release the pain of so many years of bitter anger knotted in her throat.

At a knock on the door they sprang apart. Elizabeth and the coachman were in the hallway when they opened the door. The coachman had a worried frown on his face, while Elizabeth looked relieved. "Mary. Mr. Harcourt." A grimace briefly contorted her lovely face.

Mary stepped forward and touched her arm. "Are you all right?"

Elizabeth glanced at the coachman. "I'm just fine. I—"

The coachman shook his head. "She needs a doctor." He walked away muttering.

Jesse took Elizabeth's other arm. "Come in." Elizabeth entered and sank onto the seat. A sheen of perspiration moistened her forehead.

Jesse took her pulse. "Are you sure you're all right?" he asked, eyeing her closely.

She bit her lower lip like a naughty child before answering. "Just a pain or two."

Jesse glanced at Mary, then knelt beside Elizabeth. "Pains in your back, circling your body?"

Elizabeth gave him an apologetic look. "Something like that." She insisted she was fine and would make it to Oakland without giving birth.

Jesse shook his head. "You can't stop nature, Mrs. Jamison." He stood and left to see if there was a doctor on the train.

Mary slipped the coin and silk into her pocket. She glanced at Elizabeth and felt a moment of panic, wishing Jesse would return.

The coachman knocked and stuck his head inside. "Breakfast in a snowshed this morning, Miss," he said to Mary, ignoring Elizabeth.

Jesse returned with a tall blond woman carrying a black bag. "Miss Sherwood and Mrs. Jamison, meet Dr. Louise Morgan; Dr. Morgan is on her way to Petaluma to start her practice."

As he and Mary left the chamber, they entered a snowshed, which branched off in a vee and widened like a mine tunnel. The train stopped in front of a little house, its door wide open and a breakfast bell ringing. Beside it were fields of snow, and the forest was close behind. Jesse held Mary's elbow as they walked to the dining room over icy rock.

"You don't seem worried about Elizabeth having her baby." They entered the cozy room and were seated. "Does your medical knowledge tell you it's not going to happen soon?"

"Everything happens in its time, Mary. You just take whatever comes along, do the best you can, and trust that things will work out for good. And they usually do."

"But bad things happen! Horrid things you never expect. They don't always work out for the best." *Like your family being scattered or meeting a wonderful man you can't be with.*

Jesse's eyes searched hers tenderly. "There are lots of promises to believers that things work out for good; you can walk through a dark valley, and God will be with you; be in a flood, and you won't drown; even in a fire, and you won't be burned. He doesn't say you will be spared some troubles, but He does say things will work out if you have faith to trust."

Mary almost believed there would be a way she and Jesse could be together; then she frowned at the realization that this was one dream that was never meant to be.

"Why the gloomy look?" He leaned forward, his eyebrows raised.

She fought an overwhelming need to touch him. Tearing her gaze away she said, "It's nothing. I just wonder if we'll return to a newborn baby."

Jesse sat back, smiling. "I don't think so. But Dr. Morgan has the situation in hand."

Mary felt a sorrow that after this evening she'd never see Jesse again and ate quietly, in spite of his attempts to make her smile.

Back in their room, Elizabeth and Dr. Morgan sat, calmly sipping tea and finishing sandwiches, looking as if they'd been chatting about the latest fashions. Dr. Morgan said, "She's just fine, but I'll stay with her for a few minutes, if it's all right with you."

Jesse and Mary agreed and left to stand out on the platform to watch the scenery. The moment they stepped outside they were rewarded with the sight of a blue sparkling lake on their left.

"Donner Lake," said Jesse with reverence, his voice close behind her.

His hand, next to her, gripped the rail. If she leaned back a little, she'd be enclosed in his embrace. If she turned to face him. . . She left off that perilous line of thought.

He moved to her side, and she felt a familiar pull, drawing her to him. "You've been quiet all afternoon. Are you having troubling thoughts?"

She continued soaking in the raw beauty of the lake. "It's a bit daunting to think I'll be seeing my father *today*." She smoothed her hair. "What if it turns out badly? What if it turns out well? I don't know when I'll be able to come back."

"You could stay," he said so softly she almost didn't hear him.

"But I've accepted the position in Boston. I must return immediately."

"Mary, your father isn't as healthy as he once was. Remember, it's been many years since you've seen him." The train lurched around a curve, throwing her toward him. He embraced her, and she rested for a moment with her cheek pressed against his chest, listening to the quick beat of his heart. He leaned his chin on her head. She savored the moment—so she'd never forget.

As if they'd both accepted this new dimension of their relationship, they turned to watch the view, his arm on her shoulder. She relaxed in the sweet moment of quiet communication. The train began to descend, the brakes holding them back, lest they roll too fast.

Back in their room, Elizabeth was alone, lying on the seat, looking tired and pale. "We're in California, aren't we?" She craned her neck to see out the window.

"Yes. We're heading downhill toward Sacramento," said Jesse.

"How are you?" asked Mary, crouching down beside Elizabeth.

"I've been better. But the baby is fine. Dr. Morgan says it's going to be soon." She smiled through a grimace of pain.

Dr. Morgan returned with good news. The engineer had wired ahead, and the train would be stopping in Colfax where a doctor was waiting. She also said he'd wired the Oakland station to inform her husband. Soon the train screeched to a halt, and they helped Elizabeth get off. She looked back and laughed triumphantly. "My baby will be born in California!"

Back on their journey, Mary's anticipation grew as she wondered what it would be like to see her father after all this time.

The mountains had receded back to the horizon. The train now rolled through fields of grain and grass, and colorful flowers beckoned on all sides.

Jesse invited her to sit beside him. "We'll be arriving in Sacramento soon, then it's going to be lively and bustling from there to Oakland. If you have any last minute questions or worries, we can dispose of them now."

He waited while Mary sat stroking the burnt ribbon and silk square. "I can't think of anything to ask. I only hope it turns out well."

"It will." Jesse reached out his two hands. "Let's pray about it." Mary put her hands in his, and they bowed their heads.

He began, "Father, You know how deep a father's love is. Please direct this meeting of Mary and her father. Make it a happy, satisfying reunion."

She continued, "And I ask that there be no trace of unforgiveness or uneasiness. Please direct our meeting and help me to be the daughter he expects."

They continued their prayer until the final "amen." Mary opened her eyes to see his shining back at her full of hope and affection, and she drank it in. After a moment she stood, nervously glancing around. Outside, low, curving hills with soft outlines rose and passed.

"We're coming into Sacramento. We'll be in San Francisco by twilight." He turned with a smile. "You are going to make your father so happy."

Mary sighed. "I read adventure stories, and this is just like being in one. But in those stories, the heroines always know what to do."

"You *are* a heroine, Mary Sherwood. Your father loves you and—"

The brakes screeched, blocking out what else Jesse was saying. It almost sounded as if he'd said "so do I." But that must have been hopeful thinking. As she watched sparsely placed windmills and houses pass by, she abandoned herself to the fantasy of Jesse loving her. It would be all she'd have of him. Just her fantasies.

The train rolled on, over a long trestle, through the Sacramento suburbs, and along the levee with the river on one side and a slough on the other, its half-submerged roofs and timbers revealing the ravages of a flood. She felt complete with Jesse sitting beside her as they passed a machine and repair shop with the words Central Pacific on them and rolled slowly by roundhouses and car sheds, then through the Chinese Quarter.

"It's amazing! Five hours ago we were in the mountains. And look at this." She pointed to the tidewater from the Pacific, a steamer on the river, and a long train on the other bank.

The train lurched to a stop, and Jesse grabbed her hand. "Let's get a picnic to eat here in our room. It will be fun!"

"Let's!" The thought of a quiet dinner, their last, sounded so romantic she laughed.

They hurried through the noisy Sacramento station

full of rushing people, hacks, hotels, daily papers, food stands, shoe shine stands, and a line of ticket windows. They bought bread, sliced meat, cheeses, pickles, and fruit juice. As they headed back to the train, they heard a loud voice calling, "Mr. Jesse Harcourt! Mr. Harcourt!"

The teenaged boy calling Jesse's name ran through the station with his hand up so he'd be seen. Jesse stopped him. "I'm Jesse Harcourt."

The boy grinned from ear to ear, as if he'd struck gold. "Stay right here, please! I was given a gold coin to find you and promised another if I could convince you to wait a moment." He ran off through the crowd.

Jesse turned a quizzical gaze to Mary. "What on earth?"

She looked around, saw only hurried passengers and families, and shrugged. She glanced up at Jesse and found him looking past her, eyebrows high, his eyes wide in surprise.

She turned to see a tall man with dark but graying curly hair walking toward them. His shoulders stooped forward, and he leaned on a cane. She glanced back at Jesse, who was grinning broadly as he approached the man with his hand extended.

As the man slowly drew near, he gazed keenly at her. His blue eyes. . .

"Mr. Sherwood!" Jesse grabbed the man's hand and looked back with joy at Mary.

Her father! Her head felt suddenly light, and she took a quick breath, fighting to control her churning emotions. He had aged so much in the last thirteen years that she didn't recognize him. His once handsome face was lined with evidence of worry and fatigue, and though still tall, he seemed shorter now.

But his quick blue eyes shone out from that lined face. "Mary." A sheen of unshed tears brightened his eyes. "You're more lovely than I'd dreamed." He held her with his intense gaze.

Love unexpectedly overflowed Mary's heart, but she didn't know how to respond. Her father handed his cane to Jesse and opened his arms to her. He was taking a chance. She might refuse to embrace him. But she walked into his arms and let him hug her for a long time, making up for the years they'd missed.

He broke the hug and held her at arm's length. "I couldn't wait for you to come to San Francisco. I've been searching for you for a long, long time."

"I didn't know."

"I'll be back in a moment," Jesse said and left them to talk. Her father told her how he'd almost lost hope, but Jesse kept it alive. They laughed and cried happy tears. She told him of her home in Massachusetts with Mrs. Palmer, Eugenia, and Lolly.

"Eugenia was with you!" His relief made him sag for a moment; instinctively she reached out to steady him. "May God bless her for that. She kept you safe."

The conductor called, "Courtland, Pittsburg, Oakland, and points west! Departing in ten minutes."

Mary looked for Jesse and saw him coming through the crowd boarding the train. She wanted him never to be far from her again. Glancing at her father, she realized she could not get back on that train immediately as she'd planned. There was so much more to say.

Her father, still smiling, leaned both hands on his cane and said, "I have my coach and driver out front, and I am ready to take you to our home in Eureka. But now this old man needs to sit a moment." He moved toward a bench left vacant by the departing passengers.

He moved slowly, and Mary followed him, again glancing back at the train. Jesse stood beside her father and looked at her, a question in his eyes.

"Jesse, I must speak to you for a moment." She moved a few feet away from the bench. He bent his head to hear her above the noise. "There is so much my father and I need to talk about. I don't think I can go right back immediately as I'd planned."

Jesse's face lit up in a wide smile, then he looked up and laughed. "Thank You, God!"

"But my things!" She pointed to the train. "They're going to San Francisco!"

He hugged her, lifting her off the ground, and twirled her around. "There are things you and I need to talk about." He set her down, then hugged her to him again.

"Mary, I knew when I saw you that day in Kimberly that you are the woman God made for me. You are my heart—the one I've waited for."

His gaze, tender and full of love, sent her pulses racing. "I think I knew it too when I saw you standing there on our porch. It was as if I'd been waiting for you to arrive."

He held her face reverently, searching her heart. "Mary. I love you. Will you give me a chance? Will you give your father, and Eureka, a chance to win you over?"

She looked back at him with longing. "My home is where you are," she said softly. The school in Boston would easily find a replacement.

He lowered his head to hers, and she trembled as he kissed her sweetly, tenderly. He crushed her to him in a tight embrace, then loosened her. "I've got to get our bags off the train!"

On the bench, her father was watching them, his tired eyes twinkling and a smile on his face. Jesse, holding her hand, led her to him. "Mr. Sherwood, may I have the pleasure of courting your daughter?"

Her father smiled affectionately. "Looks like you've already started, Son."

Jesse squeezed her hand and looked at her with pride in his eyes. "That I have, Sir. That I have. Oh! One more thing." He reached into his pocket, pulled out a small box, and handed it to her.

The conductor called, "All aboard!"

She opened the box to find the moss agate she'd admired in the window at Laramie. Her voice was choked up with emotion at his thoughtfulness. "Thank you."

Jesse grinned and ran to get their bags from the train—so they could begin their journey and their life on the West Coast.

JANE LAMUNYON

Jane lives in California with her husband and designates much of her time to writing and the business of writing. She is the author of *Me God, You Jane,* her autobiography, and two **Heartsong Presents** novels, *Fly Away Home* and *Escape on the Wind.* She has written short stories for adults and children, how-tos on a wide range of topics, and a stage play. Her work has encompassed many genres, including newspaper stories, book reviews, corporate newsletters, technical manuals, and prize-winning poetry. She is a speaker and workshop leader in many different areas.

Perfect Love

by Terri Reed

Chapter 1

Jamestown, California—Spring, 1898

R eally, Mr. Shaw. This is highly unnecessary." Despite the flutter of excitement coursing through her veins, Evelyn Giles dug in her heels, forcing people to dodge her as they hurried about the train depot. She had to raise her voice over the din of the baggage handlers tossing luggage into the waiting cargo bins. "There simply is no need for you to accompany me."

The big, warm hand cradling her elbow tightened slightly as the handsome, dark-haired Dirk Shaw propelled her forward toward the next Pullman car. "I beg to differ, Miss Giles," he replied in cool tones. "It isn't safe for a young lady to travel the railways alone."

Smoke billowing out of the tall, black, funnel-shaped smokestack hit the overhang and rolled down around them, stinging her eyes. "Oh, come now. Aren't you the one who sang the praises of the Sierra Railway, saying that this line was the best?" Evelyn retorted to his back. Though she was tall for a woman, Dirk's towering frame still overwhelmed her, adding to the thrill of his presence.

She nodded and smiled at the other passengers as she allowed Dirk to lead her along the awaiting train. Why did he feel compelled to accompany her? He wasn't a relative, just a sometime boarder at her family's inn. Granted, they'd spent many hours talking about subjects ranging from literature and the arts to science, but that wasn't reason enough for him to insist on joining her on this journey.

"It is the best, Miss Giles, though you'll have to take the Southern Pacific rail from Oakdale." He stopped them beside a short, empty car and released her elbow. With a sweeping gesture and a slight bow, he motioned for her to enter.

Evelyn swallowed. A shiver slid along her limbs. She wasn't sure if it was from alarm or anticipation. "First class?"

"It will be much more comfortable than general seating."

"But I can't afford this."

"It's not costing anything. It's a benefit of my job."

Surprised, Evelyn gazed at him intently. "Why are you doing this?"

Dark brows arched over chocolate eyes. If only she didn't have a weakness for chocolate.

"Because I want to," he drawled.

"Do you always get what you want, Mr. Shaw?"

His brows lowered, and to her surprise sadness crept into eyes that usually danced with amusement. "Not always, Miss Giles."

What had suddenly haunted him? Evelyn realized she knew very little of his life, save that he worked for the railroad and traveled a great deal. "So this car is for my protection?"

"Yes." He gave her a smile that sent her pulse tripping over itself.

And who is going to protect me from you?

Sweet affection unfurled in her chest, and as always, she fought against the caring that had somehow rooted itself in her heart from their very first meeting. With a mental shake, she shut down that emotion. She wasn't free to have feelings for this man, no matter how much his broad open smile and gregarious personality beckoned to her. She was already taken.

"If you'd prefer I didn't ride with you, I won't."

His kind words made her smile. Always the consummate gentlemen, that was Mr. Shaw. She didn't doubt her person would be safe with him. Her heart was another matter, but his thoughtfulness didn't warrant the rudeness that would be needed to send him away. She bit her lip. "It's not so much a matter of preference as propriety, you understand."

He considered her for a moment, then turned to look at the throng of travelers hurrying about the depot. He then flashed her a brilliant smile and dashed away. Evelyn clutched her bag to her chest and watched him as he darted through the swarm of people. His size coupled with his confident stride made him stand out in the crowd. His russet waistcoat and matching trousers seemed to barely contain his powerful build. The mere sight of him, even at a distance, made her heart pound against her bag.

He stopped and swept his bowler hat from his head. Evelyn went on tiptoe to see what drew his attention. A small, elderly woman dragging two bags struggled to make her way toward the coach car. Dirk bent and spoke to the woman. Her wrinkled face creased into a beaming smile as he pointed toward Evelyn. The older woman's head bobbed eagerly. After replacing his hat, Dirk plucked the bags from her small hands as if they weighed no more than feathers, and together they made their way back to Evelyn.

"Your chaperon, Miss Giles," he said into Evelyn's ear as he came to a stop beside her. "This is Mrs. Keller."

Evelyn smiled. His thoughtfulness was endearing. "Thank you, Mr. Shaw." She held out her hand, which the other woman grasped. "Hello, Mrs. Keller."

"Oh, dear me, just call me Millie. I was so thrilled when your Mr. Shaw invited me to ride with you. I've never ridden in first class." Millie withdrew her tiny hand and shifted her black shawl tighter around her shoulders. "This will be such a treat."

"Your company will be the treat, Millie," Evelyn said with a smile.

Dirk helped Millie into the car then offered his arm to Evelyn. She placed her hand on his forearm. Heat soaked into her palm. She nervously stepped inside and turned to thank Dirk again, but he disappeared with Mrs. Keller's bags.

"Oh my, this is so grand," Millie stated in a voice full of awe.

"Indeed it is," Evelyn replied, admiring the polished wood and gleaming brass decorating the car. Two sets of four plush padded benches lined the walls. "This is my first time on a train."

"Where are you headed, Dear?" Millie asked as she sat on the sofa at the far end of the car.

"San Francisco. And you?"

"The same. My son and his family live there," Millie replied.

Evelyn stood in the center aisle, unsure whether to sit with Millie or wait for Dirk and sit with him.

Millie settled back, and as Evelyn decided it would be rude not to sit with the older woman, Millie's eyes closed. Heaving a sigh, Millie said, "It has been such a trying day. If you don't mind, I'll just take a little rest."

"Everyone all set?" Dirk's voice filled the car as he stepped in carrying his hat in one large hand. Evelyn put a finger to her lips and pointed to Millie.

"Shall we?" he whispered, indicating the set of benches across the aisle from the dozing woman.

While Dirk secured her small traveling bag in the overhead sleeping compartment, Evelyn seated herself by the window and pushed back a stray curl. Through the thin layer of dust covering the window, she could make out the main thoroughfare of Jamestown. Strange how people went about their business like any other day.

Mrs. Taylor stepped out of the mercantile, loaded down with her bundles, and headed down the plank sidewalk. Two men lounged outside the National Hotel, the Giles family's competitor. A horse and carriage turned the corner and stopped in front of Doc Keenas's office. Evelyn sat up as she watched Jordan Ames help his very pregnant wife, Ann, down from the carriage.

Longing hit Evelyn smack in the middle of her chest. That's exactly what she wanted. A husband and a child to care for. She wanted what her parents and grandparents had. A home and a loving family, here in the town she grew up in.

That was the reason for this trip.

"Nervous?"

She looked at Dirk as he took the seat across from her. He stretched out his long legs and ran his fingers through his thick dark hair.

A sudden urge to feel its texture raced through her. She clenched her fist, crushing her reticule. "I–I must admit I am a little nervous. This is the first time I've traveled away from home."

Dirk steepled his fingers over his broad chest. "I'm surprised your parents allowed you to make this trip unattended."

Heat, born of guilt, flushed her cheeks. "I'm a grown woman. I don't need an escort."

Amusement tipped the corners of his full lips. "They don't know you're going, do they?"

She fiddled with her reticule. "I left them a note, if that's what you mean."

A deep chuckle rumbled through his chest. "How very responsible of you."

The jab stung, and she bit her lip. She should have told them, but they wouldn't have allowed her to go. And she needed to do this. *Lord, please forgive me.*

"Perhaps you should send them a wire when we arrive in San Francisco, letting them know you've arrived safely?"

Evelyn started. "How did you know?"

"How did I know where you're going?" He shook his head in mock admonishment. "Really, Miss Giles. Any person with half a brain would realize what you mean to do."

She bristled and brushed at the dirt clinging to the skirt of her navy traveling dress. "And just what do I mean to do, pray tell?"

He arched a single black brow. "Why, you intend to fetch your runaway fiancé."

"He did not run away, Mr. Shaw." She lifted her chin. "He went to San Francisco to build a nest egg for our future."

"That was over a year ago."

"It has taken longer than expected." She turned her attention back to the view of the town, hoping he'd drop the subject. She wasn't about to admit her misgivings to Mr. Shaw. He didn't need to know she feared that Allan Ryder had indeed left to get out of marrying her. Their families expected them to marry. Ever since they were babes, they'd been told they would marry one day. The town expected it. She expected it.

The more time she had allowed to pass, the more gossip flowed. People were speculating that Allan would never return, that he'd found someone else on his journey, or worse, that he'd been killed. Evelyn knew the latter was untrue, for Allan's parents received a small bank draft every month along with a wire from Allan. But he never answered his parents' inquiries as to when he was returning, and Evelyn could not wait any more. As to the rest, she shied away from analyzing possibilities for fear of what it would mean to her life. She had to know what Allan intended.

"I admire your patience, Miss Giles." Dirk's voice drew her attention again. His brown eyes twinkled. "Not many women as beautiful as you would wait so long for their man to return to them."

Evelyn blinked. He thought her beautiful? She couldn't remember Allan ever telling her that. "I made a commitment, Mr. Shaw. I intend to see it through," she said evenly.

"Even if the outcome is not what you want?"

His gently asked question sent apprehension sliding along her limbs. She wanted to get on with her life. She wanted Allan to return home, and the sooner they married the better. But she couldn't quite muster the enthusiasm that had kept her going for the past year. Doubts filtered in, clouding her plans for the future. When she closed her eyes at night and tried to picture Allan, she saw only a tall, dark-haired man with cheerful brown eyes. She saw Dirk in her dreams, and that was what had spurred her to this bold move. She couldn't betray Allan or her family.

The train whistle blew, saving her from replying. The floor vibrated as the wheels started to turn, moving the train forward. Evelyn sank back into the cushion of her seat. She was really leaving.

Suddenly, Dirk eased in beside her, his strong hands

closed over hers, stopping the tremors she hadn't noticed. She looked into his expressive eyes and noted his concern. Some of her fear abated. "I—would you mind retrieving my Bible from my bag? It's in the outside pocket."

Dirk released Evelyn's hands, unfolded himself, and stood to reach for her bag. He found the black, leather-bound book, then testing its weight, he wondered what she found in God's Word. He shrugged. He had no use for a God who took mothers away from their children and turned fathers into lunatics.

Handing Evelyn the book, he reclaimed his seat across from her. Though he was now a safe distance away, he still found her presence unsettling. Her scent filled the small, enclosed car, making him think of warm fires and cozy nights. Evelyn was hearth and home, everything he tried to avoid. Everything he couldn't risk having. She was beauty in the rare form of innocence, yet there was a pure wisdom in the young lady who haunted his dreams.

The rhythmic *clickety-clack* of the rails soothed his inner turmoil, as it usually did. He had no business accompanying Evelyn on this quest, but he didn't like the idea of her traveling alone. When he'd been filling out his report at the station that morning and discovered Miss Giles had purchased a ticket for San Francisco, his heart had nearly seized. This wild-goose chase upset the balance of things. Her place was with her family, in their inn, not off gallivanting after some idiot of a fiancé who didn't have the sense to cherish such a wonderful treasure. A fiancé who would no doubt break sweet Evelyn's heart.

From beneath hooded lids, he watched Evelyn as she

read. Her blond curls were piled high on her head today. He much preferred her hair down, the uncontrolled ringlets bouncing around her shoulders. The blue, stylish dress made a sharp contrast to her normal garb of white shirt, serviceable skirt, and white apron. She looked grown up and sophisticated, not at all like the young lady who helped her parents run their inn.

A grin tugged at the corners of his mouth. He'd never forget the first time he laid eyes on Miss Giles. She'd been hanging out the laundry in the fresh morning air, the sun creating a halo of gold around her glorious, unbound hair. She'd stopped and tilted her heart-shaped face toward the sky, her body stretching unself-consciously. He'd reveled in her beauty. He'd staunchly told himself he stayed at the Giles Inn instead of the National Hotel simply because the rooms were cheaper and that his choice certainly had nothing to do with the winsome innkeeper's daughter. She was too prim and proper by half and much too settled. She made him think of things he shouldn't, like the kind of life that belonged only to dreamers. She made him long to whisper sweet nothings into her ear and place little kisses along the creamy column of her throat.

Evelyn's verdant gaze suddenly captured his. "Is something amiss?"

Dirk cleared his throat, uncomfortable with where his thoughts had wandered. That was a path he shouldn't travel. He was here only to see to her protection and to be there for her when she faced her undoubtedly recreant fiancé, not to stir up feelings that would only lead to heartache. Searching for a safer explanation for what must be a frown, his gaze dropped to the book in her lap. "I was wondering what you find so interesting in that book."

One blond brow rose with indulgent humor. "You mean the Bible? Do you read?"

He grinned, amused by her question. "I'd be hard-pressed to do my job if I couldn't."

A blush heightened the color on her cheeks. His chest grew tight.

"I didn't mean to suggest you couldn't read." She marked her place in the Bible with a thin pink ribbon. "I meant, do you read this?" She indicated the Bible before settling the book in her lap like a security blanket.

"No," he said more sharply than he needed to.

She gave him her full attention. "What exactly do you do for the railroad, Mr. Shaw?"

He stroked his chin. "Officially, my title is that of spotter."

A little crease appeared between her bright green eyes. "What does a spotter do?"

"Detective work."

Her eyes grew round. "Like a Pinkerton?"

He hid his smile. "Something like that. I observe conductors and ticket takers, making sure they aren't selling tickets directly to passengers and then pocketing the money for themselves."

"My, that's a very important job. How ever did you come by it?"

Her eager, interested expression made his chest expand. A foolish part of himself enjoyed the way she made him feel special. He did his best to subdue the sentiment. "Just happened to be in the right place at the right time."

That cute little crease appeared again. He fought back the urge to reach out and smooth the line away. "Doing what?"

"I was a passenger on a train when I saw a conductor pocketing fares."

"And you turned him in."

The approval in her tone pricked his conscience. "Not exactly. I picked his pocket." Now why he'd go and admit that? Maybe if he took off some of the shine she had put on him, leaving her would be easier this time.

She gaped. "You didn't."

He lifted a negligent shoulder. "He was a plum mark. For every three tickets he sold he skimmed one fare. The train was full, and I needed the money more than he did."

Indignation sparked emerald fire in her eyes and stained her cheeks red. "Really, Mr. Shaw. I don't know what to say."

She looked adorable, all spitfire and righteous indignation. He held up a hand. "Now, before you wrinkle your nose at me, let me say I have reformed my ways."

"One would hope so," she said, prim and properlike. Her gaze narrowed. "What do you mean, you needed the money more than he did?"

"Seeing how I didn't have a job, pickpocketing was a profitable endeavor." He'd learned to filch as a boy. Sometimes it was the only way he and his father survived.

"How old were you?"

"When I picked the conductor's pocket?"

"Yes."

He thought for a moment. "That happened about thirteen years ago, so I'd have been fifteen at the time."

"What were you doing on the train?"

"Living."

"You were living on the train?"

He leaned forward, his gaze locked with hers. "Not everyone grew up as blessed as you, Miss Giles. Not everyone had a mother and father to care for them."

Her pink lips formed a silent "Oh." Her hand reached out toward him. "I'm so sorry, Mr. Shaw. I had no idea you were an orphan."

Such a simple thing, to reach out and partake of the comfort offered in her slender hand. Such a simple thing, to pull her to him and hold on tight, to let her keep him in one place. Such a simple thing, yet so dangerous. She was grounded, rooted, settled in, and he wasn't stupid enough to think a life like that would ever last for him. God had snatched that kind of life away from him during his childhood. How could he be sure God wouldn't do it again?

He met her gaze and sighed. No matter how much he wished it; there was no security in caring for Miss Giles. She was as untouchable as the sun. He'd never been more sure of anything in his life.

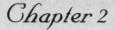

Chapter 2

An orphan.

Evelyn blinked back sudden tears. That explained so much. Mr. Shaw had always seemed slightly uncomfortable when he'd join her family for meals. Her parents, and her grandparents before them, opened not only their home but also their hearts to those who sought lodging within the shelter of the Giles Inn. Their inn was so successful because her family treated everyone as if they were related.

The anguish in his eyes tore at her heart. Compassion filled her to overflowing. She wanted to offer him comfort and care. To heal the wounds that life had inflicted upon his soul. But she had to be careful. Self-consciously, she dropped her hand back to her lap and took comfort from the Bible she still held. She wasn't free to give more than her friendship. Though friendship she most certainly could give. "Were your parents killed in an accident?"

He sat back, his large arms crossing over his chest as his legs bent slightly at the knees. To the world he appeared to be a man set to enjoy his train ride, but his brown eyes darkened to rich earth, and the tight lines around his mouth revealed to Evelyn that he was far from relaxed.

He glanced at the sleeping Mrs. Keller, then turned back to her. "My mother died of tuberculosis."

Evelyn's heart twisted with sympathy. Consumption. What a horrid disease. She knew what that illness did to a body, how long it tortured and wreaked havoc. There had been an outbreak in Jamestown years ago. Her mother braved the disease and helped care for her friend. Thankfully, her mother had not contracted the disease which ended up taking her friend's life. "Did your father contract the disease as well?"

He shook his head. "No, neither he nor I became ill."

"Were you with your mother at the time?" Why hadn't his father kept him away from his ill mother?

"I cared for her until it was over."

She felt sick with grief at what he'd endured. "How old were you?"

"Eight, when she first became ill. Two years later she died."

"Oh, you were so young. Too young for such a burden. And your father? What of him?"

He stared at her, but his eyes were unfocused, like he was looking inward at something from the past. "My father attempted everything to save her. Any crazy idea someone had, he tried. He used his clout as the president of Boston Bank to bring specialists from all over the world. Nothing helped." His gaze focused back to her. "Not even prayer."

Evelyn sucked in a breath. Surely he didn't blame God.

He laughed, a hollow, bitter sound that she'd never heard from him before. "Oh, yes. We prayed. My mother was a strong believer. Though not once did she pray for healing." He frowned as if puzzled by that. "She prayed for my father and me, that we stayed in good health." His puzzlement cleared and was replaced by a profound bitterness. "God answered *her* prayer but not mine, nor my father's. I would sit by her bed and sob, asking God to make my mother better. She suffered all the more. My father. . ." He closed his eyes briefly. "I can still vividly remember him standing by Mother's grave, shaking his fist at the sky, cursing God for allowing this to happen."

Feeling his pain of loss as clearly as if it had been her own, a tear slid down her cheek and landed on the back of her hand. "Where is your father now?"

"Without my mother, he couldn't function. He lost his job; we lost our home. One day we simply hopped on a train and kept going. From train to train we went, never stopping in any town long enough for people to wonder why I wasn't in school. But my father continued getting worse. Only on the trains, only when we were moving did he seem content with life."

Concern clogged her throat, making speech difficult. "How did you survive?"

He shrugged. "I did whatever I had to. The trains became our home."

"But you were a child. Your father should have. . ." She trailed off as his earlier words registered. She swallowed. "You said he got worse? What did you mean?"

294

He sat up straighter and turned to stare out the window at the passing countryside. "Losing my mother took his will to live. I think he didn't end his own life when she died because of me. But his grief overwhelmed him. Every day he slipped further from reality."

Evelyn swallowed back the aching that threatened to undo her. She couldn't imagine the heartache and pain Dirk had grown up with. "When did he die?"

His finger traced the ornate carving in the armrest. "Three years after my mother. His heart gave out," he said in a rough voice. His tortured gaze lifted to hers.

Evelyn held on to her composure by a thread. She wanted to sob for him, for the anguish he'd suffered and was still suffering. She wanted to open her arms and her life to him, to give him back what he'd lost, but that was impossible. She was not free to give him any of those things. *Dear Father God, what do I say? How can I help him? Please guide me.*

She had faith He would answer her prayers.

Dirk watched the play of emotions on Evelyn's sweet face. Her dark blond lashes were wet with tears she'd shed on his behalf. Something warm unfolded in his chest.

She cared.

Or pitied him.

He searched her green eyes. No, he didn't see pity.

There was compassion and gentleness and an inner strength that affected him deeply. This adorable woman with her softly asked questions drew him out, making him speak of things he'd never spoken of before to another

295

living soul. Despite that, Evelyn made him feel safe and comforted. She made him want what he couldn't have—someone with whom to share his life. He had to remember that she was betrothed and, therefore, had to keep tighter control over his emotions, not to mention keep his distance. He knew, however, that this train ride would forever be embedded in his heart and soul.

"You asked me earlier what I found so interesting in the Bible." Evelyn indicated the black book she held in her slender hands.

"I did ask," he acknowledged, thankful the subject turned away from his parents.

"What I find, and you could find, too, is hope, comfort, and peace."

He tipped one corner of his mouth up. Her earnest expression was quite endearing. "You believe that book is true?"

"Yes, it's truth." She held the Bible close to her heart. "The Bible is full of promises. Promises of peace. Promises that will heal your heart."

He chuckled and resisted the urge to push back a wayward blond lock that rested at her temple. "That is if I have a heart."

"Oh, you have a heart, Mr. Shaw."

The tender expression in her gaze made his heart pound. What did she see when she looked at him?

"And it's hurting," she added softly.

Uncomfortable with the truth of her words, he ran a hand through his hair. "You think you know me so well?"

Her chin lifted slightly. "Well enough to see that

anger and grief are strangling the life from you."

Dazed by this new twist in the conversation, he leaned forward. "Do I strike you as a man who doesn't enjoy his life, Miss Giles?"

She drew her brows together. "You strike me as a man who is running from the pain of the past."

He set his jaw. He should be accustomed to her challenging ways by now. They'd spent numerous evenings arguing the finer points of art and science. What made this subject any different? She'd always been one to question and delve deeper into the subjects they'd discussed, forcing him to look beyond the surface each time.

And she was doing it again. Only now she was delving into *him*.

He didn't want to look too deep into his own heart for fear of becoming like his father, overwhelmed and ultimately overcome by the emotions so deeply buried in his soul. Yet, with Evelyn, he couldn't hide. He didn't want to hide from her, which was dangerous because only more heartache lay down that path. "Am I not entitled to mourn my parents?" he challenged.

"Mourn, yes. It hurts terribly to be separated from those we love." Sadness reflected briefly in her eyes. "I miss my grandparents every day. Their words, their gestures, everything."

He realized he shared the same sadness. He missed his mother. Missed the gentle, loving woman she'd been. The way she'd sung him to sleep, the way she baked delicious breads and cakes. He clung to the good memories.

The only clear, positive memories he had of his father

were the few lucid times they'd spent on the trains. His father had been an intelligent man, full of knowledge. Dirk cherished those moments when his father shared his wealth of information.

Evelyn shifted in her seat to accommodate a curve in the rails as the train tipped slightly. "But you aren't entitled to blame God."

Anger pricked him. "He didn't care about me or my mother."

"He did and does," she protested. "He answered both of your prayers."

"By letting my mother die?" What kind of God would answer a prayer by doing the opposite of what was asked?

Compassion softened her expression. "I know it wasn't the answer you were hoping for, but He did heal your mother. He just didn't heal her frail, sick, human body."

His heart thumped against his ribs. "What are you going to tell me, that He healed her in heaven?"

"Yes." Her eyes glowed bright with conviction. "She's in heaven where there is no pain or sickness."

He scoffed. "Nice sentiment."

She stared hard at him, her expression turning thoughtful. "Your father chose to allow sorrow and bitterness to consume him rather than clinging to the hope of one day seeing your mother again. Is that what you want to choose?"

Deep in the recesses of his memory, he could hear his mother's voice telling him they'd be together again one day. He hadn't realized how comforting that thought had been as a child. But could he, as an adult, dare to hope that was true? "You promised me I could find peace in the Bible."

"Not my promise, God's."

His gaze went to the book still clutched in her hands and then to her face. Her passion and certainty beckoned to him, demanding he look deeper into what his own mother had believed. Evelyn made him want to be so much more than he was. Too bad she could never be his to care for or his to. . . He cleared his throat and held out his hand. "If you please."

Her smile could have brightened the gloomiest of days. She placed the leather-bound book in his hand. "You'll find what you need." She stood.

He scrambled to his feet. They stood inches apart. She placed a hand flat against the middle of his chest. Heat spread out from the point of contact, and his gaze flew to hers. She blushed so becomingly.

"I. . .uh, need to stretch my legs." She removed her hand and stepped away from him.

Dirk watched her flounce neatly down the aisle.

"That is a very wise young woman."

He spun around to face Mrs. Keller. Her kind eyes regarded him steadily.

He hadn't realized she was awake. How much of the conversation had she heard? "Yes, she is wise," he agreed.

With a sage nod, she said, "She's a keeper, Mr. Shaw."

An invisible band tightened around his heart. He tried to smile but couldn't quite manage to. If only Evelyn was his to keep. He snorted beneath his breath. There was no use in thinking "what if?" All he had were these remaining few hours with Evelyn. But read the Bible?

Years of hearing and believing that God was to blame for his mother's death rose to clog his throat. He wanted to resist, to put the book down and walk away. He wouldn't. For Evelyn, he'd put aside his doubts and look at what she found so interesting.

He ran a hand over the smooth leather of the Bible and slowly opened the jacket cover. The sprawling pen of Catherine Giles graced the first page. Not wanting to pry into an undoubtedly sweet sentiment from a loving mother to her daughter, he prepared to turn the page but stopped as the writing at the bottom caught his attention: 1 John 4:18.

He flipped through the pages until he came to the correct book and chapter. His finger skimmed down until it stopped on verse eighteen. He read the passage. A shiver born of confusion and an unfamiliar sense of awe overwhelmed him. For a moment his vision dimmed, and he was a child kneeling beside his mother's bed. Her pale skin and sunken eyes scared him. She'd clung to his hand with what little strength she had left, her voice soft and imploring, "Do not be afraid. Love casts out fear. We will be together again one day in heaven. You must believe, Son."

Dirk shook the memory from his mind and stared at the black words on the page. "There is no fear in love; but perfect love casteth out fear: because fear hath torment. He that feareth is not made perfect in love."

He sank to the bench, feeling an odd combination of

excitement and disbelief. The fact that his mother's words mirrored the first words he'd ever read from God's book was a coincidence. Wasn't it?

Evelyn found herself easily adjusting to the sway of the train as it moved along the track. On her walk she'd passed through the coach cars and noted the lack of shiny brass or rich colors. The benches were wooden and looked terribly uncomfortable. She was grateful to Mr. Shaw for making the whole train experience one she would always remember.

She sighed and headed back down the aisle of the first class Pullman car. Her steps slowed as she watched Mr. Shaw hand three tickets and some money to the conductor.

"Miss," the conductor tipped his blue hat to her before moving on down the aisle and to the next car.

"Is everything all right?" she asked Dirk as she came to a stop beside him.

"It is so kind of your young man to pay the difference in my ticket." Mrs. Keller's faced beamed. A pink hue tinged her weathered cheeks, and little lines crinkled at the corners of her eyes.

"Kind, indeed." Evelyn smiled at Mrs. Keller, before turning her gaze once more upon Mr. Shaw. Her heart swelled with pleasure. "And generous."

"I am well paid for my work." For a moment he looked almost embarrassed by her assessment, but his face broke into a grin that sent Evelyn's heart thumping. The man was positively charming, on top of being kind, generous, and smart. Oh my, she could think of so many reasons why she liked this man. And only one reason that she couldn't allow herself to care too much about him—Allan. She mustn't forget that she was betrothed. She'd made a commitment, and she intended to see it through.

Uneasy with the direction of her thoughts, her gaze slid away from Dirk and came to rest on her Bible lying open on the bench next to Dirk's bowler hat. Delighted, she smiled. "You've been reading?"

He regarded her steadily, his grin dimming. "I'm finding it. . .interesting."

Evelyn squelched the little burst of disappointment. What did she expect? Renewed faith in one reading? He had only begun his journey of faith. His soul would be healed in God's timing, not hers.

Now that her chaperon was awake, Evelyn moved to sit across from the older woman. She gazed out the window, trying to ignore the hum of awareness buzzing along her limbs as Dirk slid onto the bench next to her.

Dark, jagged cliffs of porous rock dotted the terrain. She'd never seen such strange formations. "What is that?" She pointed out the window to the passing countryside.

Dirk leaned close. So close she could see where his beard would grow in along his strong jaw. Evelyn inched back to allow him room. She shakily breathed in and caught a whiff of his scent. Spicy, earthy, and male. She smothered a feminine sigh.

"That's lava," he stated.

Surprised, Evelyn turned to stare out the window again. "I didn't know there'd been a volcano here."

Mrs. Keller sat forward. "Look, that one mountain is flat on the top."

"That's called Table Top Mountain," Dirk offered.

Evelyn stared at his strong profile. "You made that up."

He turned to face her. A mere breath of space separated them. "No, I didn't."

Evelyn swallowed as longing hit her, and her gaze dropped to his lips. What would it be like to be kissed by him? She had no experience to speak of. Allan had kissed her on the cheek several times and only once on the lips before he'd left town. But she inherently knew the chaste kiss she'd received from Allan would somehow be much different than a kiss from Mr. Shaw.

"Dear me, look at the stone wall the lava made. Do you suppose that volcano could erupt again?"

Mrs. Keller's voice jolted Evelyn from her thoughts. *Oh my, what was I doing thinking about kissing Mr. Shaw?* She met his clearly amused gaze and blushed. Surely he couldn't tell what she'd been thinking—could he?

He sat back and stretched out his long legs. "Not to worry, Mrs. Keller. There hasn't been any volcanic activity in this part of the state for many, many years. We'll arrive in Oakdale soon. We may wish to dine on board before we change trains."

Not having eaten before leaving home, Evelyn was thankful for the suggestion. Besides, it would provide a good distraction from her growing attraction to her male traveling companion.

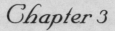

Chapter 3

Dirk nodded his thanks to the waiter clearing the table of their empty dishes, then focused his gaze on Evelyn. He smiled with amusement as he listened to her animated tales of her family's inn. Mrs. Keller hung on every word, occasionally interjecting, "You don't say," and "Oh, dear."

Though he was familiar with many of her stories, having heard them at her family's table, he found enjoyment in watching Evelyn. She was so quick to find good and so willing to overlook flaws in people but not herself. He found that an endearing quality. Evelyn humbly accepted her own shortcomings and strove to better herself. He was amazed by how well-read she was. He used reading, not necessarily to further his knowledge, more to take him away from his pain and loneliness.

His smile faded as that last thought slammed into his consciousness.

Lonely? Him? Was that why he'd so often stayed at the Giles' Inn, when he'd made a point of never staying in the same place more than once in any six-month period?

He liked his life. Liked the adventure, the anticipation of never knowing what was waiting for him the next day. He liked deciding what he would do and where he would go when he wanted. The trains were his home.

Only he couldn't deny he didn't feel any connection to the people of the railroads. How could he, when he was paid to keep watch and to report other employees?

He didn't need a connection. He was fine on his own.

At least he had been until Evelyn stepped into his life.

Dear, sweet Evelyn. She'd slipped under his skin, breached the barricades to his heart. The pip of it was she'd done it without even trying. With her natural grace and beauty, her unself-conscious way of speaking her mind. . .her convictions, her faith. . .

The woman had no idea how she affected him. She'd encouraged him to read from her Bible, something he'd never thought he'd do. Not when he'd spent so many years believing that God had taken his mother away while also believing God didn't love him.

We love because He first loved us.

The line of Scripture that followed the one written in the front of Evelyn's Bible made Dirk's insides quake. Could it be that God did love him? Were the words he'd read, the words of love, faith, and eternal life, true?

The cynic inside his brain laughed, taunting him, effectively shutting down his speculations. Nothing would bring back his parents; nothing could convince him that God was for real and that He cared. He would not trust in God.

The booming sound of the train whistle brought

305

Dirk out of his thoughts. "Ladies, shall we return to our seats before we arrive in Oakdale?"

Dirk slid from the booth and rose to offer Mrs. Keller his arm. She placed her weathered, blue-veined hand on his jacket sleeve and rose. "Thank you, young man. You sure know how to make a lady feel special." Her gray eyes twinkled up at him.

"My pleasure." Dirk nodded with a broad smile.

Mrs. Keller snorted. "Don't waste your charm on me, young man." She tapped his arm and gave a pointed look toward Evelyn.

Dirk winked at the older woman before stepping forward to offer his hand to Evelyn. Evelyn brushed back a stray tendril and blinked up at him before slipping her hand into his. His gaze riveted to their clasped hands. Her slender, petite hand looked vulnerable against his large, blunt fingers.

He promised then and there that he would protect her from whatever lay at the end of this journey. He gave her hand a gentle squeeze. She lifted her dark blond brows in question as she allowed him to help her to her feet.

"Have I told you today how lovely you look?" He steadily met her gaze. Her eyes reminded him of the lush rolling pastures of Kansas.

She blinked, and her cheeks turned a soft shade of pink. "I—why, thank you, Mr. Shaw."

Behind him Mrs. Keller giggled a soft, girlish sound.

He and Evelyn stared at one another for a moment longer before breaking into wide grins. He regrettably released her hand and ushered the ladies back to their car.

The train began to decelerate, the wheels grinding on the track as the brake was applied.

"Oakdale," called the conductor as he entered their car through the vestibule separating the coaches.

Outside, dust and steam swirled around the car, making the window smudged and dark.

"Ladies, shall we wait a moment for the dust to clear?"

Mrs. Keller patted at her hair. "Oh, yes, please."

As Dirk met Evelyn's gaze, he knew when all was said and done, when Evelyn was either married to Ryder or back home with her family, if he wasn't careful, she'd be taking a piece of his heart with her. And he didn't have that much heart to spare.

The change of trains in Oakdale had gone very smoothly, and now they were headed for San Francisco. Evelyn settled back into the seat of the first class Pullman car of the Southern Pacific railroad. She'd thought the first class car of the Sierra Railway handsome, but it paled in comparison to the one she now sat in. The seats were a tad more cushioned and the plush, deep blue material very soothing. The shiny brass lamps sparkled as if someone had recently polished them, and the beautiful woodwork was infinitely more intricate and lavish. But the biggest difference, she noted, was the ceiling. An elaborate painting of a city street adorned the roof. Evelyn stared up, mesmerized by the amount of detail and effort that had gone into the work.

"That is amazing, isn't it?" Millie Keller sat beside her, her hands busy with the knitting she'd retrieved from her bags while they'd waited for their next train.

"Yes. I've never seen anything like it," Evelyn commented, still studying the rich colors and scenes above her.

Voices drew her attention. Ladies with plumaged hats and gentlemen with high, starched collars filed in, filling the seats. This ride would not be as quiet or as intimate as the previous. She didn't know whether that was a good thing or not.

Biting her lip, Evelyn watched the doorway for Mr. Shaw. He'd ushered them in and told them he had something to do. Was he watching the ticket takers? A thought suddenly occurred to her. What would the conductors and ticket takers do if they realized that Dirk was a spotter? Did he live with the constant danger of being discovered?

Mr. Shaw was a big man, perfectly capable of taking care of himself, she consoled herself. Still, the thought that he could be in danger at any given moment sent rivulets of anxiety sliding clear to the tips of her fingers. She shivered.

Mrs. Keller paused and glanced up. "Cold, Dear?"

Smoothing the skirt of her traveling dress, Evelyn tried to force her anxieties away. "A tad nervous about the trip, I suppose."

"Whatever for, Dear?"

She couldn't very well tell Mrs. Keller she was going to San Francisco to find her betrothed. The older woman would want to know where Dirk fit in. Evelyn couldn't contemplate where he fit in. Friends? Yes. But the feelings she was fighting seemed so much more than that.

"I wonder where Mr. Shaw has gone," she murmured.

Mrs. Keller patted her hand. "Not to worry. I have a feeling your young man won't let himself wander off too far from you."

"He's—e's not my young man." Heat crept into Evelyn's cheeks.

Millie raised a brow. "I think it's quite plain that you two are smitten."

Oh, my. Evelyn put her hand to her throat. Had she somehow led Mr. Shaw to believe. . .had her feelings been that transparent? "I assure you, we are merely friends."

Millie gave her a knowing smile before resuming her knitting.

Could what the older woman said be true? Was Dirk Shaw really smitten with her?

She shook her head. No. He'd never been anything but a gentleman.

Then why did he insist on accompanying you on this trip? a little voice inside her head whispered.

He was worried, she reasoned. *He said it was unsafe for a woman to travel alone.*

Ah, but you're traveling with Mrs. Keller now aren't you?

Be quiet, she thought crossly.

She sat up straighter and placed her hands in her lap. This trip was about securing her future. Bringing Allan home and starting a family. . . She would not let herself be sidetracked by. . .by. . .well, by unmerited feelings for Mr. Shaw.

Dirk scanned the crowded car and spotted Evelyn sitting

primly at the back. His gaze narrowed. The expression on her face was slightly pinched, as if her shoes were suddenly too tight. She'd been so relaxed and seemingly carefree earlier. What had changed?

He strode through the car, mentally counting the passengers and quickly figuring the totals that should be collected. He shook his head wryly, throwing the numbers away. He wasn't on duty today. He'd wired the home office and told them he was taking a vacation. Something he'd never done before.

"Ladies," he said as he slid onto the bench across from Evelyn.

She nodded at him then averted her gaze to stare out the window. He noted her tightly folded hands and the tips of her dark, dusty shoes that were snapped together. The blond curls that had earlier escaped were now controlled beneath her properly placed bonnet. She looked every inch the refined and collected lady.

Only the rapid beating of her pulse visible at the base of her lovely throat belied the calmness. Undoubtedly, she was worrying about what she'd find at the end of their ride.

He sat forward, placing his elbows on his knees. "Miss Giles, would you like for me to retrieve your Bible?"

She smiled at him gratefully. "Yes, thank you."

From the overhead sleeping berth where he'd placed her one bag, he took the black leather Bible out of the side pocket. Momentarily, he felt an unexplainable comfort holding the book. He held it out to Evelyn.

As she grasped the book, he watched the way her hand flattened across the cover, much like the way her hand had earlier flattened against his chest. He stepped back, away from the memory of her touch, and bumped into Mrs. Keller in the process.

"Oops." Her knitting tumbled from her lap.

"Mrs. Keller, I'm so sorry." He bent to pick up the stray yarn unraveling across the floor, and his hip knocked against something soft. He snapped up when he realized Evelyn was on her knees scooping up yarn.

"Please, sit, Mr. Shaw," she said gently, her grassy green gaze twinkling. "I have it."

He flopped back onto the bench while Evelyn helped Mrs. Keller gather her things. Suddenly she giggled, and his heart squeezed at the musical sound.

She pointed. "You have yarn snaking up your leg, Mr. Shaw."

Indeed he did. Red, fuzzy string clung to his pants. He plucked the strands away as Evelyn reeled it toward her using the ball of yarn. "Thank you, Miss Giles."

"You're welcome." She held his gaze, her meadow-soft eyes temperate and illuminating, then abruptly she moved back to her seat. Once again she sat rigid and stiff while clutching her Bible. Some part of him wished he had the power to offer her comfort.

The train whistle signaled their departure as the floor beneath their feet rattled and the wheels began churning. The train inched forward, picking up speed. They were on their way to San Francisco. Normally, Dirk found great peace in the going. It didn't matter where the trains were headed as long as they were moving. But as the familiar hum of the rails filled his senses, the contentment, the peace remained elusive. Unsettled by the lack of solace, his gaze rested on Evelyn. Once again she stared out the window, her pulse less visible in the lovely column of her throat.

"The Bible is full of promises. Promises of peace, hope, and comfort."

Now Evelyn was in his head.

He stared at the Bible in her hands. His heart rate picked up speed along with the train wheels. He didn't want to feel this compelling pull toward God and His Word, but it was there, taking root. The more he tried to pull away, the more it beckoned.

You'd be setting yourself up for a painful fall if you go down that road, sneered a different voice, the voice that always brought him to his senses.

Dirk checked his pocket watch. "Less than three hours and we'll arrive in San Francisco."

"Really?" Evelyn glanced away from the window. He nodded, hoping to talk, but she turned away. Why did he have this feeling she was closing him out?

"I can hardly wait," Mrs. Keller said, her hands still busy with her knitting.

"You have family there?" Dirk inquired.

"My son and his family. John and Dora have two little girls. My grandbabies, you know."

"That's nice. Isn't that nice, Miss Giles?" He wasn't going to let her shut him out when they only had a short time left together.

Evelyn turned to smile at Mrs. Keller. "How old are your granddaughters?"

"Eight and four. Little angels, they are."

"I'll bet they can't wait to see you," Evelyn commented, clearly focused on Mrs. Keller.

Mrs. Keller grinned. "Want to show me the sights, they do."

The sudden sting of jealousy caught him unaware. It was ridiculous for him to feel slighted by the attention Evelyn was bestowing on Mrs. Keller. He cleared his throat. "Ah, yes. San Francisco has many sights to behold," he pointed out, looking at Evelyn. Her expression continued to be distant. "The zoo is amazing. It's filled with the most interesting collection of animals from all over the world."

A spark of curiosity flared in Evelyn's eyes, but she quickly looked away.

He pressed. "You surely wouldn't want to miss that. Nor would you want to miss the park. Beautiful landscaping. Sculpted hedges, flowers of every color, water fountains, and the most incredible trees I've ever seen. That McLaren chap has done a marvelous job."

"Sounds lovely." Mrs. Keller glanced at Evelyn. "Don't you agree?"

"Yes, lovely." Evelyn picked up her reticule and fiddled with the drawstring.

Dirk realized she was trying to appear uninterested and smiled inwardly. Perhaps there was more to the way she was acting. "You can't miss the bay. Magnificent. It stretches forty-six miles across and from the sea looks like arms open wide, welcoming the seafarer. It's called the Golden Gate to riches because so many have passed through its waters on their way to seek gold."

Evelyn's hands stilled. "You've been out to sea, Mr. Shaw?"

Ah, so he had her attention now. "Yes. I've sailed from the bay down to the southern part of the state."

"I would like to see the ocean," she admitted softly.

He smiled, thinking of the additional time he would have with her. "That can be arranged. The wharf is unbelievable. The ships are huge and the vendors loud."

She bit her lip and averted her gaze.

"But there's nothing like standing on the top of Telegraph Hill and watching the fog rolling in over the Pacific Ocean like a fluffy blanket of cotton being stretched out over the water."

"It sounds as if you've spent a fair amount of time in San Francisco," Mrs. Keller commented.

"I have." Though he responded to Mrs. Keller, he was aware of Evelyn's sidelong glance. "I love the architecture of the city. Especially the homes on Nob Hill, the ornate decorations and beautifully done balustrades. The Victorian homes are referred to as the Painted Ladies." He wagged his brows.

Evelyn turned her full attention on him, amusement crinkling the corners of her eyes. "You made that up."

He grinned. "No, I did not."

She eyed him dubiously.

Tenderness rose, making his chest ache. Instead of giving in to the desire to wipe the doubts from her eyes with his kiss, he said, "The Mission of Dolores is another sight not to be missed. A handsome building with ornate, tiered towers and arched doorways and windows. The grounds are splendid."

"It all sounds wonderful," Evelyn commented, her expression turning wistful.

"That's just San Francisco." He wanted to show her his life was good, that it held so much. "There are amazing sights and experiences waiting out there. New York, Boston, New Orleans, the Great Plains of the Dakotas. Now, with the railroads expanding daily, there's no place that cannot be explored." He longed to show her his world and see the glow of discovery in her eyes as they rode the rails together. He was a fool to harbor such thoughts. He'd have to settle for her delight when she got her first glimpse of the Pacific Ocean.

"You've been to all those places?"

He nodded. "I've lived a good life." Her gentle smile reminded him that he'd shared his past with her. "Okay. An interesting life," he amended.

"I had no idea. I assumed you worked only for the railroads in California."

"I rotate regions around the country. Gets a little risky if I stay in any one place too long."

Understanding showed in the depths of her gaze, followed quickly by concern. He'd never felt so cared for. The feeling was overwhelming yet comforting. It scared him, but he gladly tucked the goodness of Evelyn's care away in his memory. Care was not love, but it was close. Close enough for him because that was all he could allow.

She was not his, and even if she were, he couldn't risk having, then losing the kind of settled life that came with running an inn. Besides, she'd never be content with the kind of life he led. The interested, wistful expression she'd worn when he'd talked about traveling gave him pause. Or would she?

The possibility grabbed hold of his imagination and caused tentative hope to unfurl. Perhaps he should find out.

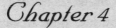

Chapter 4

Evelyn had guessed his job held danger, but having Dirk's confirmation set her nerves on edge. She didn't like the thought of him being in danger. Even if he did get to see such wonderful places that she would only read about.

Imagine, traveling clear across the country, seeing the history of America and meeting people who were the same, yet so different. What would her contemporaries in New York be like? Or the South? Would women there see her as dull and timid because she was content to live a quiet life sheltered within her family's inn? Or were there women elsewhere who were like her, who thought family and home were more important than independence?

She'd never dreamed of nor wanted anything more from her life than to marry, have children, and run the inn.

While she'd certainly contemplated what the ocean would look and feel like, what a really big city would be like, she'd never given it much more than a passing thought. Until now.

The way Mr. Shaw had described the sights of San

Francisco made her ache to see the city with her own eyes. Knowing that soon she would be there let loose a restless twinge inside her. Suddenly, just having read about the world wasn't enough anymore. Part of her wanted to see it, touch it, and experience it.

She glanced up at Dirk and met his intense, probing gaze. It was his fault. Once again she was allowing herself to be distracted from her goal. Guilt pricked at her that she could be so easily diverted from her intentions.

Turning to stare out the window, she tried to conjure up an image of Allan, but as the train passed beneath a trestle, effectively blocking out the sun, Mr. Shaw's reflection was the only thing she could see.

He was engaged in a conversation now with the gentleman who was sitting next to him.

She loved to watch him, to see the quick intelligence in his warm, brown eyes, to hear the amused undertone in his voice. She enjoyed the way her heart tumbled when she caught a glimpse of his charming grin.

Sunlight burst through the window, and Evelyn closed her eyes against the brightness, against the bittersweet pain of caring about Mr. Shaw. She rested her head on the window frame and allowed the humming of the train whizzing along the track to lull her senses.

No matter how appealing Mr. Shaw's life sounded or how her heart responded to him, he had no place in her life. Her dream of the future was set. A life running the inn, raising children with Allan, that was what she wanted. But as sleepiness claimed her, she couldn't erase from her mind the sorrow and the world of hurt in Dirk's eyes as he'd talked about his parents. Nor could she drive away the need to give back to him what he'd lost as a child—family, belonging, and love. Neither could she banish the desire to be the one to teach him that God's love was unconditional.

"Miss Giles. Wake up."

Evelyn sighed. In her dream, Dirk called her "Sweetheart." They were walking through the meadow that bordered one end of Jamestown. Yellow monkey flowers rustled about their knees, and the warm sun kissed their faces with a light, smooth touch.

She nestled into the hand stroking her cheek. She loved this dream. She loved the gentle way Dirk brushed his knuckles over her skin. It felt so real, so right.

She blinked open her eyes. It was real. Evelyn sat up with a start. Dirk had touched her cheek. *Had* he called her "Sweetheart"? Her blood raced, and she gazed up at him.

His full lips curved into a tender smile. "We've arrived."

"Oh, my," she breathed out, suddenly aware that the train indeed had stopped moving, and people were bustling about.

Adjusting her traveling dress and smoothing her hair, she let the moment sink in. She'd dreamt about Mr. Shaw, but she was on her way to see Allan. It made no sense. She should be dreaming of a romantic reunion with her childhood friend. Instead, her senses were filled with another man. Surely, once she saw Allan again all this nonsense in her head and heart with Dirk would stop. It had to.

She accepted Dirk's offer of help as she rose, then

allowed him to lead her and Mrs. Keller out of the car, through the vestibule, and down the stairs to the platform. A chilled breeze whipped by, blowing stray strands of hair into her eyes. The coldness wasn't what she was expecting. Hopefully, this was the only unexpected thing she'd encounter.

"Brrr," exclaimed Mrs. Keller as she descended the stairs behind Evelyn. She pulled her black shawl tighter around her shoulders.

Dirk flashed a quick smile, showing his white, even teeth. "Summer in San Francisco."

There was a decidedly different quality to the atmosphere. The air was not fresh in the piney way like in the foothills of the Sierra Nevadas, but there was a crispness that tantalized Evelyn's senses. Excitement quickened within her. She was in the big city—far away from Jamestown and everything she knew.

Mrs. Keller let out a joyous squeal as two little towheaded girls came barreling toward her, yelling "Nana," followed by a handsome-looking couple. The scene of Mrs. Keller being reunited with her family clutched at Evelyn's heart, reminding her of the reason she'd come to San Francisco. She ached to start the family she'd dreamed of having.

Mrs. Keller made the introductions then said goodbye. Suddenly she was gone, leaving Evelyn and Dirk standing on the platform. People hurried about, the noise of the baggage handlers loading and unloading the cars filled the air, and a ticket taker roamed the crowd selling tickets.

Dirk took Evelyn's arm. "Miss Giles, you should tele-graph your family that you've arrived safely."

"Yes, of course." Her parents would be upset, but she felt certain they would understand, especially when Allan returned with her. The thought dropped like a stone into the pit of her stomach. *This is what you want, remember?* she scolded herself and promptly lifted her chin. She was committed to Allan, committed to her dream.

Dirk directed her to the telegraph office then excused himself with the promise he'd be back momentarily. Evelyn ignored the empty sensation his departure caused and directed her attention to the business at hand. She made the telegraph brief. There would be time enough to explain her reasons for this trip when she returned home.

Once that was done, she stepped out of the little office onto the street side of the train depot.

Several carriages rolled by. A few stopped to unload passengers who then hurried past her toward the trains. Evelyn watched in rapt fascination. The smartly dressed women in rich colors with hats sporting poufs of lace, yards of ribbon, and bouquets of flowers hardly spared her a glance as they passed by. The men, she noted, dressed much like Mr. Shaw. Clean lines to their coats, bowlers or top hats resting jauntily on their heads.

Evelyn shifted uncomfortably in her homemade dress. Her mother had done a fine job of sewing the heavy navy blue cotton, but still Evelyn admired the fineness of the other people's fabrics and the discernible quality of the tailoring.

She looked like what she was—a simple country girl.

She didn't belong here. A little burst of panic sent her searching for Mr. Shaw. What had she been thinking to set out on this trip alone? *Thank You, Lord, for sending Mr. Shaw.*

As she headed back inside the office, Dirk rounded the corner from the train yard, carrying her small bag in his large hand. Her heart lurched at the sight of his tall, lean, and masculine figure. He stood out not for his clothing but for the way he carried himself. So self-assured and confident. He made her feel safe. He grinned, and she felt faint.

"All set, then?" he asked as he drew abreast of her.

She nodded, afraid to speak for fear words wouldn't leave her dry throat. He tucked her hand into the crook of his elbow, and they started up the street. As they walked, Evelyn realized that the street had a rather steep incline. They slowly crested a small hill. Evelyn stared. The city was a rolling mass of buildings, streets, and houses constructed on hills. "I had no idea the city would be so. . .hilly," she puffed.

Dirk's low chuckle curled her toes inside her not-made-for-serious-walking shoes.

They walked for several blocks, and excitement built in her with each aching step. Evelyn's gaze couldn't capture everything at once. There was so much to see. The buildings were nothing like those back home, and the people were nothing like those back home and. . .well, nothing was like home. Her pulse clanged in her ears from the thrill of it all, making her head pound.

Suddenly, Dirk pulled her to the side. The clanging she'd heard grew louder until she realized it wasn't trapped inside her head but coming from a strange contraption that looked similar to a train car but different, lacking a visible engine. It ran on rails and had a dark cable attached to lines that ran overhead. Bemused, she turned to Dirk.

He beamed. "That, my dear, is a cable car. A clever invention that has saved many pairs of feet, I am sure."

"It's amazing."

"Would you like to take a ride?"

"Yes, please." Anticipation made her giddy, while her sore feet made her grateful.

Dirk waved at the operator. The cable car slowed, finally lumbering to a halt. He paid before helping Evelyn aboard. He then set her bag on the floor in front of a wooden bench seat. "Sit here, Miss Giles." He indicated a vacant spot next to a beautifully turned out woman.

Evelyn couldn't help but stare. The woman's porcelain skin and light blue eyes made a striking contrast to her dark, stylishly coifed hair. Sitting, she noticed the woman's attention riveted on Mr. Shaw. The woman smiled a soft, interested smile at him.

Something hot and unfamiliar twisted inside Evelyn's chest. She quickly glanced up to see Dirk politely tip his hat to the woman, then turn his attention back to her. The intensity in his eyes cooled the burning in her chest. With nothing more than a look, he assured her that she alone held his attention.

The car began to move with a rattle and hum reminiscent of the big locomotives. Evelyn sat back and watched the scenery go by as her mind tried to understand what had just happened.

She was stunned to realize that for a fraction of a second, jealousy held her in its grip. She had never been jealous of anyone before, not even Allan.

Before she could come to terms with that little bit of knowledge, the cable car began to grind up a steep grade. She clutched the edge of the seat to keep from leaning into the woman at her side. How did Dirk balance so easily? His long legs were braced apart, and his large hand wrapped around a gleaming brass pole. He was steady and sure. She liked that. It was amazing to her, that with all the upheaval in his life he could still be grounded and solid.

She felt privileged to have seen a glimpse into his heart. She ached for him, yet it wasn't only compassion that made her heart pound, or her pulse race, or jealousy burn hot. She jolted her thoughts away from such dangerous ground and concentrated on the sights going by.

Why, there were steps built into the sidewalk, going all the way up the hill. Ingenious. When one lives on hills, one makes provisions.

When Dirk's free hand came to rest on her shoulder, she tore her gaze from the pedestrians taking the stairs. He urged her to stand, despite the fact that the car still rumbled along. Cautiously, she rose, then gasped as his arm curled around her waist and brought her tight against his side.

"Mr. Shaw?" she declared, unsure whether to feel indignant or pleased.

He leaned in close, his breath tickling her ear. "Look. Over the rise."

The cable car crested the steep hill, and the horizon came into view. Evelyn pulled in a sharp breath. The

Pacific Ocean. Joy surged at the sight of rich blue water with crisp, white-capped waves. The ocean stretched out as far as her eyes could see and met an even paler blue sky. "So beautiful."

"I agree." Dirk's deep voice rustled in her ear.

A charged silence passed between them.

Evelyn didn't know if it was the delight she felt at the sight of the ocean or the look in Dirk's eyes, but suddenly she forgot all about being proper. She went on tiptoe to place a kiss against his slightly stubbled cheek. His whiskers felt like soft bristles against her lips.

Surprise widened his eyes, then they darkened to simmering chocolate before he grinned. Tiny shivers raced down her spine. She forced her gaze back to the horizon for one last glimpse of the blue water before the cable car began its descent.

"Thank you," she whispered as she extracted herself from his grip. She hurried to reclaim her seat. Several seconds passed before her racing heart slowed and her wildly out of control thoughts could be brought back to order. She folded her hands in her lap as calmly as she could. It was time for her to find Allan before she completely forgot about her commitment.

Dirk couldn't stop grinning.

She'd kissed him. And for one crazy moment he was tempted to pull her close and kiss her back. Knowing he couldn't because the gentlemanly thing to do was push away his attraction for her, he'd let her pull away and become all properlike again. His grin deepened. Had her impulsive action stunned her as it had him? And what did it mean?

The kiss meant nothing. His grin slowly died. She'd been caught up in the moment, excited to see the ocean, nothing more. He wouldn't fool himself into thinking she cared for him other than as a friend.

He wanted her to care. His insides clenched, and he gritted his teeth against the longing filling him. How was he going to manage handing her over to Allan Ryder? Every instinct he possessed screamed that heartache lay at the end of this journey. Undoubtedly, his heart would be left crushed and abandoned.

A tugging on his coat brought his attention to Evelyn. She stared up at him, her expression closed. In her hand she held a piece of paper which she was holding out to him. He took it and read the address written in Evelyn's fine penmanship. She wanted to find her betrothed.

Even though he'd known this moment would happen, he wasn't prepared for the anxious need to prolong the inevitable. Regretfully, he reached up and pulled the cord, indicating to the grip operator that they wanted to disembark. The car slowed until it came to a halt at the bottom of the hill. Dirk hopped off, then helped Evelyn step down.

"I'd like to finish what I came to do." Evelyn's voice wavered slightly.

Dirk forced his expression to remain even, though inside he wanted to growl with frustration. He didn't want to let her go. "Why don't we take a tour of the wharf first? Have a little bite to eat and see the docked ships, feel the water. . . ?"

Interest glimmered in her eyes.

He pressed, "I know the skipper of a fine sloop. We could take a quick ride across the bay. What do you think?"

Her pearly teeth tugged on her bottom lip. Indecision warred in her eyes. Slowly she shook her head.

Disappointment unfurled in Dirk's gut. He bound the aching in his heart and pushed it deep down inside of himself where he kept all of his pain. He'd get through this like he had everything else in his life, through force of will. And alone.

He hailed a hackney, and soon they were on their way to the address on the paper he held in his fist. Evelyn's hands moved restlessly in her lap, and Dirk chalked it up to maidenly jitters. After all, she hadn't seen her betrothed in over a year; it would stand to reason that she'd be nervous.

The cab came to a halt in front of a three-story Victorian townhouse on the edge of Nob Hill. He paid the driver, and they stood on the sidewalk staring up at the house. It was no boardinghouse.

Dirk gave a low whistle. "Your fiancé has done well for himself."

When Evelyn made no response, he grew concerned. Her wide eyes and pale complexion spoke volumes. She looked beyond nervous, more like scared witless. He placed a reassuring hand on her arm. "We don't have to do this right now. You could send him a message, let him know you've arrived."

She squared her shoulders and lifted her chin. "No.

I'm here. It's best to get it over with as quickly as possible. I need to do this." She marched forward.

Dirk arched a brow. She made it sound like a distasteful chore rather than something she'd been dreaming about. He puzzled over that as he hurried to catch up with her. She'd already used the huge, lavish knocker and stood waiting with her head held high and her back ramrod straight. She did not look like a woman about to face the love of her life. There was no primping, no girlish giggles.

From through the heavy oak door came a masculine voice. "Coming."

Evelyn gave a little start and stepped back as if to retreat, but then the door was pulled open. A blond man with a straight nose and square chin blinked at them owlishly through his round, wire-rimmed glasses. The man's gaze shifted from Evelyn, to Dirk, and back before recognition widened his eyes. He quickly grabbed the door handle and pulled the door closed behind him.

Apprehension crept up Dirk's spine. This was going to be bad. Even though he'd suspected something fishy was going on with Ryder, he'd hoped, for Evelyn's sake, that he was wrong. He stepped closer to Evelyn.

Allan Ryder swallowed, his Adam's apple bobbing. He looked stunned. "Evelyn? What are you doing here?"

A visible shudder rippled through Evelyn. Dirk winced. Obviously not the reception she'd been hoping for. She lifted her small stubborn chin. Dirk's admiration for her swelled. No wallflower here.

"I came to bring you home, Allan." Her voice

sounded young and vulnerable despite her brave stance. "We are, after all, engaged, and you've been gone much too long."

A deep flush spread over Allan's face. "Uh. . .well, about that. I. . .you see. . ." He scratched his head. "I've been meaning to write and tell you, but I—"

"Tell me what?" Impatience tinged her words.

Dirk hid his smile.

Ryder glanced nervously over his shoulder, as if expecting the door to open. "This isn't a good time. You should have told me you were coming. I could have met you somewhere else."

Dirk clenched his hands at his sides. "She's traveled a long distance to see you. You aren't going to be putting her off like this."

Ryder scowled. "Who are you?" He turned his frown on Evelyn. "What's going on here?"

"Look, you." Dirk stepped closer but stopped when Evelyn placed a restraining hand on his forearm. That gentle hand held his rising temper. The man had no call to be rude to Evelyn. Dirk searched Evelyn's expression, wondering at her calmness.

In a strong, steady voice, she asked, "What are you hiding from me, Allan?"

Allan's gaze slid away, and he shifted his feet. "I feel very bad about the way things have turned out." He met her gaze, his expression imploring. "I really was going to send word. I just didn't know how to. . .everything happened so fast and. . .I. . ."

"Out with it, Allan!"

Evelyn's no-nonsense tone worked. Allan straightened and squared his thin shoulders. "Evelyn, I'm already married."

Rage clouded Dirk's vision. The scoundrel was married! He lifted a fist, intent on slamming it into Ryder's face, when Evelyn stepped back and nearly missed the stair. Dirk quickly grabbed for her and drew her protectively to his side. He'd deal with Ryder later.

He was already married.

Evelyn allowed Dirk's comforting arms to hold her while she waited for hurt and anguish to suffocate her. Nothing happened. Where was the pain, the grief? At least there should be anger, rage. . .something.

She took in a deep breath and realized the lightness she felt was that of a weight being lifted from her shoulders. Relief could be a giddy emotion. She stifled the urge to giggle and concentrated on the problem that remained. They'd made a commitment, not only to each other but also to their families. She wasn't going to be explaining this on her own. Banked anger finally stirred in her chest.

"I can't believe you would do such a thing." She disengaged herself from Dirk's arms and was thankful he'd kept a hand to the small of her back. She took strength from the contact. "We made a commitment to each other, to our families."

"As children, Evelyn. We were never given the opportunity to decide for ourselves." Bitterness spilled from his words.

She cocked her head and studied him. "Is that why

you left? Because you wanted the opportunity to decide?"

He sighed. "I left because I was stifled in Jamestown. I wanted more than—"

"Me," she supplied.

"No. That's not what I mean. You and I have known each other forever. You were my best friend growing up. I. . ." He took a deep breath. "I never loved you in the way a man should love the woman he marries. And I know you never loved me in that way either. You loved the idea, I'm sure, but not me. I left so we'd both have the opportunity to find out what life held for us."

"You could have let me in on that little secret," she shot back. To think she'd wasted so much time clinging to her ideals and her dreams, when all along he'd had no intention of marrying her. What was she going to tell her family? Her eyes narrowed. "When were you going to tell your family?"

"I'll wire them today."

She shook her head. "No. Wait two days. Let me get home and inform my family first." She didn't want the gossip to flow before she had a chance to tell her mother and father.

Dirk made a noise, similar to a growl, deep in his throat.

Allan frowned. "Evelyn, who is this man?"

How could she explain Mr. Shaw? A friend, yes, but he was much more than that now. Instead of answering she asked, "Do you love your wife in the way you spoke of?"

Allan's face softened, and happiness entered his eyes.

"Yes. I couldn't imagine life without her. She's my whole world."

Evelyn's soul responded to the love shining in Allan's expression. She understood what he felt. Her mother and father shared that sort of love. Oh, how she wanted a love like that. Her pulse quickened, and with a start she turned to stare into Dirk's intense brown eyes. She did love like that. She loved Mr. Shaw. Her heart smiled. Perhaps her journey wasn't in vain after all.

Chapter 5

After a hasty good-bye and a "wish you well," Evelyn had practically been forced to drag Dirk away. The dear man wanted to defend her honor. His genuine outrage on her behalf made her heart swell with feminine satisfaction.

She'd finally persuaded him to take her to the wharf where they'd dined on cracked crab and the most delicious sourdough bread she'd ever eaten. The salty air, devoid of fog on this crisp clear night, mingled with her buoyant sense of freedom and kept her smiling. Several times by the golden glow of the gaslights she found Dirk staring at her as if she'd lost her mind. She didn't blame him. He expected her to be crushed. She wasn't. She was in love. With him. Only how was she going to declare her love?

"You must think me a complete ninny not to be heartbroken," she ventured as they now stood waiting for the train to take them back to Jamestown.

His dark brows drew together. "Not a ninny. I suspect you're in some sort of shock."

She shook her head. "No. Quite the opposite."

He drew back. "You aren't angry?"

She shrugged. "A little. Only because I think it was very dishonest of Allan not to tell me how he felt."

Dirk narrowed his gaze. "Didn't you pray to God that Allan would be waiting for you? Didn't you pray that your dream would be fulfilled?"

He thought she should blame Allan's dishonor on God? Oh, the sweet, misguided man. *Lord, help me find the words to reveal Your character to Mr. Shaw.* She squeezed his arm and said gently, "I did pray, and God answered all my prayers."

The corner of Dirk's mouth lifted. "But not the way you wanted."

"No, not the way I *expected,*" she said patiently. "You have to understand, Mr. Shaw, that God doesn't author everything that comes into our lives."

Fierceness lit the dark depths of his eyes. "Things like disease," he stated in a rough tone.

A pang of compassion touched her soul. "Yes, things like disease, death, and dishonesty. Allan was dishonest with his family and me. That didn't come from God, but God used Allan's choices for the betterment of us both. The Bible says God uses all things for the good of those who love Him."

His mouth twisted in thought, then he asked, "So you think what Allan did was good for you?"

"Yes. He was correct when he said I didn't love him the way a woman should love the man she marries. And since he didn't love me in that way, we both would have been miserable."

"Then. . .then why did you come here?"

She answered him honestly. "Because I'd made a commitment."

He gave her a lopsided grin. "You are quite the honorable woman, Miss Giles."

His approval was all the motivation she needed. After taking a fortifying breath, she said, "I have a confession to make."

One dark brow arched in question.

She wrung her hands. *Get it out before you lose your nerve.* "I love *you*, Mr. Shaw."

He went utterly still. She shouldn't have blurted it out so shockingly, and by the grim expression on his face, Evelyn feared she'd blundered her declaration.

She loved him.

The initial shock of her words gave way to incredible joy. Dirk hadn't realized how much he'd wanted her love. His voice held a tremor as he asked, "You love me?"

"Yes. Could you. . .perhaps. . .well, learn to love me?" She sounded so young and vulnerable.

"Learn?" He dropped her bag and gathered her hands in his. "My dear Miss Giles, I'm far beyond learning."

The green of her eyes darkened, reminding him of the Redwood Forest. "You are?"

He released one hand to stroke her cheek. "I think I've loved you since the moment I first saw you."

Her smile, so filled with love, set his heart to pounding. With her by his side, traveling the railways, living each day to the fullest would be a dream come true. A

335

dream he'd never thought possible. He couldn't wait to show her his world, to take her to all the places he knew she'd read about. Taking her as his wife would only be an asset to his job. What better cover than that of a man on a perpetual honeymoon? He could even teach her how to spot. Together they'd make a formidable team.

He suddenly became aware that Evelyn was talking, her words tumbling over themselves. Warning bells, like the whistle of a steam engine, sounded in his head. He distinctly heard the words "inn" and "live" within the same sentence. "Whoa, what did you say?"

She nuzzled his hand. "I said, Mother and Father will be so happy. They really like you. I know you'll love living at the inn, and with all your travel knowledge we'll make the inn the best in all of California."

Dread seized his breath. She wasn't talking about joining his life but about him giving up everything to be with her. She didn't know how impossible that was. Ignoring the inbound train, he shook his head. "I'm not going to live at the inn."

She tucked in her chin and gazed at him. "I suppose we don't have to live in the inn. We could get a house nearby."

He pulled her to a sheltered spot, away from the other passengers and railroad employees who were busy securing the train to make it ready for its return trip. "I thought you understood that the trains are my home."

She frowned and slipped her hand out of his grasp. "The inn is my home. I want to share it with you."

"And I want to share my life with you. I want to show

you the world. You would learn to enjoy the railways as much as I do. I know you would."

"You can't seriously expect me to live on the trains. To live like a vagabond. How could we raise children like that?"

He stepped back as if he'd taken a blow to his middle. Children? He'd never contemplated being a father. The thought was too overwhelming; he wouldn't know how to be a parent. But of course Evelyn would want children. She'd be a wonderful mother. His newly bloomed heart began to wither. He couldn't ask her to give up her dreams. "This won't work between us."

Tears welled in her eyes, confusion marring her expression. "I don't understand. If we love each other, that should be enough to make it work."

"Our lives are too different."

Her hand reached out to him. "I can give you what you lost as a child. A home, a family. A place to belong. Don't you want that?"

Like a knife to the chest, her tempting offer stabbed at him. The little boy inside wanted to accept, wanted to follow wherever she led. The man inside wanted to clasp her hand and show her his world.

Don't be foolish, Boy. A settled life is too easily snatched away. But the trains, the trains will never die, they'll never leave you. His father's words brought him to his senses. "I'm sorry, Miss Giles. I can't—"

"What are you afraid of?" she asked, cutting him off. Her chin rose, and her gaze grew thoughtful beneath her tears.

Her perceptiveness goaded his defenses. No matter

how much it hurt, he had to make her understand that he couldn't walk away from his way of life. He couldn't take that kind of risk. "My future is set. I cannot leave the trains."

She wiped at her tears with the back of her hand. "Will not, you mean."

The anger and hurt in her voice ripped at his insides. Love could never be enough. She wanted what he knew he wouldn't be able to hold onto, and he loved her too much to ask her to give up what she deserved.

She grabbed her bag from the ground and clutched it to her heaving chest. "You're too afraid to trust anyone. Even God, who loves you more than I could even love you. You *are* choosing to live like your father."

"My father attempted to have the kind of life you're talking about," he protested. "Only to have it ripped out from under him. I'm never going to make that mistake."

"What a sad, lonely life you have ahead of you." She backed away from him, then headed for the waiting train.

Slowly, Dirk followed. He should have known better than to hope for anything more than the life laid out before him. He wouldn't be so foolish again. He'd do a better job of locking his heart away.

He scoffed. No need to do that, since Evelyn would be taking his heart with her.

The next morning, as the Sierra Railway locomotive drew to a stop at the Jamestown depot, Evelyn awoke stiff and physically sore, as well as emotionally drained. She'd avoided Dirk as much as possible throughout the ride back home, and now she just wanted to get off his beloved train.

"This way, Miss Giles."

Dirk's impersonal and formal tone set her teeth on edge. If he loved her, why was he doing this? Why couldn't he get beyond his fear, and trust? She forced the thoughts away and straightened her spine. She would not let him see how upset she was. She followed him out and allowed him to help her down the steps. Once on the platform, he handed over her bag.

"I wish you well, Miss Giles," he said as he took her hand and pressed a light kiss against her skin.

She extracted her hand and resisted the urge to slap him. How dare he act so chivalrous when her heart was breaking in two? Her own upbringing wouldn't allow for rudeness. "Thank you, Mr. Shaw. It's been. . .an experience."

A flicker of pain quickly retreated behind his sad smile. "Indeed, Miss Giles. This trip has been an experience I too will cherish."

"Ha!" she huffed. She'd laid her heart at his feet, and he'd kicked it away like old trash. "Good-bye, Mr. Shaw."

He tipped his hat in his familiar gentlemanly fashion. "Good-bye."

Evelyn flinched at the note of regret in his tone but hardened her heart as he turned and reboarded the train. He'd said he loved her but not enough to give up his nice safe little world within the railroad.

And what are you willing to give up?

The thought sent her staggering to the nearest bench,

as realization hit her with the force of a speeding locomotive. She'd declared her love, then demanded he give up everything he knew for her. What kind of love was that?

Conditional.

Feeling physically ill from the truth, she wrapped her arms around her middle. What had she done? She'd wanted so much to show Dirk the true character of God, and yet she'd selfishly expected him to become what she wanted. God didn't love like that. His love was faithful and true, not demanding nor selfish. He'd given the ultimate sacrifice—His Son—in exchange for the world. Could she do any less?

Please, dear Lord, forgive my pride and selfishness.

Evelyn lifted her chin. Her love for Dirk was true, and she would gladly give up all that she had for him. For without him, her life would not be complete.

She stood and shook out her skirt as if to shake off the past. Her future was on that train with Dirk, and she wasn't going to let him leave without her.

Dirk sank to a seat and closed his eyes, taking in the pungent smell, the familiar feel of the railroad. As the steam engine sounded its warning whistle, signaling the train's imminent departure, and the wheels began to rattle and hum as the locomotive warmed up, Dirk found no comfort. He felt oddly empty, much like the passenger car he now sat in.

Once he returned to his way of life, he'd be fine. He'd be free from the pain of loving Evelyn, free from the pain of knowing they could never be together.

"What a sad, lonely life you have ahead of you."

Evelyn's voice bounced around his head and settled in the pit of his stomach. He'd hated seeing the pity in her eyes. Hated that what she'd said was true. Could it be any other way?

Love casts out fear. The soft echo of his mother's words rambled around his head, making his pulse race and his palms sweat.

What had the Bible said?

There is no fear in love.

We love because He first loved us.

Evelyn's voice piped in, *"You're too afraid to trust God."*

Little lights sparked behind his closed eyelids, and his temples throbbed. What was happening to him? He felt a need building inside, a longing for something he couldn't explain.

Don't be a fool, Boy. You listen to me. Don't you ever talk to me about God. God took your mother away. He doesn't love you. He doesn't love anyone.

Dirk's heart slammed against his ribs, and suffocating fear engulfed him. Jerking his eyes open, he expected to see his father standing over him, his large fist raised and ready to strike. He let out a noisy breath. He wasn't a child any longer, cowering in the corner of an empty box car, half hating, half loving his father.

He forced the voice to be silent. No more. No more would he listen to his father's bitterness. He didn't want to end up like that, angry and alone. He wanted to know the God his mother had believed in. The God Evelyn believed in. But how?

I love you. A gentle whispering soothed his inner turmoil. A refreshing peace eased over him, and in that moment he felt the presence of God.

"You *are* real," he breathed out.

The train began to move. Evelyn! He scrambled to his feet. *God, Evelyn said Your Word promises You work out all things for the good of those who love You. Well, she loves You, and well. . .I want to love You. Please, don't let it be too late for us.*

Dirk hustled through the vestibule and jumped off the train. His feet hit the platform running. Evelyn was nowhere in sight. He headed toward the road.

"Mr. Shaw!"

He pulled up short, wildly looking for Evelyn.

"Dirk, here!"

Swinging around, his eyes widened to see Evelyn clutching the rail of the top step between the last two cars. She was on the train! He made a mad dash for her. Thankfully, the steam engine was slow to pull out of the station. He ran in alignment with Evelyn. "What are you doing up there?" he hollered.

"Looking for you," she shouted back.

"Jump off," he cried, holding out his arms as well as his heart to her.

Evelyn gaped, her heart pounding in her throat. "No! You jump on!" With her free hand she held fast to her hat. "I love you, and I'll go anywhere as long as you're with me."

He grinned, that grin she so loved. "I love you too, Evelyn. Marry me!"

Happiness surged in her heart. "What?"

"Evelyn, hurry! Jump! I'll catch you."

He was almost to the end of the platform. There was only one thing for her to do—trust him to catch her. Closing her eyes, she let go and flew through the air, her traveling dress billowing out around her.

Still running, Dirk caught her, his muscular arms wrapping securely around her. He stumbled to a halt. With her still enclosed within the safety of his arms, they watched the train chug away.

After setting her back on her feet, his gaze searched her face. He swallowed tightly. "Did you mean what you'd said? You'd go with me anywhere?"

The uncertainty in his chocolate eyes touched her soul. "If you'll have me," she replied with a shy smile.

Relief and love replaced the doubt in his expression. "Ah, my dear. Will you forgive me for being a fool? I *was* afraid. Afraid to love you too much and risk losing you. I was afraid to trust. To trust God to be there for me, but I know in my heart that what you've taught me about His love is true. I need you to teach me more about love."

Dirk's words made her heart soar. "It takes courage to face your fears." Even as the words left her mouth she knew she had a few fears of her own to face. Like the fear of change. But with Dirk guiding her with his love, the fear would die a quick death. She lowered her gaze. "I too must ask for your forgiveness. I had no right to expect you to change your life for me."

With the crook of his finger, he lifted her chin. "I propose a compromise."

She melted into his intense rich gaze and made a noise of assent deep in her throat. She never wanted to leave the shelter of his love.

He took possession of her hands and brought them to his lips. She sucked in a breath at the featherlight kisses gracing her knuckles.

"Jamestown can be our permanent residence, and together we'll make the inn the best in all of California," he murmured.

Her mouth went dry. "And. . .?"

"On occasion we can take a trip. There is so much out there I want to share with you."

A deep and brimming joy filled her to overwhelming. She pulled him closer. "Whenever you feel the need for an adventure, I will gladly hop on the nearest train with you," she solemnly promised.

His deep, joyful laugh washed over her, and Evelyn thought it the most wonderful sound she'd ever heard. He sobered, and a decidedly amused gleam entered his gaze. "So, Miss Giles, will you marry me?"

Tears of happiness welled in her eyes and love, perfect love, filled her soul. "Yes, Mr. Shaw. I will."

TERRI REED

Terri grew up in a Christian home nestled in the foothills of the Sierra-Nevada Mountains of California, and now she resides in the Pacific Northwest with her husband, Shel, two young children, Malone and Caden, and an Australian Shepherd named Blueberry.

Since childhood, she has had stories and characters dancing in her head, vying for attention. In the sixth grade she wrote her first romantic story, so when she seriously committed to putting pen to paper, it was natural to inter-wine her faith in God with her love of romance.

A Letter to Our Readers

Dear Readers:

In order that we might better contribute to your reading enjoyment, we would appreciate your taking a few minutes to respond to the following questions. When completed, please return to the following: Fiction Editor, Barbour Publishing, Inc., P.O. Box 719, Uhrichsville, OH 44683.

1. Did you enjoy reading *Romance on the Rails?*
   □ Very much. I would like to see more books like this.
   □ Moderately—I would have enjoyed it more if _____
   _____
   _____

2. What influenced your decision to purchase this book?
   (Check those that apply.)
   □ Cover   □ Back cover copy   □ Title   □ Price
   □ Friends   □ Publicity   □ Other

3. Which story was your favorite?
   □ *Daddy's Girl*   □ *The Tender Branch*
   □ *A Heart's Dream*   □ *Perfect Love*

4. Please check your age range:
   □ Under 18   □ 18–24   □ 25–34
   □ 35–45   □ 46–55   □ Over 55

5. How many hours per week do you read? _____

Name _____

Occupation _____

Address _____

City _____ State _____ Zip _____

If you enjoyed

Romance
on the Rails

then read:

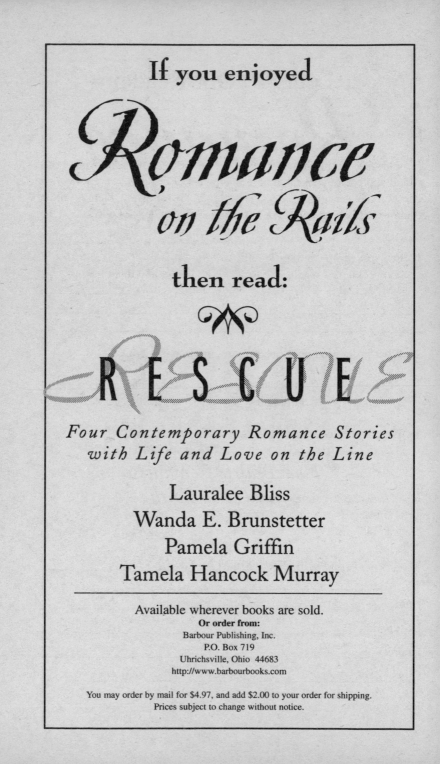

RESCUE

*Four Contemporary Romance Stories
with Life and Love on the Line*

Lauralee Bliss
Wanda E. Brunstetter
Pamela Griffin
Tamela Hancock Murray

If you enjoyed

Romance

on the Rails

then read:

the *Sewing* *Circle*

*One Woman's Mentoring Shapes Lives
in Four Stories of Love*

**Andrea Boeshaar
Cathy Marie Hake
Sally Laity
Pamela Kaye Tracy**

INTRODUCTION

Daddy's Girl by Wanda E. Brunstetter
Glenna Moore has grown up following her father from one gaming table to the next and never putting down roots. When her father is caught cheating at cards on a train, he is forced to jump off at gunpoint, leaving a hysterical Glenna behind. The Reverend David Green befriends her, and it just so happens he is in need of wife to help him at his new church appointment. Could such a pair be partners for life?

A Heart's Dream by Birdie L. Etchison
Charlotte Lansing has taken a teaching position in Traer, Kansas, and must take along her only living relative, her little brother Robert. Robert quickly makes friends on the train with Frank, a handsome doctor. Frank insists on escorting them to her post. Will she ever see him again if he gets back on the westbound train?

The Tender Branch by Jane LaMunyon
Separated from her father during the Civil War, Mary Sherwood is now forced to travel from New York to Oregon by train to reunite with him. Over ten years have passed, and Mary is wary of her father's friend, Jesse Harcourt, who was sent to accompany her on her journey. Numerous railway delays still don't make Mary anticipate the end of her journey. Can there be a peaceful reconciliation for her heart?

Perfect Love by Terri Reed
Evelyn Giles runs her family's inn and is ready to settle down and marry her fiancé. But he has not returned from fortune hunting, and Evelyn is determined to look for him. She begrudgingly accepts Dirk Shaw as her escort on the train trip. Could his presence be a lifeline for the days ahead?